Born in the mid-West in 1949, Keith Heller for many years taught English Literature, most recently at a Californian University. Together with his wife and daughter he lived abroad for seven years, three of which were spent in Madrid. He has also lived in Japan and Argentina. A published poet, he is the author of a highly acclaimed trio of crime novels set in eighteenth-century London, which first appeared in the UK and America in the mid-eighties. SNOW ON THE MOON is his first work of general fiction. Now retired from university teaching, Keith Heller lives in California where he writes full time.

Snow On The Moon

Keith Heller

review

First published in 1996
by HEADLINE BOOK PUBLISHING

First published in paperback in 1997
by HEADLINE BOOK PUBLISHING

A REVIEW paperback

10 9 8 7 6 5 4 3 2 1

ISBN 0 7472 5378 1

Typeset by
Letterpart Limited, Reigate, Surrey

Printed and bound in Great Britain by
Clays Ltd, St Ives plc

HEADLINE BOOK PUBLISHING
A division of Hodder Headline PLC
338 Euston Road
London NW1 3BH

Every door to left and right of the road is shut. All the lamps have gone out, all of them. And one only moves forward by falling!

Wolfgang Borchert

By the time the monastery guards found Evelyn's purse lying on a shelf by a locked Bible, the last bus to Madrid was halfway down the mountain, and the sky above the north courtyard was gray and moving. It was too late to hurry now. She would have to stay one more night in the bleak town of Escorial, even though it meant walking back again through the slate streets and the sudden snows and sleeping in her cold hotel room. When she had finally found a way through the hungry afternoon shoppers, she rested for a while before going down to the late dinner, her shoulders wrapped in a blanket and her eyes fixed on the bedroom wall as if they were memorizing some message scribbled invisibly across it.

The dining room was dim and freezing, the brown wallpaper shaggy with grime, but there was a working radio shining on a sideboard, and the stove inside the nearby kitchen roared with charcoal. Evelyn would have much preferred to sit alone at any of the dozen tables, but the guests had all been gathered together at one closer to the kitchen door, and she had to join them there. The only empty chair was beside a tall man, who rose now to greet her with a nod that made the top of his hair flash beneath the bare ceiling bulb.

'Miss Winter, you're just in time for the soup.'

The other men at the table stood and sat down again.

Evelyn smiled vaguely at everyone.

'We all thought we should have lost you by now.'

'That's right. We supposed you'd be back in Madrid.'

'Mr Dearing here was quite upset at his loss.'

The Englishman colored, glancing apologetically at the woman beside him, at her oval face and the brown hair worn curled down along her neck. Evelyn looked back at him with the blind stare of a woman alone in her thirties and thanked him for his concern.

'Well, Señora Liot exaggerates a little . . .'

The woman from Barcelona, stuffed into wool beside her grown son, Antonio, teased the two awkward foreigners.

'I tell only the truth. We all missed you. Whatever happened to your plans? Does this mean that you won't be able to take all those exciting military flights you were telling us about? What a shame that would be. And to miss all the coming holidays, too.'

As well as she could in her schoolgirl Spanish, Evelyn told them that her schedule was flexible and that she had no reason to rush anywhere. As she spoke, she tried not to address any one guest in particular, as if by spreading a fan of conversation she might be able to disappear behind it. Eventually, those at the table turned to other topics, and then to the *olla* of smoking soup that the hotel proprietor was carrying into the room.

He apologized for the dry garlic broth, then for the day-old bread, the handful of rice, and the few beets set out by the young maid. The war, he explained.

'Not to mention the years of drought,' Martin Dearing said.

'Oh, of course. Escorial hasn't seen an orange in years.'

The oldest man in the room spread his hands graciously over the frayed oilcloth and spoke diplomatically.

'Lorenzo, don't torture yourself on our account. I'm

certain that none of us has eaten any better since this fearful nightmare began. Everything will return to normal, now that it's all behind us at last.'

'You're too kind, Herr Heuter. And to help hurry that along, especially during this sacred season,' the proprietor added, 'let me pour you all a taste of this fine *tinto* that I've been saving since the fall of the Republic. If we can't enjoy it now, then I don't know when we ever will. Lulú.' He motioned to the maid, and the two of them began to circle the table.

The warm wine, followed by potatoes and onions, soon had all the guests more relaxed, and the room grew quieter as when a fever in a hospital ward has finally broken. The travelers dined as slowly as they could, sharing and conserving, as if they might add something to tomorrow's rations by dawdling long enough over tonight's. Even fallen bits of rice were unconsciously dabbed up on the tips of fingers, while the old man from Bern sat cleaning his teeth with a shard of crust that he finally gummed into mush and swallowed. Lengthening the last of their wine, the guests sat back and smoked, not listening to the window behind them that was whispering with accumulating drifts.

The historian from Toledo who was visiting Escorial for its monastery assured Miss Winter that the storm would end by morning and that she should be able to find a place on tomorrow's bus.

'Julio's right,' the proprietor said. 'The storm won't last. Up here, we usually only get some powder, with ice in the shadows, and then in the morning the sun rises high enough to clear almost all of it away.'

The maid said, 'But I've never seen it come down so heavily. I was just at the back door, and the stones of the pathway have all vanished.'

'It was getting deep even when Antonio and I were out,' the woman from Barcelona declared.

'Lulú's from Sevilla,' Lorenzo informed the others about the maid. 'To her, winter is a dozen flakes in the street. I've lived here all my life, and I tell you the roads will be fine. In these times, I know, many strange things are possible. But even snow is only snow.'

The guests discussed the weather, the Englishman missing his traditional Christmas back home and Evelyn Winter dreading her return to the brutal December winds of Wisconsin. Someone wondered aloud if the couple from Switzerland shouldn't know the most about cold and winter.

'Frau Heuter and I are a bit disappointed, actually,' Alfred said. 'We were hoping to escape the worst of it and enjoy a warmer holiday for a change. But I gather we should have gone on farther south. Andalucía is said to be lovely this time of year.'

'We could still go,' his wife suggested in a child's voice.

'Perhaps. Perhaps.'

'You should,' Lulú advised as she began to clear the table. 'It's so much nicer down there this time of year. Not so hot.'

'In here, at least,' the proprietor said heartily, 'we could keep warm and fed even if it came down all night and buried us in an unmarked grave. We should all just be thankful that we're not out in the open on a night like this. Sometimes the frost can do things to you that you would never have thought possible.'

To reassure his guests even more, Lorenzo suddenly agreed to grind and brew some rare coffee beans that he had been saving for the New Year. Then a peaceful, blurring restfulness overcame the room, numbing everyone's private worries and letting them forget about the freezing rooms upstairs. Beneath the table, their limbs stretched out lazily and crossed until no one could tell who was who, and even the uncomfortable American woman let herself relax a bit and listen more closely to the changing conversations. She still talked very little herself, taking refuge in her inability to speak the local language well, but at least the two men beside her could feel the body between them growing a little less rigid.

As the night deepened, Lorenzo finally consented to turning up the radio, and the buzzing of the music soon put the wife from Bern to sleep against her husband's shoulder and made Señora Liot's bored son Antonio wish he were back home in Barcelona where he felt more needed. The Englishman tried to talk in private with Evelyn, but he failed, and he was forced to listen to the Toledo historian's parchment voice urging him to come and see his city's wonderful cathedral.

'I probably will, if there's any chance of my selling these tractors of mine around there. Otherwise—'

'But why wouldn't there be? After the Civil War, the people in the countryside need all the help they can get.'

'It's still all quite a mess, isn't it?' Martin said.

'It is,' Julio nodded. 'But now at least the rest of Europe is safe again.'

The others around the table sat eagerly forward.

'It's been a long time since anyone could say that,' Martin Dearing said.

'Too long.'

'You should see London. Or, rather, you shouldn't. Not yet.'

'We should all thank God,' Lulú said simply, 'that we lived to see the end of it.'

'While so many others didn't,' young Antonio replied.

'That's right.'

'I left a lot of good friends in France.'

'And I,' Herr Heuter murmured, 'in Germany.'

'But now,' the maid insisted, 'it's time to move forward.'

'Easy enough to say.'

'But we've all come so far,' the proprietor exclaimed. 'And the greatest threats lie defeated behind us.'

Yet the woman in wool only shook her head.

'We're not out of the worst of it yet,' Carlota Liot said. 'In our city, we have old problems leaving every night, and newer problems arriving every morning. Just like before.'

'Yes, I suppose the food shortages and labor—'

'The economy—'

'Oh, the banks are suffering horribly—'

'I mean,' the woman from Barcelona maintained darkly, 'from the north.'

'Mother!'

'What are you saying?' the maid asked her.

'I think,' Herr Heuter said quietly, careful not to wake his wife, 'that Señora Liot must be referring to the refugees.'

A new stiffness came over the group, as if they were posing for a portrait of the table that would take years to paint. But Señora Liot said that he was right.

'What else? Refugees from every country have been littering our streets like animals for over ten years now. In the past few months, it got to be more than I could bear, until coming here to look after some property left me in thirty-seven was the only thing I could think of to keep my sanity.'

She swept a black triangle of hair out of her eyes and put both hands against her side of the table as though she wanted to push it up against the Englishman's chest.

'Do you know how many of us who were born in

Barcelona have to hang onto the beach with our fingernails? There's hardly any room left anymore. There are more of *them* than there are tables and chairs outside some of the cafés. And at the market, my maid has to wait for hours in a line behind someone who hasn't taken a bath in a decade. I think if it doesn't get better soon, Antonio and I might have to move here to hide out until it's all over, if such a day ever comes.'

'Oh,' Lorenzo said mysteriously, 'even we have two of those same problems here in Escorial, believe me.'

'What I can't understand,' the historian said, 'is why Spain should have to spend the little money it has in trying to protect itself from all these refugees. We should use it to restore some of our treasures, like the monastery here, before termites or Time itself eats them up once and for all.'

'The monastery?' someone objected. 'We need money for bread first.'

'History is bread.'

'Try telling that to the children in the streets. Like that little sick boy who spends all his time drawing diagrams on the stone courtyards around the Escorial. What do you want him to eat? The walls of the building?'

'I've seen him myself, early in the mornings. It's so sad.'

'So have I,' someone else suddenly remembered.

'What little boy?'

'That damned little troublemaker,' Lulú put in and frowned.

'What do you mean, troublemaker? What's he done?'

Lorenzo glanced stealthily off to the sides of the room and then lowered his head and his voice.

'He's given us all a little hope, that's what he's done. In a few short months, he's started to make this corner of Spain more bearable for honest men and women. That boy helps us all to keep going in his own small way, even if the Church and the city fathers want him to stop what he's doing. They say he's a danger. But anyone would be a danger to them, if he was teaching the citizens how to live again.'

'What does he do?' a few of the others asked, but Lorenzo's eyes were shut, and the subject soon disappeared into the dining-room shadows and was entirely forgotten.

From the kitchen, the stove sent off waves of heat while, behind the window, snow piled up like sand dunes. A high wind could be heard in the pauses between songs, and as soon as a deeper announcing voice took over, the wind changed its tone to a harsher whine. The power was too weak and the mountains were too near for the signal to be steady, leaving the dial to flicker as uncertainly as a candle in a blizzard.

'Well, it's going to get worse before it gets better,' the proprietor warned as he gazed down at the single coffee bean that he was trying to split apart with blackened fingernails. 'There are more refugees now than taxpayers, more wounded than well. And Spain just happens to be the most convenient escape route for all the runaways from Europe. It seems,' he sighed, 'that everyone is looking for a way out of somewhere.'

'And just when we thought all our troubles were over, too.'

'It can't be helped, I suppose.'

'People always say that,' Antonio objected.

'That's because it's usually true,' the Englishman said.

'Of course it is. Once you say that.'

Suddenly, Carlota Liot turned on the American who had almost succeeded in fading completely away beneath the waning light bulb.

'Your country has more room than ours. You should be taking some more of this riffraff off our hands.'

Evelyn Winter leaned back again and fumbled for an excuse.

'The Americans won't be able to,' the Swiss gentleman put in gallantly, 'if Truman signs his rumored Executive Order.'

Alfred Heuter looked slowly around the table, making sure of everyone's complete attention. He was gray in color, translucent, as if his flesh were composed of paper or ice. Over his mouth, a moustache of white straw fluttered with his breathing, while the hair on his head and hands was childlike and pink under the brown room light.

'You'll permit me, Miss Winter, but I used to work in Geneva with Gerhart Riegner and his World Jewish Congress there. Our job was to watch what was happening to the European Jews, and I heard most of the news about all the Displaced Persons. Just now, there are so many refugee camps in the different occupation zones that no one can predict what might become of all the people. All we do know is that they are filled to capacity, and yet more are coming in every day. Some people think that as many as seven million are uprooted and homeless on the Continent right now. Some would put that figure at half as many again.

'But most of them,' he assured the Spaniards, 'want nothing more to do with Europe and are hoping to go to the United States. I know many in that country might welcome them, but many more may not. At least some of the Displaced Persons are young, strong men who could work well anywhere at any task—'

'Like those in our camp at Miranda de Ebro,' Julio put in.

'—but many others are sick or with families or have nothing to bring. They might become burdens to whatever country they move into, so quotas have been set for limiting their numbers. This is what Truman will probably do in two or three weeks. He's going to let in only those who are in the US occupation camps no later than the twenty-second of December. Anyone who comes after that,' Herr Heuter sympathized, 'will simply have to be excluded.'

'And,' someone said, 'go elsewhere.'

'But where?'

A muted *crack* sounded as the proprietor finally broke the bean and started to crunch it morosely between his back teeth. The guests seemed to have exhausted themselves, and hung their heads wearily as the wind outside chattered against the roof and the window. Even the kitchen fire had run out of breath, and now the two rooms were growing colder and darker as if they were falling into the same sleep that the people around the table should have been enjoying hours ago.

In the dirty light of the dining room, the pale face of the young man from Barcelona stood out as he looked about him.

'Has anyone heard,' he asked softly, 'anything more of what the liberating soldiers found in the German camps?'

The American woman abruptly clawed her chair back across the hardwood floor and stood away from the table.

'I'm afraid I'll have to turn in now,' she said to everyone. 'I have to make an early start tomorrow.'

'Let me walk you up,' the historian offered.

'It's all right. Really. Thank you, anyway.'

'I'm coming, too,' Martin Dearing said in English, rising.

'Good night, all,' Evelyn said, and turned away before anyone could answer.

The stairs were narrow and shaded, and the two almost had to face each other as they sidled upward. The Englishman's door came first, but he refused to allow Evelyn to walk to her room alone. Outside her door, a dingy green couch stood against the wall, and it seemed only natural for the two English-speaking visitors to sit together for a few minutes for a shared smoke. The woman's attention was elsewhere, but Martin's uncombable hair and crooked glasses gave him a flustered look that made him seem trustworthy and harmless.

'So,' he began, 'do you think you'll be able to get down to Madrid tomorrow?'

'I hope so. I have a friend down there who might be worried if I don't.'

'A friend? Another American?'

'No,' Evelyn said. 'Clara's a Spaniard I met in London at the end of the war. She's the reason I came down here at all. She said that as long as I had some time before being shipped back to the States, I should have a vacation here before I hurry home for Christmas. I've never been to Europe, and I always wanted to come to Spain, so I pulled a few strings and traveled down with her.

'Then, of course,' she went on more coldly, 'as soon as the two of us get here, Clara runs off with her boyfriend and buys me a bus ticket to Escorial so that I can do some sightseeing until she gets back. I can't imagine why that man of hers couldn't have waited for us to finish our trip together before he had to stick his nose in between us. After all, I'm the one who should be home in a week or two, not them. They're already where they wanted to be.'

The Englishman hummed quietly in support, then tried to set her anger off to one side.

'I heard that you worked for the war effort in England. You weren't stationed near Ipswich, were you, by any chance? Who knows – we might even have met before in a pub or at some function.'

Evelyn frowned across at him in the quiet gloom of the hallway.

'I was with the US Army's Eighth Air Force, first at High Wycombe and then at Bassingbourn,' she said. 'But only since June of last year. I never had the time to get out very much.'

'The AAF? You don't mean to tell me you were an airgirl, do you?'

'Nothing so glorious, although I did start out at one of the AWS stations on our East Coast.'

Evelyn spoke reluctantly, but Martin was gentle with her and patient, like an old friend, and he was able to thaw some of the numb reserve she had maintained throughout the crowded meal downstairs.

'AWS?' he asked, already knowing. 'What was that?'

'Aircraft Warning Service,' she explained. 'There were a lot of volunteer civilian women at the stations, at least for a time. Then I joined the Women's Army Corps, trained at Fort Des Moines, and was lucky enough to be assigned overseas with the Eighth. But that was as far as it went.'

'You sound disappointed.'

Evelyn stared at the floor.

'It's just that I was so excited about finally getting away from the Midwest and coming over to do whatever I could to help,' she went on. 'Yet all I did was the same secretarial duties that I'd always done – only this time in white, green, yellow, and pink copies. Everything that happened seemed to be happening *around* me and not *because* of me. I suppose it sounds selfish, but I wish I could have worked as a translator or a cryptographer, and then I might have felt that I was making a real difference.'

'Well, we all contributed.' Martin Dearing sat back against the couch and reasoned with her. 'I myself may have only handled motors at a munitions factory, but I like to think that no matter how small my part was, it was still necessary.'

'I understand that.'

'It all came out well enough in the end,' he replied. 'We've got plenty to be grateful for, all of us here at the hotel. In a week or so, you'll be back safe at home, and I hope to be placing orders for tractors that will help all these people here get back on their feet. I don't know what else any of us might be looking for. You weren't,' he asked Evelyn, 'dreaming of any kind of excitement from the war, were you? Because that's not what it was about, you know. Not at all.'

'No, of course not.'

'And it wasn't an individual matter, either.'

'I know that,' she said, offended.

'Well,' Martin continued, 'what then?'

They finished their cigarettes in silence as the building vibrated with the storm outside and the feet and voices of the other guests making their way to their rooms. A tired expectancy hung in the air, as if the hotel, the town and the surrounding mountains all awaited her answer.

'I'm not too sure.' Evelyn hesitated. 'It's just that all my life, I've gone along and done everything I was supposed to do. I quit school early to help support my family. I took the first job that came along and became a secretary. I even stopped taking my piano lessons so that I could spend all my time doing the solid, sensible work the rest of the world told me I was supposed to be doing. I was never doing what *I* really wanted to do – because I had no idea what that might be. Eventually, I started to feel that I was living everyone else's life instead of my own, or at least a life that everyone else thought should have been mine.'

'Well, we all have that problem to some degree,' Martin said sympathetically. 'What with the way the world economies were failing just before the war, we had to do the best we could with what we had.'

'I know, I know,' Evelyn answered. 'But in forty-three, the Army started sending the WACs into noncom training, and I began to hope that now there would be a real point to what I was doing, both in the war and in my own life. Everyone back home was pretty sure I was crazy, putting a good position in Milwaukee on hold for who knew how long, and running off like that. But I did it. I signed up and took the training and did the kind of things I never thought I'd ever be capable of doing. And I felt as if I were finally heading somewhere – no, not just that – as if I finally had somewhere plain and obvious to go to that no one could even see but me.'

Animated by the memory, Evelyn placed her knees together and propped her elbows on them, poised like a figurehead bringing her face around toward an open horizon.

'Then,' she recalled, 'when I came over to England and added my contribution, everything seemed so important and final, and I felt bigger than I used to. I think I even sat up straighter in a chair, and I was more serious about stenographing and teletyping than I'd ever felt about anything else in my life. I guess I knew what I was here for – but not only in England – and I could finally start to see the shape my life was taking on, and it wasn't what all the people back home expected it to be. God, it wasn't what *I* would ever have expected it to become, either! I mean, there were still no children or husband or career or anything like that, but I felt that I was coming into focus somehow, that from then on nothing in my life would ever be quite the same again. Can you understand what I mean?' Evelyn asked him desperately.

'I think I can,' the Englishman said. 'I suppose there was a special significance in what we were doing, and that helped each of us make it through. We had less time to think about ourselves, and that always tends to make one's life better, don't you think?

'But,' he went on, 'as I said before, we've come to the end of it, and I think we can all take quite a bit of pride in how it turned out. So . . . what is it that's worrying you now, Evelyn? What do you feel is still wrong in your life?'

The woman waited for a long time. Then she said: 'I guess I'm just wondering what I should do next. Right now, the only thing I can think of is to forget that any of this – any of the only worthwhile years I have ever lived – ever happened. But what kind of a life is that going to leave me, over the next thirty or forty long years? What will I be when I'm not even an Eighth Army secretary anymore?'

They sat together through another cigarette as the hotel corridor grew colder and darker and the building around them became quiet enough for them to hear the smothering flakes massing on top of the roof. In a while, there followed a clumsy game of gestures and excuses as the two stumbled their way through halfhearted embraces and an accidental kiss. Their mouths met wood, and it was a tired relief for both of them to part at the door with promises for breakfast.

Before climbing alone into her steel bed, Evelyn stood at the window for a while, trying to squeeze some warmth out of the dull radiator. Outside, the night was moving invisibly downward as the flakes fell quietly onto the black railings and the even blacker streets below. A few lights burned out from random corners, and somewhere in the distance a late café wavered with suggestions of heat and laughter. But here, only the snow gave off any radiance as it fell, and that was no more than what far stars might have emitted, had they started plummeting silently out of the air. Even the rare cars had been put to bed, leaving behind a frieze of tracks that faded just as Evelyn started to watch their ruts being erased by the storm.

She lifted her eyes over the houses and toward the monastery where it stood grim as winter on the edge of town, holding up its stone gridiron to catch the softly falling sky, falling faintly. Through the night, she could feel its harsh stillness and all the comforting purity of its granite and its gray age. A temperature too low to feel began to spread upward from the dead radiator and through her thighs, until she finally shivered into her bed and turned her face away from the window's draft. As she did so, the building closed down about her, and the night burying the village reached all the way into her dreams, and she was able to sleep through until morning without even dreaming that she was sleeping.

Outside, the thin moon broke free of some clouds for a moment, edging them with subdued, dark light. Through a film, its changing face shone gray, a mixture of dusty colors that might have been found in a kitchen or around an abandoned campfire. Anyone watching could see on its surface the outline of a horse, its hooves rearing in the air . . . or the face of a man turning his eyes aside as if in shame . . . or even the topography of a city that was too foul and frozen to live anywhere on earth.

Breakfast was tasteless and uncomfortable, and Evelyn hurried it along as quickly as she could. She muttered her way through some toast and heated milk, sitting coldly across from Martin Dearing and Julio, the historian from Toledo. They were the only two other guests eager enough to be up this early. The door that Evelyn had opened last night between herself and the others still stood open – though she tried hard to close it by keeping quiet, saying only that she had to be at the bus station by eight. But when she got up to go, the two men rose with her.

'I should be going, too,' the Englishman said. 'I've got one or two clients to meet today.'

'And I'm off to the monastery to get on with my researches,' Julio added.

'Isn't the bus station in that direction?' Evelyn asked him suddenly.

'Why – yes, it is.'

'Then I'm with you,' she said, and took his arm before Martin Dearing even knew what was happening.

Stepping out into the street was a revelation. The snow must have rained down fiercely all night, for the town had been buried in a muffler of cold cotton which blazed in the kind of frozen sun that can be found only among mountains. Hovering gray threatened more of the same, while the streets lay mostly still unmarked and inhuman at such a cold hour. The two guests struggled panting to the bus station, where Julio did all he could to convince the bus driver, who wore two sweaters, that the morning roads would be passable. But even with all their begging, the only place Evelyn could get was on the afternoon bus to Madrid, and so she was left with another long, idle day, alone in the isolated mountain village.

Anything, she reflected, would be better than sitting all day in the hotel, where by now the maid would be throwing open every window for the morning airing. So she started walking with Julio toward the enormous monastery at the bottom of the street, hoping today to see its outside as completely as yesterday she had seen its interior. From the historian she learned that, to some, even the strangest studies might be made meaningful, and she listened to his account of his research work on the delegation of four Japanese teenagers who had been invited by Philip II to tour the palace on its completion in September, 1584. He wondered why they had come from Nagasaki, why they had been given such a grand reception, and what legends they must have told on their return. His totally pointless enthusiasm intrigued her and made her slightly jealous of the restful way he could escape from himself in such a flurry of impersonal data about the great building.

'Not to mention,' Julio told her, 'the two thousand or more windows and the twelve hundred doors. There are eighty-four miles of corridors and courtyards, eighty-six staircases, sixteen courts, and fifteen cloisters. The entire complex is one single, vast parallelogram, some two hundred and seven metres by one hundred and fifty-two—'

'Any people?' Evelyn interrupted him in mid-stride.

'Oh, of course. Nearly a dozen kings, almost one hundred and fifty heads, and twice as many limbs. The relics alone must reach seven thousand or so in number.'

'I meant, does anybody live in it now?'

The question had obviously never occurred to him before, and Evelyn wondered at the heartless precision some people brought to their work to keep themselves too busy to feel.

Furred in white, the immense monastery looked suddenly frail and sly in the morning, as if last night it had burrowed its head in its paws to sleep the rest of the winter away. In the metallic cold, its skeleton stuck out like ice from beneath a white shell, while in places the gray *escoria* – the lava from which it had taken its name – showed through like bald patches or squares of burnt skin. Evelyn and the historian approached it from the west where the main gate and its overlooking statues framed three arched doorways, now the darkest black against the surrounding light. A stray wind stopped them and made them contemplate the great severity of the building and feel some of the loneliness buried inside its ancient stones.

'You're not coming in?' Julio asked as Evelyn held back.

'No, I think I'll take a walk around it instead.'

'Through all this?'

'I'm from Wisconsin, remember?' she said, wandering off. 'A few measly drifts like these are nothing to me.'

It took Evelyn nearly half an hour to wade through the broad courtyards and walkways and gardens that were almost invisible in their carapace of packed snow. The brilliant cold made her mouth tingle, while the endless stretch of the walls and towers helped her forget most of her regrets and fears. Even when her shoes filled with wet, she took her time over the pools with their cream waves and the arches that coiled like a serpent above the banks. Except for some slight damage left over from the Civil War, the monastery was unchanged, a monstrous fossil that had died and then been planted here long before memory began. She had never seen anything so motionless and calm, and when she had completed her circuit she had to remind herself not to forget her afternoon bus and next week's flight back home, or she might find herself rooted beside this desolate colossus for ever.

Rounding the last tower, she stopped in the north courtyard and looked at a boy kneeling down on the ground. He had stationed himself where the sweeping gnomon of the tower would keep him in shadow all day and where no trampling tourists could disturb him. She noticed first his wrinkled clothes, the rag of a jacket and the short hair under the fur hat, and only then did she hear the scratching and see the stick vibrating in his hand. The boy's back was to her, but when her shadow began to grow out of his, obscuring his sharp outline, he turned and trained his dark eyes on the intruder looming above him.

'*Bitte*,' his bat's voice said. '*Mehr Licht*.'

The words startled her, and she suddenly remembered most of the German that she had spoken on the farm until her first day of school.

'*Es tut mir leid*,' she said, backing away a step.

The dark face beneath her smiled upward.

'What are you doing?' Evelyn asked, craning around the boy's back to see.

'*Nichts*.'

But he was, in fact, drawing. Using a short stick that could cut into the crust as delicately as a razor, the boy had drawn an outline, a perfect labyrinth, that lay clearly on the white page of the ground. The woman saw a small miracle of lines and spaces, a geometrical blueprint of a building that included outcroppings and alcoves, smudges of windows with flicks of the stick that any viewer might mistake for doors, a nimbus of blurred gardens, and a general grille pattern that at first resembled the wings of some wounded bird. Evelyn stared at the design for a moment, then she stood further back, suddenly breathless.

'My goodness,' she cried. 'Why, this is the monastery!'

They both reared back and took in the monastery in a glance, and the boy nodded proudly over his impossible creation. Because Evelyn seemed as astounded as a child, the boy softened a little toward her and began lecturing with his wand.

'Here's that door right over there,' he indicated, 'where in the afternoon a lot of people start to go in and out. Then comes the tower down at that end, and around that corner are some big doorways with stone men standing halfway up the wall. And then as soon as you go through these arches here,' he scratched at a few semicircles, 'there are all these gardens running all along this opposite side to the third tower over there. And then the gardens turn the corner and have to go a little off to the side to get by the big bump that's in the middle of this wall here. And then the last tower is right over there and going around it brings us back to where we are now and to this little door right here.'

With a final flourish of his stick, the boy stabbed down at his illustration and accidentally poked the door wide open.

'Oh!'

Evelyn was about to comfort him when she heard the real door swing open and saw a guard dip his head out to test the winter's air.

'I'll fix it,' the boy said.

As deftly as a surgeon, he closed it up again, and the guard retreated into the warmth of his post.

'That's a neat trick,' Evelyn observed. 'How did you do it?'

The boy waved the question aside.

'Do you like my palace?' he asked her as he returned to his work.

'Oh, I do. Very much.'

'It's not quite finished yet. I need to add some more closets and curtains and other places to hide.'

'How long have you been working on it?' she wanted to know.

'Since last night.'

'But it was still storming last night.'

'I know.'

'And it was dark,' Evelyn persisted.

The boy stopped fussing with his sketch and stood up to face the stranger who miraculously spoke his own language.

'No, it wasn't. It was just dirty out. Because of the moon.'

Evelyn frowned down at him out of adult ignorance.

'Haven't you ever seen the moon,' he asked her, 'when most of its face is buried in soot? It's all gray or black, like the ground gets around a chimney. You can still see it, but it's hard, the same way wire is hard to see in the dark. It's because the blizzards up there haven't started yet and most of the moon's land is still bare and flat. But then, in a couple of weeks, more will start to fall up there just like it does down here, and then the whole moon will change. You'll see,' the boy concluded with a confident nod. 'It happens over and over all the time. You should really try to notice such things better. Then you can do more.'

'I'll try,' she promised.

'*Gut genug*,' he said, pleased.

Standing tall, Evelyn studied the boy as he resumed his icy sculpturing. It suddenly occurred to her that she had no idea how old he might be. She had been an only child herself, with few friends, and she had never been married, so she knew next to nothing about children and their special lives. This boy kneeling before her was short, with a poorly fed body and weak white skin, and in her eyes he might just as easily have been nine or ten as twelve. His simple honesty charmed her, while the open trust he gave her even before she had earned it was the first she had seen in years. But such total innocence worried her a little, and now she tried to correct the boy's misunderstanding of the moon and its regular phases.

'But there's no snow up on the moon,' she informed him.

'Not yet,' he answered patiently. 'I told you, it takes time to pile up high enough so we can see it from way down here.'

'But I don't think there's any weather up there at all.'

'Well, that's just because the moon is still too near to the sun. Once it goes its own way, then you'll see it grow colder and whiter. Just like around here,' he added, swiveling his bird head about and inviting her to compare.

Evelyn looked with him at the plain vellum of the courtyard, whiter than blindness, and she noted the increasing numbers of tourists and locals who were coming to admire the monastery in its new finery. None of them seemed to wonder at the dark child scrabbling across the ground like a crab and the woman who stood over him as if she were tending some plant that was threatened by an early frost. In fact, some of the town's oldest citizens even orbited past to nod over his efforts or bless him with a flurried gesture in the air. If he were the troublemaker everyone was talking about, he was obviously known and respected by most of the townspeople, though a few did regard him with the kind of superstitious dread that they usually reserved for gypsies and escaped prisoners.

As the boy sat back for perspective, the woman bowed down to bring their faces closer together.

'What's your name?' she asked him.

'Herschel.'

'Herschel What?'

He was suddenly guarded. 'Just Herschel.'

'Mine's just Evelyn,' she conceded.

'Eva?' he said, giving it an extra European syllable.

'If you like.' She peered down at the facsimile once again and said, 'This is really very good. You must love drawing.'

'More than anything.'

'It's such hard work,' Evelyn observed. 'Why do you like it so much? Most kids your age would rather make angels or fortresses or igloos. I know I did.'

The boy pondered for a moment as he sharpened a corner.

'I think because it's so clear,' he finally said. 'The world is always so blurry and hard to make out, like when you look out at things in moonlight or through a curtain. They don't have any edges, so sometimes you can't really tell if they are there or not. Do you know what I mean?'

'I think so,' the woman said uncertainly.

'But when you draw a line, you know where it's going to end up even before it gets there. You even get to point it where you want it to go. It's straight and fine,' the boy ended in a quiet voice, 'like a dark stream running out between piled drifts. You can see where you are when you draw, and you don't have to wonder what might come next. And even when you look back at where you've been, everything is still right where you left it, right where it should be.'

He had spoken so gravely that Evelyn looked down at him to see if he were pouting or crying, but his face was as untroubled as if he were asleep.

'Don't you ever curve your lines?' she asked, checking over his layout of the monastery and finding none.

'Never.' He looked offended. 'If I bent even one of them, I would never be able to know where it might lead or what all of them might make together. And where would I be then?'

Evelyn asked him what else he liked to draw.

'Oh, I like to draw trees and houses and streets and chairs and stuff like that. But mostly I like to make maps of big places so that I can look down at them when I'm done almost as if I were a bird flying over.'

'Or,' the woman suggested, 'the man in the moon.'

Now Evelyn had made a friend for life.

'The snowman in the moon, you mean.'

'The snowman,' she agreed.

She looked up and considered the clouds gathering over the distant hills.

'I hope you don't lose all your hard work,' she said. 'There might be more storms coming in tonight.'

'If I do,' he said, 'I'll just have to draw it all over again. That's easy.'

'Do you think you could do it the same?' she asked.

'I have the outline already. Look.'

The boy motioned her to bend down, and he erased a slice of garden to reveal a charcoal sketch on the stones underneath.

'You see, I started this a long time ago because I knew some snow would fall eventually and when it did it would fall onto the lines and start the picture for me from below. It's like when you rub a pencil or a piece of dirt across a paper on a person's face when he's sleeping. You get a picture of what he looks like. It's never the same as a real photograph, but here at least no one can take it away from you and beat you for doing it,' he said, neatly repairing the wet smear he had made and concentrating on his work again.

'Don't you ever draw people?' Evelyn asked him a bit later, after they had exchanged opinions about winter for a while.

'Not usually,' he said. 'They always move around too much.'

'What about your parents? They might like it if you made a portrait of them.'

'They're gone.'

The war, Evelyn thought. She was sorry.

'Then what about brothers or sisters or friends? Other kids your own age?'

'There aren't any.'

'I know,' she sympathized. 'I'm new here myself.'

'That's all right.'

'Well,' she suggested, 'you could always draw yourself.'

'I do. I did. You, too. We're right here. Can't you see?'

He pointed and she looked, and there in the small courtyard just outside the miniature building stood two stick figures, one short and one tall.

'Should I wave at us?' Evelyn laughed.

'If you want to,' the boy said happily.

She did, and a swirl of flakes waved back at them, and then the morning gray grew lighter all around them.

For the next few minutes, in the bright cold and bright air, the two of them worked comfortably together. The boy was still as reserved and hidden as before, and the woman was still wrapped up in her heavy coat, but they met somewhere over the diagram as if they were two relations at a reunion, idly pruning a winter bush in a white garden. Only here all their branches were ice.

The boy added some finishing touches to his work, then stood up and suddenly reached out for Evelyn's hand.

'Let's go for a walk,' he said.

'Well, I suppose so,' she hung back, 'but not for very long. I still have a bus to catch. Where do you want to go? Home?'

'No,' he shook his head. 'Just around.'

The woman surrendered her hand reluctantly, never having had such a frozen monkey's paw in hers before. As eagerly as a guide, the boy tugged her across his completed design, and she cried out in horror as her foot crashed through a smooth wall.

'Oh, I'm so sorry!'

'Don't worry,' Herschel said. 'We'll fix it later.'

They set out, scuffling across the courtyards to circle the palace anti-clockwise as the building's shadow crawled beneath their feet and the surrounding village grew livelier in the warmer air. This was the same tour Evelyn had just finished making by herself, but now the child added a fresher, keener pair of eyes to hers. Soon, she learned how to estimate the height of turrets by the edges of their shadows on the ground and how to measure the curves of the arches by sighting over the boy's lifted fist. In no time, Evelyn had picked up some of his passion for exactness, and for his part he seemed to enjoy having someone he could help to see things as precisely as he did. The awkwardness between two strangers in a foreign town soon settled like drifts into a common peacefulness between them, until even talking became unnecessary to tell each other what they should both look at next.

Rounding the third tower, they passed through the dust of a collapsed wall and then came back to where they had started. Next to her, the woman sensed a feeble trembling similar to what she sometimes felt upon waking from an afternoon nap.

'You're shivering. Are you cold?'

'A little,' the boy answered.

'You should have something hot to drink.'

'Wait, I have to fix this first.'

Scooping chips of ice with his bare hands, Herschel patched the wall the woman had kicked down, then he pointed helpfully at a storefront across the street.

'They have really good hot chocolate in there. You could dry your feet and your coat. You don't want to catch cold, you know.'

She hesitated, but he was already pulling her across the way as if he were running out of time to save her from freezing, and she had to go along.

The bar was overheated with an early crowd of locals warming themselves over brandies, but Evelyn and the boy claimed a table against the wet window and ordered two hot chocolates. As they wordlessly slurped up the weak brown water, they warmed their hands on their thick mugs and watched the townsfolk circling the monastery like arteries about a bone. The quicksilver white of the road outside reflected a faint blue into the bar that made them too sleepy to talk much, and for a time they sat restfully together between the hot center of the bar and the refreshing silence of the cold out in the street. The warped wood of their table felt old and human under their melting hands.

Evelyn finished first, then searched through her pockets

for a cigarette, but found nothing and was about to ask a waiter.

'I'll do it,' the boy offered.

He snatched yesterday's newspaper from an adjacent chair and tore off a corner. Then, after squeezing out tobacco from some of the ends in the ashtray, he rolled a tube and licked it shut with a tongue still sticky from chocolate. He even lit it for her with a borrowed match.

'You're pretty good at that, Herschel. You aren't a smoker, are you, by any chance?'

'Not much.'

'So where did you learn to do that so well?'

'I used to do it for my father.'

'What happened to your father?' Evelyn asked as she smoked and he carefully watched his good work turning to ash.

'I told you before,' he said casually. 'He's gone.'

'Your mother, too?'

'Her, too.'

'You must miss them a lot,' Evelyn said with feeling.

'I do,' he said. 'But people come and go,' he added, with a shrug that seemed to be his favorite gesture. 'You can't start missing anybody too much or, when they leave you, it hurts too much for you to get over it. It's easier just to think about what color they were when you saw them last.'

'What color?' Evelyn was puzzled.

He nodded. 'Some of us are snow, white or gray according to how much time has passed us by. Some are brown, just like trees. Some are burnt red and look like bricks, and their skin is rough like frozen dirt. It always helps to notice people's colors, and then when they disappear – like they always do – at least you have some pretty shades to remember them by. Like sunsets.'

She gazed at the face that was now aged by seriousness, and observed aloud that most people stay with their loved ones as long as they possibly can, but sometimes circumstances win out.

'People are smoke,' Herschel maintained as the room began to fill with the moving phantoms of cigarettes and cigars. 'They're like the soot on the moon. It takes a lot to cover their tracks once they're gone, but it can happen overnight, and then in the morning you find new people in their places, and you just have to learn to accept them as if nothing has changed.'

As they talked, the child kept glancing out the window as if he were willing the curious and the sun away from his drawing in the blank courtyard across the street. The village grew more and more busy with all the buried excitement that sometimes overcomes survivors, children ricocheting from frozen puddles to icicles as their parents desperately hunted for the tracks they left behind. But no one seemed to be interested in the clear blueprint in the shadow of the monastery, and as far as the two friends could see from a distance, Herschel's masterpiece lay as isolated as if it really had been carved on the dusty surface of the moon.

When Evelyn finally had the boy's attention again, she tried to learn a little more about him.

'You're not from here, are you?' she said. 'I mean, you must be from somewhere where you learned to speak German so well. I'm sure we're the only two people in Escorial who can do that, *nicht wahr*?'

'But I can speak lots of languages,' he declared proudly and began bending back his fingers, one by one. 'Listen. Snow; *neige, nieve, nipha, Schnee, snieg . . .*'

'Still,' Evelyn interrupted him, 'you don't look much like a Spaniard. Where were you born? Germany? Austria? Switzerland?'

'I don't know,' he answered.

'You mean you don't remember.'

'Not very well. I was little,' he said simply.

'But,' Evelyn pressed on, 'you must have someone in Escorial who looks after you. A relative, a brother or sister, a friend?'

'Yes, I do.'

'Who?' she asked hopefully.

He pushed his empty cup toward her and raised his eyebrows.

'You,' he said.

She grimaced at the sweet, clever face and the sly teeth, and remembered her bus.

'But I'm afraid I'm not going to be around here much longer. Who's going to take care of you then? You?'

'No. Someone else,' he said. 'Everyone always takes care of everyone else, Eva. You should know that by now.'

'Maybe on the moon,' the woman muttered unhappily.

'No. Everywhere.'

Evelyn looked across at him and pitied his innocence.

'But I have to go in a little while,' she told him. 'Really, Herschel, even if I didn't want to. I do have to go.'

'Go where?' the boy asked.

'Back to America. I have to get back for the holidays. There are people waiting for me back home, and I wouldn't want them to start worrying about me if I don't show up.'

'Who? Your little boy or little girl?' he wondered.

Something in the street caught Evelyn's eye and turned her face away from his for a moment.

'No. Just people.'

'Then stay here for a while,' Herschel said, getting excited by the thought. 'If it really does storm again tonight, who knows how wonderful everything will look tomorrow? We could start a new drawing this afternoon, me and you. I could teach you how.'

'I really can't . . .'

But Evelyn looked into the empty cup and at Herschel's brown moustache and ordered him another hot chocolate if only to see some of his momentary disappointment fade away. Then they sat and talked some more of winter, about the boy's love of its textures and cold, and of Evelyn's own fantastic Wisconsin memories of drifts as high as barns and toboggan runs down the parlor stairs at dawn. They told tales to one another, legends that even they knew could never be true in this world, and each of them believed everything.

When Herschel was finished with his chocolate, Evelyn left a half-peseta tip on a white saucer and casually began working her chair away from the table.

'Are you ready, Herschel?'

'What?'

'Are you ready to go? I could walk you home. If we hurry . . .' But she had lost him to the window again. 'Herschel? Is there something wrong out there?'

Evelyn follows his stare across the street to the courtyard, and she sees what he sees. The yard is still preserved silver and crisp, and the tourists still seem to prefer the gray stones over their heads to the glaze beneath their feet. But now a new detail has been added. Now a rare white car has stopped at the curb, and a man and a girl have climbed out onto the boulevard. The man is dark and official, he squares his shoulders and aligns his hands across the girl's back, while she is as slim as shadow and bends in a wind that stirs her alone. She is dressed in a black cloak, the flapping wings of a raven, her hair is a boy's hair, and she turns helplessly in the man's hands; he turns her hideously from side to side as they search the courtyard from the dry street for any signs of secret movement. They see nothing but white, and the man shows his anger by folding the girl up in her cloak as if she were a folding ladder and doubling her back into the car with all the finality of a bureaucrat slipping a rejected petition through a slot. He taps the driver into motion, and Evelyn sees their car speed off in a shower of fragmented glass, and then a fresh cloud of flakes descends onto their blackened tracks as if to hide them for ever . . .

When she turned back to the boy across from her, she found a look of despair in his eyes, shards of frosted glass. He saw that she really meant to leave, so he stood up and let fall two unspoken words.

Hide me.

No one else heard him. Even Evelyn couldn't be sure he had spoken, but she had seen his bud mouth weaken and break.

I can't.

She stepped away from her chair, away.

Hide me.

She looked at the boy. Then outside. Then away. Then at all her expectations left to rust. And she felt a door somewhere just behind her breastbone quietly shut and lock itself without a key.

I'm sorry. I can't.

Then she turned and flew out of the door, leaving him alone in the male fog of the bar. And as she climbed frantically up toward the bus station, she thought how lucky she was to be here in such a quaint mountain village on such a lovely winter's day with only a pleasant ride down the mountain to look forward to. And all the time, over her head, a plainer air and a rounder sun made the sky seem bottomless, while slivers of mirrors fell across her eyes in spicules of delicate, surgical crystal.

It was the boy's fever that made her miss her bus. It was unlike any fever Evelyn had ever seen, mysterious and subtle, lying low until just that hour in the afternoon when escapes to Madrid were scheduled, and then flaming up into the boy's face like a physical humiliation. In her room at the hotel, alone with him and arguing that he simply could not stay with her, she had watched the fever overcome him like a fit of drowsiness, swaying him backward onto her bed and coinciding perfectly with her picking her luggage off the floor. Then she knew that she was trapped because she was not about to leave him delirious and alone and, after the fear he had shown earlier in the day, she sensed that some of the people in the village should probably not be told where he was. So she put her suitcase back down at the foot of the bed and did what she could for the sick child, wondering uneasily if this might not have been what Herschel had been planning all along.

He had followed her from the bar, of course, although it was not until she had checked in at the bus station and walked almost back to the hotel that she had noticed his smaller shadow caught on the hem of her skirt. She had done her best to ignore him, until a blue storefront window had shown her his maddening patience, and then she had tried to plead with him to go back to whoever might be waiting for him to come home. Nothing had worked, not threats or bargains, and she had finally had to start running toward the hotel door. She might have made it, too, if the boy hadn't cried out, 'Mama!' after her in every tongue he knew, his arms reaching after her and his voice trembling, until the scowls of passersby persuaded her to hide him behind her through the door and all the way up into her room.

Once there, the boy's stomach had begun making the crawling sounds of a mouse across a hollow floor, and Evelyn had gone down to beg some scraps from the napping maid. These had seemed to be enough to carry him through most of the afternoon, along with one or two sips of stolen water, but as soon as the woman had decided to leave, the fever had held her back and made the room feel cold and windy. She didn't know much about children, but she could see that the fever was real, so real that she had led the boy at the end of the day to the window to cool off his forehead against the glass. It was the only remedy she could remember from the fevers of her own childhood, when her mother would wipe the frost off a window with a cloth and lay it across her face, as if some of the winter's crust could help cool the fire within.

At the window, rubbing his face across it as if it were an inkpad, the boy had suddenly stopped and pointed out across the roofed village toward the darkening horizon.

'There it is again, Eva. Just like I told you. And it still looks ashy.'

Rising now, the waxing crescent of the moon rode silently on a linear cloud across the purple of the sky, its right edge white and the unlit portion gray and black and silver with earthshine.

'It's the new moon with the old moon in her lap,' the woman said.

'No.' The boy frosted the window with his breath. 'It's just the start of another winter.'

Before she led him back to bed, Herschel had etched a circle on the window's rime at the level of the moon in the sky. Then he had insisted on lying down only in the position where the two dim rings would fit together, and he had finally fallen asleep gazing through their lenses into the night that was promising even more flurries and a deeper freeze. Evelyn had watched over him in the dark, regularly pressing her forehead against his or puffing cool air across his face, until the corridor outside her room began to grow loud with hunger for the typically late Spanish dinner. Then she hurried to make an appearance in the dining room before some other guest came up to find her, locking the door behind her more carefully than any door she had ever locked before.

Tonight's dinner was quicker and quieter, partly because of the deeper frost and partly because the woman from Barcelona was away, embittering a relative. Evelyn said even less than she had the night before, confiding only that her friend in Madrid still had things to do and, anyway, she herself had plenty of Christmas shopping left. The table reviewed most of the old subjects, then swerved off into a discussion of the causes of the war that they had finally left behind them. Because of today's date, some asked Evelyn if many Americans still thought the memory of Pearl Harbor would live for ever, but she seemed too distracted to have a thought to spare. Tonight, most of her mind was taken up with the meager bread and cheese, as her hands were with shielding coughs and dropping food repeatedly into the folds of her gray dress. After a half hour, she excused herself, saying she felt feverish, and forcefully refused Martin Dearing's hopes of helping her all the way up to her room. She finally stalked out, holding the front of her clumsy skirt in her hands as if she were a farmgirl sneaking contraband crumbs across a barnyard to her pet calf.

Evelyn hated to wake the boy, but she was worried about his fever and the papery withering of his arms and legs. Yet when she got back to the room, she found him already awake, his eyes white in the dark as they stared through the ring on the glass that had captured the moon.

'Why didn't you turn the light on, Herschel?'

'I can't.'

Evelyn looked at the switch high on the wall.

'Oh, I understand. But I think it would have been all right. No one would have noticed. They're all downstairs eating.'

He repeated that he couldn't, his voice slurred by the heat of his fever, so she left the lights off to save his eyes.

'I've brought you something. It isn't much, but you need to keep up your strength. Here.'

He took the bread, but he hesitated over the pieces.

'What's wrong?'

'I could use these,' he said vaguely, 'for gloves.'

'What?' His German must have confused her. 'No, go ahead and eat. I can always sneak you up some more.'

They sat together on the bed while the boy gnawed at the dry food and Evelyn kept checking his temperature with her cheek. Out in the night sky, the slice of moon still hung over the low hills leading down into the plains, and the rippling waters of the tiled rooftops with their white-caps seemed to lead off into mid-air. The two on the bed spoke in whispers, accidental and private thoughts on winter and the moon and the frost flowers glowing on the pane. As the crescent gradually dissolved the sky in a wash of mercury and the mountain stars stood taller, a fine gauze of illumination fell across the boy's hands like cream, furring him with night's light, until finally sleep overtook him again as water wears away at a stone. It cost the woman whole minutes to fold over a corner of the blanket across his waist, and she took even longer to rest her hands more lightly than cloth on his tiny shoulders. Then she lay down beside him and watched through the circle on the window the shadows of the horse plowing its way through the white fields on the moon.

But even sight has weight. In his sleep, the boy could feel her eyes on him, and he folded himself away from her like a slat of wood. To keep him asleep and warm, the woman shut her eyes and curled her body behind his in a faint crescent, and in her lap he finally calmed down and began to snore childishly. Evelyn went to sleep, too, with the memory of the real moon still hanging like a medal in the boy's fingernail tracing on the black window. And as she slept, she dreamed.

She dreamed that she lay down in a bank that was sculpted all around her like sheets or moonlight. The boy was standing next to her, shaping the cold, granular fabric in his hands, then backing toward a red barn that stood behind him. Beyond, a simple village was still going about its winter business, the streets liquid and the yards before the kitchen chimneys smoking merrily. Up in the morning air, suspended as if in glass, two crescent moons floated in perfect alignment and shed a gray dust over everything beneath them so that even the people and the people's actions were gray.

She lay naked on the earth, except for a torn striped shirt, and now the boy covered her tenderly as a circle of women came to take her away. They lifted her upward, calling her Ester and then Rifka, and they carried her through the village, past the closed windows, each with its etchings of buildings and farmlands. They brought her at last to a place of steam and foul smells and laid her where she heard weeping and voices telling stories. And then the boy leaned forward and began to tell her of birches made from frost, and then he closed her eyes with a touch of his white twig fingers.

He sleeptalked in her sleep of winters in the village when a stranger would come walking backwards down the street, intent on seeing only what had been left behind. And he told her news of a world cool and faraway like ice, of mountains and paradises like sugar, of men on fire and of women with wings in their mouths. As he whispered, she could see beyond him the wet planks and the wet windows of the town flowering with new drawings, until the weight of the lines grew to be too much, and the windows shattered under the burden of remembering too much at once. The children and the parents pictured on them broke inward, and they stood uncertainly in the gray moonlight, gray themselves and as unreal as crystals frozen in the air. They surged forward toward where she lay back in cold, and she sobbed and begged not to be taken away, she had no strength to give, she could not bear their pale eyes. But then the boy stood beside her again, sprinkling flakes of paraffin and tobacco around to distract the dogs, and he promised her that she could sleep again, because although brick and wood were too sharp to hold, the shadows of trees were soft, softer than life itself, and all our lovely memories of snow and death are round . . .

Evelyn woke just before dawn. The boy lay at her side again, no longer flushed, but warm as breath. The drawn moon still hung in its circle, and the etching of the village on the window still rode through the changing sky without a streak. The room felt hot and lighter, as if the child's healthier sleep had somehow washed the air clean and turned the musty smells of rugs and iron into a scent from a boy's skin. The frozen hotel lay about them as quiet and whole as a nut, and the weather outside the window shone calm and white, ready again for its daily cycle.

Only once more did Herschel squirm half-awake to ask when he could drink hot chocolate again, and Evelyn said, *'Morgen früh,'* tomorrow morning. Then, for some reason that she could not know, she had to lie back helplessly and listen to him weeping himself to sleep as if his wintry heart would break.

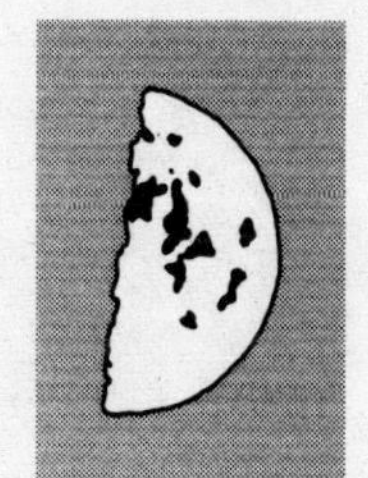

Evelyn was the first one down for the simple breakfast, but most of the rest of the hotel's guests appeared before she was able to finish and go. As always, the group congregated around a table by a window, the latecomers pulling chairs from nearby tables to add places for themselves. By the time Evelyn had eaten the bread and drunk the warm milk colored with last night's coffee grounds, the Englishman was sitting on her left and the historian from Toledo on her right, although the Spaniard had politely allowed a chair to remain empty between them. Everyone else seemed to avoid that place, embarrassing Evelyn, and until the end of the breakfast it stayed vacant, as if one more companion were always just about to arrive, but never did.

This morning, after a night of lighter snow, everyone seemed to be resigned to the season's having settled in for good.

'Why fight it?' the unshaven proprietor remarked. 'We might as well get used to trudging through all this muck until the end of the month or even into the New Year. At least the little ones should enjoy it.'

'Our *Kinder* back home wouldn't know what to do without it,' the old Swiss gentleman smiled, and his wife Frau Heuter cheerily agreed that nothing could be more lovely than the crust hanging over the edge of a chalet roof.

'It's so strange-looking,' the maid observed. 'Like flour.'

'Like powdered sugar,' one of the guests added.

'Or a landscape from some other world.'

'Well, I still think it's all a bother,' said the proprietor again, not to be defeated in his own dining room. 'It makes such a mess of the roads and the walkways.'

'My son would give an eye from his face for such a wonderful playground.' At this Antonio protested, but his mother babbled on: 'Where do you think he went on his last vacation with his friends but up into the Pyrenees? At his age, too! Running uselessly around like a pack of polar bears. I can't imagine what such young boys could find to do with themselves way up there.'

'Nothing good, I'll bet,' the Englishman said with a wicked grin meant for Evelyn alone.

'Stop it,' the historian said as Antonio turned red in the face. 'You're making him melt.'

'Perhaps he's even more naughty than any of us can imagine,' Herr Heuter murmured.

Staring hard at him, Antonio Liot assured everyone that none of his pleasure excursions had the least impropriety about them. 'My friends and I enjoy the mountain passes, that's all.'

'This is nothing compared to Wisconsin,' Evelyn mentioned, to save him from further discomfort.

'So it snows a lot where you live?' Antonio asked her.

'It seems like all the time.'

'Then you must be used to this.'

'How could anyone get used to this?' someone else groaned.

'Is it pretty cold over there, too?'

Evelyn shivered. 'Oh, very. Sometimes it gets so cold that the tires of cars can barely turn. And when you walk outside, your nose gets pinched closed just by the frost in the air. Icicles used to form on my father's moustache, and he would let me break them off, one by one.'

'I've seen them do that up in Norway,' the historian said.

'I've always liked that when it's happened to me,' the older man from Switzerland chuckled, and he made a crackling motion with a hand over his mouth.

'That's too much winter for me,' one voice protested, while most of the others hummed in agreement.

'It has its own beauty,' Evelyn said thoughtfully. 'There's a special color to it and a special shape, and even the cold has its own personality in a way. It's almost as if you could get to know it the way you get to know a person. Better, maybe.'

Such a morning's burst of lyricism embarrassed her, and she retreated behind her plate as some of the other guests smiled at the softer change the weather had caused in the visitor. For some few minutes more, the conversation focused on climate in general, until Martin Dearing had clearly had enough.

'Samuel Johnson said that the only man who wouldn't already know about the weather is a man in a cave or in jail.' He turned toward Evelyn who was just finishing her coffee. 'I'd much rather hear about Miss Winter's new plans. It seems terribly impulsive of you to change your schedule so drastically. Are you thinking of missing all the buses and staying in Escorial permanently?'

'You should,' the proprietor said. 'There are worse places.'

'No,' Evelyn replied, 'I guess I just grew tired of running around from place to place in the past year or so. My time is my own now. What's the rush? Maybe I'll take the long way home. I've got no one to take care of now but myself,' she added evenly.

'You must have a very understanding employer,' the maid said – with a hard look at Lorenzo.

'Actually,' Evelyn hesitated, 'I'm between jobs just now. I guess the Depression hit us all pretty hard in the Midwest.'

'I thought you told me,' the Englishman said in an intimate tone, 'that you were keeping that position on hold?'

'On hold, turned down,' the woman shrugged. 'What's the big difference?'

'It should be much better by the time you do get back,' Herr Heuter assured her. 'Wars always have such a tragic way of giving a boost to struggling economies. I sometimes wonder if that might not be why we keep on fighting so many of them.'

'Well,' the historian complained, 'I only wish the same were true for Spain. Neither war seems to have helped us much. Unless you count not being able to trust anybody and not daring to think for ourselves as improvements. And I, for one, don't.'

The room experienced a momentary stillness as the Spaniards and the foreigners alike tried not to voice too loudly any loose, unpatriotic opinions. The proprietor seemed offended by the young man in the messy shirt, as if the historian had taken his secret, while Carlota Liot stared about her frankly, expecting someone to be struck dead for blasphemy.

'Do you have any hopeful prospects?' her son asked Evelyn in a concerned voice.

'A few. My father knows a lot of businessmen who might need an experienced office manager, even though now I'm not so sure if I really want to keep doing what I've been doing all my life.'

'Why not?'

'It's just that I hate to start a new year without having a new start for myself, too. Is that so selfish of me?'

'Of course not,' the Englishman assured her.

The rest of the circle chimed in.

'You should do what you think best. It's your life.'

'I think,' the historian said, 'we could all use a new start every once in a while. Especially in these times.'

The diplomat joined his hands across his belly and told her not to hurry. 'You youngsters are always rushing after tomorrow, when tomorrow always comes anyway. *Ohne Hast, aber ohne Rast* – that's what Goethe said. And that should be the smart way for all of us to live, don't you think?'

Evelyn thanked Herr Heuter in German, and the old Swiss was delighted to hear her speak it. They conversed separately as the others ate their slices of bread dipped in olive oil or wiped the milk froth from their lips and wished there were more. Then some of the men lit cigars, and the winter window glared with indirect light, and the women admired the perfumed lace on Señora Liot's sleeve that had come all the way from Barcelona.

'Even in these nightmarish times,' Carlota Liot sighed, 'a civilized person has to stay civilized. It takes a lot of work to stay clean and proper, but I wouldn't compromise for worlds.'

She waved her arm over the table at everyone, and the guests pecked forward like chickens for a sniff, but Evelyn was suddenly distracted by the shadow of an arm reaching for her coffee cup.

'Do you want something?' she asked, turning toward the historian, but Julio was facing the other way, and Evelyn saw only the deep emptiness of the chair beside her.

She asked the clattering maid if there was any hot chocolate in the kitchen.

'I could make some,' Lulú said unwillingly.

'For me to take up to my room?'

'Lorenzo?'

The proprietor signaled with his head for the maid to see to it, and then he regarded Evelyn, sincerely hoping that everything would work out for her once she got back home.

'I had a daughter who would have been your age if she'd survived the Battle of Madrid,' he said grimly. 'Take my advice. Don't let your life go by without you. None of us gets any other life than this one, and it's a shame if you don't make it happen the way you want it to, the way it should.'

'No other life?' The woman from Bern came alive, her wedge-shaped face turning violet. 'Then what about heaven and hell?'

'We've already been through hell,' he said. 'And our priest told me that my Rosita wouldn't be allowed in heaven because she fought against Franco and the Church. I told him to choke on his goddamned paradise. I don't want any part of it without Rosita.'

The gray window shivered with the man's sudden fury, and the guests all busied themselves over their breakfasts. Only the American woman glanced at the proprietor with understanding.

'I'm sorry,' Evelyn said. 'But life's not always that easy, is it?'

'It's not supposed to be easy, *chica*. It's life.'

'What I mean is that sometimes there's not much we can do to stop things from getting away from us. It's like an avalanche – is that how you say it?' She groped for the Spanish. 'Once it starts rolling, once you make your first mistake or even just your first real decision, there's not much that you can do after that. Even God, they say, can't change the past.'

Lorenzo relented a bit and sighed. 'Still, God must love us a little for all that.'

'How do you know?' Herr Heuter said skeptically. 'Because of *Schadenfreude* – the joy we take in the pain of others? But how can you call that love?'

'Because,' Lorenzo answered, 'at least He doesn't force any of us to live it all over again.'

'None of us except His Son,' Frau Heuter corrected him.

'That's right,' the proprietor nodded. 'The crucifixion must have seemed like child's play compared with having a whole second life.'

From the kitchen, a brown scent of chocolate seeped into the dining room on the heatwaves from the oven, and the guests began making some of the insect gestures of straightening their clothes and glancing toward the door that reluctant leavetakings require. In the window beside them, exotic animals and ferns of ice peered jealously through the glass at the orange warmth within, and from the floors above them sounded the groans of a building waking up to a December sun that was too cold to help.

As Evelyn pushed herself back from the table, her right hand fell on the vacant chair beside her, and she winced at the moving heat of its fabric. Then she heard the historian saying, 'Oh, and here I am forgetting today's big news. Have you heard what's happened to our little troublemaker?'

'Who?'

'Do you mean that boy over by the monastery?'

'Our precocious artist?' the Englishman sneered.

'I knew something would—'

'I haven't heard a thing,' Lulú said. 'What about him?'

Julio of Toledo sat forward to hold the guests together with the thrill of tragic rumor.

'Well, it seems he's nothing more than a common criminal.'

'No!'

'Mother of God!'

'That doesn't surprise me,' Carlota Liot said, and then she asked the proprietor, 'Who is he, again?'

'He's the tiny boy who's always scratching around in some of the palace's courtyards,' the historian reminded everyone. 'Well, it turns out that he's disappeared and the police are asking around for him, turning over every stone, looking everywhere.'

'What's he supposed to have done?'

'I'm not sure, but I do know that yesterday they had to pick up his sister and use her to try to find him. Apparently, it didn't work, so now they're searching high and low for him and keeping his sister locked up as bait to lure him out into public again.'

Evelyn returned her hand to the empty chair beside her and asked why.

'I can tell you that,' the proprietor said slowly. 'Everyone in town knows a little of the story, and together we all probably know it all. The poor boy and his sister don't belong here, it's as simple as that. And anyone who doesn't belong gets found out, sooner or later, and taken care of – if you know what I mean.'

'Refugees?' Herr Heuter assumed.

Lorenzo nodded. 'At least, that's what everyone thinks. The children showed up here a few months ago and went to live with a family in an apartment over on Libro Verde Street. Their name is Piña, I think – an old couple with a married daughter and all her family living with them. These two youngsters came from somewhere up north – Germany or Poland, some say – and moved right in. These Piñas are some sort of distant relations, and they'd promised to look after the kids until their parents could come get them. Whether their parents are still alive or are on their way or even know where the children are, who can tell? These days, a lot of people are loose on the road, coming from or going to some other place. Here in Spain, almost every town has at least a few Displaced Persons hanging around, waiting for their lives to get back on track. Madrid knows about most of them, keeps tabs on the worst, and turns a blind eye to the others. That is, they have so far. Up here, we're so far off the beaten track that these strays are just about the only ones we've ever had. Maybe that's why no one here has bothered much about them. Until now, they were just one small reminder of the millions who were waiting for our help through all these years, but who didn't get nearly enough.'

'But what do they want now?' Martin Dearing interjected with bitterness. 'Only to barge into another country that already has its full roster of its own natural-born citizens? That shouldn't earn them much of our sympathy or respect, certainly.'

No one agreed or disagreed, and Herr Heuter only shrugged.

'Are there really so many of them in Spain?' Evelyn asked as quietly as she could.

'Far too many, to my mind,' Carlota Liot maintained. 'Franco should never have replaced Serrano Suñer with Count Francisco. It encouraged too many gypsy parasites to take advantage of our good hospitality. And, needless to say, we should never have remained neutral in the first place,' she accused the Swiss diplomat.

'Whoever said we really were?' her son put in.

'The trouble is,' the historian said, 'their legal situation has always been up in the air, decided by each case. If a refugee had an important sponsor and enough money, he could probably stay in Spain quite a while. If not, he could be detained and, in some cases, deported. It's always been hard to guess which way it was going to go.'

The proprietor added, 'I suppose the civil authorities were just waiting to see if the parents would ever show up to collect them. Now that everything's over and most of the refugees are in the camps or on their way home, there's no reason why these *niños* should be allowed to stay with the family any longer. They're not theirs, after all, and they're not ours either. Besides,' Lorenzo went on reluctantly, 'the Piña clan has always been distrusted in Escorial, ever since some of its members got caught up in political activities during the Civil War. While these children have been living with them, the entire house over there on Libro Verde Street has been watched, infiltrated, and raided. It seems to me that the family would be glad to get rid of anyone who brought that kind of misery to their door.'

'You said the sister was detained,' Evelyn said to Julio and turned to include the proprietor. 'But why should the police have acted now, instead of before? Just because the war is over? What have the children done to deserve that kind of scrutiny now?'

The three who were the most familiar with the town – Lorenzo, Lulú, and Julio – silently conferred for a moment before both men started answering at once.

'The thing is,' the historian began, 'this boy is not quite like any other normal child. He's strange somehow—'

'That's what I meant that night,' Lorenzo addressed Evelyn, 'when I said that the boy gives us all hope. Since he's been here in Escorial, he's worked wonders among us, wonders that even some of our priests think might come close to being true miracles.'

'Satan's miracles, you mean,' Lulú scoffed and stepped away.

'I don't understand.' Evelyn shook her head.

'It's those drawings of his,' Julio interrupted. 'Some folks think he can do things with them – weird, unnatural things . . .'

'People talk,' said Lorenzo. 'And sometimes the talk grows bigger the farther away it gets from the truth. You should know, Señorita Winter, that in his time here among us, the boy has been up and down almost every street in our small village. I've never seen him in action myself, but from what I've heard, he's always left behind little mementoes of his visits on the sidewalks, on the walls, sometimes even on the coats of the townspeople or the jackets of the soldiers when they're not looking.'

'Mementoes?' someone echoed.

'Drawings,' the historian repeated. 'I've seen some of them, both around the monastery and near the shops and houses. Sketches of empty streets, layouts of buildings lost during the war, whole designs of towns that are probably no more. They're really quite remarkable in their conception and execution. They'll appear with no warning in the strangest places – in the mud in the gutter, on the window of an abandoned apartment, in the ashes at the back of a bakery or a tinsmith. Few of them seem to include people, only the places where people used to go to enjoy themselves in times of peace. I hear that no one can really identify the places with any certainty, but the pictures are general enough to belong to everyone at once. Perhaps that's his secret,' Julio mused softly. 'The boy knows instinctively that he'll move the most people with scenes that no one could call exclusively his own, but which none of us could ever fail to recognize.'

A random discussion erupted about various artists throughout Europe, but Evelyn hurried the conversation back to Herschel by asking why a mere boy's doodles should ever affect anyone.

'The funny thing is,' Lorenzo spoke quietly, 'from what I've heard people saying, they think his drawings can change things in the town. If some woman's husband is being unfaithful to her, one of the boy's illustrations might appear in her garden soil, showing the other woman getting on a train. Then, the next day, the wife will find her husband back in his own bed again. Lost heirlooms have been found in walls, even Death itself has been held off for an extra month or so by a few lines on a frosty doorstep. Or so people say. There have been more unexplained windfalls in Escorial since that child got here than since the days of Santa Teresa. I myself,' he added with sorrow, 'once thought of asking him if he could let me have one more glimpse of my Rosita. But, no, I expect it's all just talk – and, anyway, one such loss in a man's lifetime is more than enough. More than enough.'

A gray pain overcame him, and it took him a minute to return to the table and his guests.

'Still,' he had to concede, 'the boy has been a godsend for this town, no matter how suspicious the police and the churchmen might be. His sketches remind us of what we had before the Civil War, before Franco took it all away from us – the joy, the freedom to be who we were. At the end of such dark years, the boy's drawings tell us how it used to be before we forgot what it means to be human.'

'But why in the world should that make him a troublemaker?' Evelyn said to Lorenzo. 'I should think that everyone would want to keep such a special treasure around as long as possible.'

'You don't know yet what Spain's become in the past five or six years,' he told Evelyn, defying Lulú and the watching walls to keep him from telling the truth. 'Strange, awful things take place for absolutely no reason at all. Decent people disappear, and no word of explanation is ever given. Orders come down from above, and even those who pass them along have no idea why they're doing what they do. A man can be living for years on the best of terms with the government and the police – like these children in Escorial – and suddenly he'll find himself in a prison or worse, and no one will ever tell anyone why. This is what goes on in Spain all the time now. Sometimes you can't even be sure if you'll make it across the street without vanishing from sight. And your family will live on for years and never even know that your bones have been broken and buried under the street right in front of your own home. It's insane, I swear. And so sad, especially for the innocent children.

'In a way,' he concluded, wagging his rough head in anguish, 'our daily lives have become supernatural. When nothing makes sense, everything that happens is magic. A woman gets lost in an alley and is never seen again. A man talks in his sleep and is found strangled in a field with his bedclothes around his throat. The way everything is now, it's no wonder that the boy and his drawings are seen as a curse to some and a blessing to others.'

The proprietor's gloom infected the whole table, while even Lulú became quiet and morose, remembering something that she had not yet been able to forget. Herr Heuter muttered a few comments that meant little or nothing, and the rest of the table brooded separately over their own homelands and the changes that might be waiting for them there.

As for Evelyn, she was staring at a dribble of liquid on the table top in front of the empty chair, at its dripping movements and the copy of her room upstairs that was beginning to shape itself . . .

'There's something more,' Antonio Liot said after a lengthy pause. 'I was having a drink down in a bar when I overheard talk of a stranger who came to Escorial in the last few days and made contact with this girl whom the police have picked up. Apparently, this newcomer is some kind of subversive, an outside agitator, even a Communist or radical whom the authorities in Madrid have followed from town to town. Once someone learned that the girl had met up with this anarchist, I suppose the police in the capital forced the police here in town to work harder on a problem that should have been solved long ago. That's usually the way it works, isn't it?' the young man asked his elders. 'No one does anything really evil until someone else tells him how much good it will do.'

'So what's going to happen to them now?' Evelyn asked before the table could splinter aimlessly apart.

'Who knows? The police have the girl, and eventually the boy will be found, too,' the historian said. 'Escorial isn't that big a town. They might even be keeping her in the hopes that she can lure her brother out of hiding. They do that sometimes.'

'And then?'

No one had any answers, or none anyone dared to say aloud.

'Can't they keep on at the same place they've been living in?' Martin Dearing spoke up. He had noticed the

American woman frowning his way before, and now he tried to redeem himself in her sight, but she was not looking. The empty chair beside her had her attention now, as she braced herself on its frame and leaned eagerly across it.

'What would happen,' Evelyn began, 'if they *don't* find this boy, but they still have his sister? What would they do to her?'

'That's hard to say,' Julio declared. 'But I doubt if she'd ever be allowed to stay here alone. The children would just have to be broken up for good.'

'Usually,' the proprietor explained, 'they're put into some hospice or orphanage and then pretty much forgotten. I even heard of one girl who, when her parents finally did come to claim her, refused to go with them. The nuns,' he added bitterly, 'have ways of keeping their own.'

'But I've heard talk of worse,' the historian whispered, his voice a ghost.

'What?' cried Lorenzo. 'Deportation?'

'Worse.'

'Not imprisonment!' Lulú objected. 'Surely not of children!'

'Worse . . .'

A quarreling sound from the kitchen hurried the maid to her feet, and in a moment she brought back a steaming cup of chocolate and set it in front of the vacant chair. Evelyn turned the cup so that she could hook a finger through the handle, but she delayed picking it up and taking it upstairs. She sat feeling the warmth seeping through the porcelain and into her hand as if someone had not yet let go of it, and she felt something loosen within her.

'That's impossible,' Evelyn said. 'They're only children.'

'Worse has happened,' Herr Heuter consoled her. 'Much worse. And it will happen again. These are dark days for us all, my friends, as the world tries to pull itself back together. Has any of you ever seen a late flower blasted by the winter's cold, how its petals curl up and stiffen and then fall? Now how could a flower like that ever be put back together again, unless you could run Time itself backward?' The old man rumbled deep in his chest, and his silent wife put her hand on his arm. 'After such a nightmare as we have all lived through, none of us should expect to sleep well again for a long, long time.'

Gradually, now that breakfast was over and the day starting, the guests broke apart from the table and scattered into smaller groups to move upstairs or out the front door. Evelyn hung back, blowing across the hot drink to suggest that she was still in no hurry, that she wanted to dawdle alone with her warming cup. The historian from Toledo left with the hotel proprietor, both caught up in social observations that would waste most of their day and lead nowhere. The Englishman, after murmuring vaguely about some restaurant down the street, eventually trickled away, helpless before the American woman's moody distraction. He felt that he understood her today even less than he had before, and he asked himself in despair what he must have done to deserve such inward and unhappy women.

In a few minutes, Evelyn climbed upstairs, the cup of hot chocolate still in her hand. As she passed a closed door, she heard the woman from Barcelona telling her son what everyone downstairs had obviously overlooked.

'And what if the parents won't be coming for them,' she said spitefully, 'not because they're dead or worse, but because they just don't want the little brats anymore?

Years change people, I say, sometimes so much that not even their own loved ones can say who they are. What would happen to their little runaways then?

'And isn't it time,' her voice rasped on as Evelyn retreated down the hallway, 'for some sons to be leaving early for home and not spending any more time in cheap bars? If I ever catch you—'

By the time Evelyn reached her own door, the cup felt cooler to her touch, but that was only because she must have swallowed half of the hot chocolate without noticing. Now, the boy inside her room would have to be satisfied once again with not having quite enough.

you [illegible] people. I [illegible] so much [illegible]
families and loved ones [illegible]
would happen to them [illegible]
[illegible]
[illegible]
only for [illegible]
[illegible] you—

By the time Evelyn [illegible]
[illegible] to her [illegible] was only because she [illegible]
have [illegible]
[illegible]
[illegible]

'Her name is Rifka,' Herschel said at last, and Evelyn moved away from the bed, hearing an echo that she could not identify.

'And you're both from somewhere in Germany?'

'Brzez. That's in Poland, I think. Places change places all the time these days, you know.'

The weak chocolate had finally brought some color back into his face, and the bread Evelyn had hidden in her skirt seemed to make his small hands stronger. He sat cross-legged on her bed in a crawling angle of sunlight, his thinning jacket and trousers aged by his feverish sleep and the early morning cold.

Evelyn suddenly remembered the room at the end of the hall.

'Did you go to the bathroom?'

'I used the window.'

The woman smiled. 'So you *can* do something your older sister can't do.'

'Oh, lots! I can run faster than she can. I can talk in more languages. I can draw better. I can even remember things longer.' He sighed unhappily. 'The only thing she can do better than me is stand.'

'Stand?'

'Well, she's a lot taller than I am.'

'But she's older than you, too, isn't she?'

'Yes,' he said. 'But what if she's always going to be taller than I am, just like she's always going to be older? What will I do then?'

'She won't be,' Evelyn assured him. 'You'll catch up.'

'But what if I don't?' he persisted miserably.

'If you don't, you don't. Is it really that important to be tall?'

Herschel thought about it for a moment, and then he said, 'I think it is. When you're tall, I mean when a boy or a man is tall and big, then people respect him more and do what he orders them to do. I've even seen some boys win at games and get more to eat just because they were able to reach a pole with their heads and not have to stretch. Sometimes height counts more than anything.

'Besides,' he added, grinning, 'mothers always hide the best treats on the highest shelves, and I always have to climb up to get at them. And that's just not fair.'

In the room's shadows, Evelyn could almost see him shinning like a monkey up the sheer wall. Then she sat down beside him on the bed, and they grew serious again.

'I suppose that was Rifka you saw outside the window of the bar yesterday, being taken away by that policeman?'

Herschel nodded and said he was sorry about that.

'Sorry for what?'

'It's just that I didn't dare run out and save her. And I thought that if you knew she was my sister, you wouldn't want to hide me here. Would you have?'

'I don't know,' Evelyn said truthfully. 'The point is, what are we going to do with you now? If your sister's in custody and the police are looking for you, too, I really don't think I can keep you here any longer. Your fever's gone, and Rifka must be worried sick about you. Besides,' she addressed the clanking radiator, 'I can't tell how long I might be here myself.'

Finishing his meal, except for the wedge of bread which he slipped into his pocket like a coin, the boy tried to make Evelyn feel a little better about what she might have to do.

'It's all right. Don't worry. People come and go. I told you before, there's always someone around to take care of anybody who needs it.' He hung his wren's legs over the side of the bed as if to put his words into action. 'We've been alone before, my sister and I, and we've always managed somehow.'

'Do you have any idea where your parents are now?'

'We got a letter from our mother a little while ago.'

'Where are they?'

'Somewhere, I suppose,' he muttered dully.

The seated boy grew distant, as if they were speaking about total strangers.

'Where?' Evelyn persisted. 'In Germany? France?'

'I suppose so.'

'In a camp for DPs?'

'No,' he said simply. 'In a camp for people.'

'What did the letter say?' the woman asked him.

'That Father would be coming for us at the end of the year.'

'So they know where you are? That you're here in Escorial?'

The boy hid his dark eyes under his dark eyebrows and wagged his head in pity.

'We got the letter, didn't we?' he giggled. 'Eva!'

Evelyn laughed with him and tried to relax.

'But what separated you and your parents in the first place? How long have you and Rifka been on your own like this? It has to be hard on you two. Couldn't you tell me something about it?'

Shifting within the sun, Herschel reluctantly told her about their unsettled life in their home village of Brzez and after. As the war had wound down, the boy had developed his first fever and fallen behind in the old village as their parents had gone out to look for day work. Rifka, four or five years older, had stayed at his side to look after him and make contacts with former friends and branches of their families. Somehow, when the town fell apart for good, the children had been sent away on a long journey that had ended at the Spanish border and a smuggler who had mistakenly herded them together with some random refugees and burrowed them all into the country. In an unusual stroke of luck, one of their traveling companions had turned out to be a Piña who was a cousin of a cousin of one of their mother's cousins. The boy and sister had found themselves in Escorial and safe among a family of strangers before they knew what was going on, and since then they had waited patiently for their mother and father to rejoin them. Until now – when the local authorities must have abruptly decided to prosecute them as undocumented aliens, and had seized the girl while her brother was out working on one of his masterpieces.

As he told his story, today so much more trusting and serene than yesterday, the boy swayed slightly where he sat as if he had to time the passage of his miseries like a clock or sing them to sleep. Weaker after his night of fever, but in a firmer mood with his new friend at his side, Herschel glowed in the dark room with all the dignity of a boy who had survived an imagined trip to the moon. The risen sun had erased all but a few streaks of his scene on the window, but in the remnant he could see parts of his past recreated, and with his words he was able to make the woman see a shadow of it, too. The retelling drained him as if it were hunger and left him unhappy, but finishing it also made him clearer, and he grew a little taller where he sat in the yellowing sun.

'Look,' the boy said as he reached under the blanket. 'I did these while you were downstairs. They're for you.'

On the backs of two or three scraps of paper scrounged from the bottoms of cabinet drawers, Herschel had drawn a triptych of their night together. Evelyn marveled at the depiction of the boy writhing like a wire with fever while the woman watched over him, and she held her breath before the sketch of another child out of whose hands the smoke of buildings and trees flowed onto a frozen window. But when she saw the third, the gentle line drawing of a woman sleeping on her side with a boy in her lap, she had no more words to say. The graceful belting of the woman's arms around the boy's waist and the river's current of the four legs rippling as one struck her as genius, and the intimacy of it touched a buried ache in her that she thought had been mislaid years ago.

'I can really keep these, Herschel? For always?'

'You can, if you bring me some more paper before you go.'

'Of course I will,' she answered, standing uncertainly. 'If I ever do decide to go, that is. The way things are now . . .'

'But you have to go,' the boy pleaded with her as innocently as a blackmailer. 'Otherwise, how are we ever going to find each other again?'

'Excuse me? But we're already here together—'

'Not us, silly.' Herschel raised his voice. 'Rifka and me. I thought you were going out to get her and bring her back here to me. I can't go, can I, if everyone is running around looking for me? So you have to go. You have to!'

'What?' Evelyn stared at him and retreated a step or two. 'I really don't think *I* could do anything . . .'

'But why not? You're not going to turn me in, are you?' the boy cried out.

'Of course not,' she said. 'It's just that, well, this isn't really any of my business . . .'

'What difference does that make?' he said crossly.

'A lot, I think.'

'No, it doesn't. People always do things that aren't any of their business, and sometimes it's good, and sometimes it's bad.' As he turned more petulant, his face wrinkled, and his eyes grew cold and white. 'Why does everyone think it's so hard to do good, when they're always able to do bad without any trouble at all?'

Before the woman could answer, a bucket suddenly knocked on the door and tried to let itself in.

'Señorita Winter?'

'What is it, Lulú?' Evelyn said at the door, holding it shut with her hand.

'To clean the room, please.'

The two inside looked wildly toward each other, until Evelyn finally begged the maid to come back later, please, I'm dressing, and the bucket went grumbling down the hallway to the next room.

When Evelyn turned back, she found a different boy squatted down between the bed and the wall. She approached him, concerned that he might be hiding out of fear, but then she saw his lips in a drooping pout, and she shook her head over him.

'So this is how you always get what you want? You hide in a corner until someone does your bidding, is that it?'

'–'

'Well,' she went on, straightening a curtain, 'it won't work this time. I may not know much about children, but I do remember enough about being one not to let myself be conned into anything that I'm not very sure about. And I don't feel too good about any of this.'

'–'

'Besides,' she wavered, 'where would you hide when the maid comes back? You couldn't hide under the bed or in the wardrobe or behind the curtains. I doubt if Lulú cleans very thoroughly, but even she has two eyes in her face. She'd soon find you – and then what would you do with yourself? Tell me that, why don't you?'

'–'

She followed his look outside toward the baby balcony of wrought iron and tiles. It had never been intended for anything more than flowerpots or laundry, but a very small boy might be able to perch around the edge until the room was clear again.

'Oh, I don't think that would work.' She shook her head and trembled at the fall to the street below. 'And, anyway, how would I find the police station without everyone wondering what I was up to? And if I did find it, how could I ever make them listen to me without letting on that the girl's only brother had sent me and was waiting for us back at my hotel? I'm only a simple secretary from Wisconsin, you know. I'm no Mata Hari. How would I do it?'

The bony shoulders rose again in the customary shrug, and the voice sounded as innocent and routine as milk.

'Lie.'

Evelyn didn't return until nightfall, and then it was those last few streets that almost did her in. Her visit to the police had been long, frustrating, and eventually useless. They had quickly decided to tell nothing to the American woman who came in calling herself an unknown aunt of Rifka, the tall girl dressed in black, and of Herschel, the little street artist with a shaggy jacket. A lieutenant had wondered why she hadn't been able to remember the children's family name, and even the teenaged soldier at the desk had frowned at her unidentifiable accent. In the end, Evelyn had not accomplished much more than turning suspicion on herself and overhearing that the girl was not even being kept at the station house, but was at some other place where her brother would be more likely to come looking for her. And even that was too much for anyone in Escorial to say out loud.

The walk back had been a run of lungs burning with cold and hard, fragmented looks from passersby. All Evelyn could think of was how in the mornings all the maids threw open the windows and aired out the rooms and how wicked poor Lulú suddenly appeared in her memory. For some reason that Evelyn could not understand, the boy's being discovered and turned in was not the worst thing she could imagine. What was worse was the possibility of their having found him without her. She could not stand to think of him walking out of the hotel beside a policeman instead of herself, or to see the detached, neutral balance of his small back and know that she had not been there. She knew he would not cry, but in a way this was the most dreadful part of it, and this fear quickened her up the road and the hotel stairs as if something precious were burning out of control.

He was still at home, sprawled across the bed and at work on further studies of the room. Even from the door, Evelyn could see that his afternoon fever had started up again and robbed him of a whole night's strength. He cheered up when she gave him the Swiss chocolates she had bought at a shop on her way back, and now he handed her his latest pencil drawings with an outburst of loud exhilaration that was unusual for him.

'Here, Eva. I told you she wouldn't find me.'

'So the maid did come, after all? Lulú was here?'

He nodded and said, 'She's really quite efficient. She swept the entire room, turned the bed, shook out the covers and drapes, and brought you all those fresh towels over there.'

He pointed, and Evelyn saw a pair of flat towels piled up on top of the cooling radiator.

'Where did you hide? Out on the balcony?'

'No, she cleaned that, too.'

'Will wonders—?' The woman darkened with fear. 'Don't tell me she found you, but agreed not to tell anyone else! What does she want in return? How much?'

'No.' He indicated his sketches. 'Look.'

'Where?'

'Right here.'

She leafed through his drawings. They all showed the hotel room, each from a slightly varied angle and each containing as much of the furniture as might be seen from that viewpoint. In every scene, Evelyn saw shifts of perspective in the gradual turn of the day's light that seemed to make the murky interior revolve in a cartoon dance. Yet the one constant was a vague outline that showed up as an opaque space in the drawn background, in one as a tiny shaped door in the wall, in another as the other half of the mirror, in yet another as the fourth leg of the bed. Afraid to be too critical, Evelyn gently pointed out these gaps to the artist who sat dangling his legs in anticipation.

'What are these, Herschel? Something to be filled in later?'

'No, that's me.'

'What do you mean?'

He touched the holes and grinned proudly.

'Hier bin i', Eva.'

In an instant, Evelyn heard again the childish game that

she used to play with her father as they had teased one another with the unthinkable dread of separation.

'*Da bist du,*' she answered quietly.

'That way,' Herschel explained as he took back his drawings, 'I didn't have to go out, and I still didn't have to frighten the maid by popping out from behind a curtain or pretending to be some ghost in one of your dresses from the cabinet. Though that would have made a good picture, too, don't you think?'

Suddenly, his newfound energy left him as he mused wearily, turning his face away, 'But I've always been good at hiding. When you're small, there are so many good reasons in the world not to be seen and so many places for you to disappear.'

As much as Evelyn wanted to find out what had happened while she was gone, she could see that the child was exhausted by the fever, and she began making preparations for tucking him in for the night. While the cold dark fell and the fatter moon slid up onto the horizon, she tried to make the room as comfortable as she could by shrouding the leaky window with the curtains and by shading the bare light. Although less restless tonight, Herschel still babbled quietly about roads that got lost in forests and an escaped bear in a jacket who could sing his way through walls. In an hour or two, Evelyn had made him stable enough to sleep, and she silently slipped outside to see what she could find for him below in the kitchen. She was halfway down the corridor when a door opened and the diplomat from Bern let himself out of the bathroom as if he were afraid of waking the hotel.

'*Guten Abend, Fräulein.* Might I have a word with you?'

He had whispered in German and taken her elbow to steer her toward a darker alcove near the bathroom. For one mad moment, she thought he might be trying to kidnap her, but then she heard the genuine worry in his voice and saw his kind look.

'You'll forgive me,' he began.

'Of course.'

'Is it time for dinner already?'

'I was just going down for a snack.' Evelyn searched for the proper slang, but all she could come up with was '*Stück*,' a piece of something.

'Because,' Herr Heuter went on, 'there is something I wanted to talk to you about, something of great importance.'

'What is it? Shall we go down to the dining room?'

Instead, he held her still in the shadows of the alcove.

'I'm afraid, Miss Winter, that today my wife and I happened to see a small boy coming out of and returning to your room – the same little boy, I think, whom everyone seems to be talking about in town.'

'I can't imagine—'

'Please, please don't think that your secret isn't safe with us,' he cried softly. 'I've been working with refugees for ten or twelve years now, and I know that many times it is the police and the courts who are the greatest villains. Believe me, I would not dream of betraying your trust or turning an orphan over to people who sided with a buffoon like Hitler. I remember Guernica.'

The man spoke with a sudden passion that enlarged him in the narrow hallway and made his pink skin flare purple and thick.

'It's just that I found him,' Evelyn stammered, 'or he found me, and now he has a fever and there's no one to take care of him and they won't even tell me where they're keeping his sister. His mother just wrote them that she and their father are going to be coming for them any day now . . .'

'Of course,' he calmed her. 'I only wanted to assure you of our faithfulness and that both my wife and myself will keep your secret as if it were our own. I refuse to give any aid or comfort to those who are trying to keep the victims of the war from their rightful homes.'

'Or from finding some new ones,' she reminded him.

'That goes without saying,' the Swiss gentleman concurred.

Unbending a bit, Evelyn asked him if he thought anyone else in the hotel knew about Herschel.

'I doubt it. We wouldn't have seen him either but for luck. I haven't heard any talk about him other than idle speculation.'

'Thank goodness,' the woman said, and then she leaned toward the old man's furry ear. 'The truth is, I'm a little worried that this fever of his might get out of control. I've got my two hands full just trying to keep him fed and figure out what I'm going to do with him. You could really help me by talking to a doctor or a pharmacist about him and maybe even getting some drugs. I've got a few aspirins in my suitcase, but—'

As soon as she had said this, a change came over the man, and he grew smaller against the wall. Shrinking back, he had the appearance of a turtle shying away from a bright light.

'Oh, but I think that would be a mistake, I really do. There might be word out in those quarters, and any rash enquiries could awaken suspicion. Besides, I haven't been that impressed with Spanish medicine thus far on our trip. It might be better if you simply do as much for the boy as you can yourself.

'I'll tell you what I will do, though,' he went on, leading them both out of the alcove. 'While I'm here in Escorial for the next day or two, I'll find out as much as I can about where they might be keeping the sister and what a person might be able to do about getting these two children back together again. That's all I can do, you understand – to work behind the scenes. As a visitor in Spain myself, I don't dare step over too many lines or make too many bureaucrats wonder what I'm doing. When you've been lost in diplomatic circles as long as I have, my dear, you'll begin to see that you can open many more doors from the side than you can from the front.'

'What more can *I* do?' Evelyn asked as they reached the Swiss couple's room and she began to feel alone again.

'Well, I guess you could try to find out as much as you can about the boy and his sister, their family situation, the people they were staying with here in Escorial, what plans they have for the future, details like that. And try to keep him down. The last thing any of us needs at this point is for him to be unearthed in your room. I don't know what the penalty might be for harboring a refugee, but I suspect it's severe. Invisibility is our watchword now. The best DP,' the diplomat decided, 'is the one who is never seen or heard. That way, they have the best chance of coming back into the human community again, and the rest of us might be able to get on with our lives once more.'

He reached his door, and Evelyn felt a chill. The old Swiss gentleman was reasonable, efficient, and precise, and as he turned his face toward her she felt a brisk scent of mountain air and cleanliness wash over her as a cool shower of rain. She had smelled the same aroma before on the cheeks and necks of Army generals as they had charged through the secretarial pool on their way from an attack conference to the war room, and even then Evelyn had thought how much they had smelled like cold iron and steel. Now the diplomat was giving off the same inhuman odor, only with his round features the woman had the impression that she was watching the dark face of the moon turning its blind eyes toward her, gray and lifeless with unimaginable ice.

'And try not to worry,' Herr Heuter smiled at her. 'The boy and his sister will soon be reunited with their parents. And even if they can't be,' he said as he disappeared into his room, 'they will always have someone else to look after them, won't they?'

The next day, Sunday, Evelyn and the boy spent the entire day in the hotel room, but their staying in had less to do with fever or fear and more with the lazy quiet of a winter holiday. After the maid had been turned away for good, and once the curiosity of the other guests had been satisfied with tales of a headache, the two of them were able to regain their strength, get their bearings, and learn a little bit more about each other. With the streets and the bars of the town dulled by the Sabbath, an empty calm stole into their room and made them forget yesterday's troubles and tomorrow's new worries, letting them both catch their breath. Even the snow over the rooftops helped by filling the room with a whiter light that made even the boy's faded jacket seem velvety and snug.

Privately, by mid-morning, the jacket was beginning to bother Evelyn. Herschel would simply not take it off. Although today the room was warmer with sun, he refused to part with his jacket even long enough to have it aired on the balcony and shaken clean. He kept himself wrapped up in it as if it were his skin or as if he were some species of hibernating moth that could feed only off its own shrouding wings. When the woman offered to wipe away some of its stains with a wet cloth, or when she tried to bite off the straggling threads at the cuffs, he yelped in protest like a dog. In the end, she began to understand that for Herschel the jacket, pathetic though it looked, was all he had left to connect him with his sister and his mother and father, so she sat back and let him alone, amazed at how loyal a small boy could be to a meaningless piece of clothing.

For her part, throughout the course of the day Evelyn began to learn something about how little a child needs to fill up his time. She herself had always assumed that it was only adults who could find enough to interest them in merely sitting and thinking and remembering, as she had always done alone at work or alone in her apartment with her books, her radio, and her plants. But now she saw that a boy could amuse himself for hours with simple and inward pastimes. Herschel, of course, had his sketching to keep him busy, and she enjoyed watching him scribble different studies on every scrap of paper or cardboard that she could find. By the time evening came on, he had half a dozen rough drafts ready to show her of the room or of the view from the window. One scene impressed her more than any other – a panorama of the monastery on the edge of town, quilted with gray patches and levitating like a dream on a cloud in front of the falling valley beyond. As Evelyn held it up at the window, comparing the real with the copy, winds disturbed the powder outside and rearranged the frosted rooftops to match precisely the webbed cross-hatching in Herschel's scene. But when even the shadow of the hotel's eaves aligned itself with a chance crease in the paper, Evelyn simply had to look away.

Yet not all of the boy's time was devoted to drawing. He was just as happy scouting around the room, rearranging the furniture into rocks in a cave or into mountain ranges or into the shining, marble parlors of an Arabian palace. After some prompting, Evelyn let herself get caught up in the child's fantasies, and soon they were roasting a wild dog of a boot over a roaring scarf, crossing the headboard with Hannibal, and burning tobacco incense inside a silk-hung wardrobe paneled with porphyry and alabaster. In spite of all her doubts and regrets, the woman gave hardly a thought to her missed bus and flights or to the family waiting for her back home. She did feel one pang when the boy carried them aloft upon the wings of the bedstead over the blue Atlantic of the circular throw rug, but that lasted only until he pointed out to her some of the wonders hidden in the leafy woods of the floor, and before long Evelyn found that this one room held everything she needed.

As the afternoon wore on and his nightly fever awakened, their games grew quieter and smaller. Lounging across the bed, the boy taught her how to play with their hands, transforming them into a quartet of shy monsters with index and middle fingers for legs and an unbalanced trio of arms. Although restricted in activities by the wrists growing out of their heads, these freaks could come and go across the counterpane, stalking nobly in a parade or with foolhardiness in a vaulting attack on a fort behind a leg. Before the boy tired, he proposed a game of football, two men to a side; and then Evelyn had to scramble to defend a goal of crossed feet against the boy's flashing hands and a rolling ball of paper. Points later, as Herschel sank back into a victorious sleep, the woman covered him and sat down in the risen moonlight, deciding that today had been the fullest day she had ever spent, even though – or because – she had accomplished nothing at all.

As close as they had grown during the day, tonight repeated the boy's cycle of fever and restlessness. After Evelyn came back from dinner, she found the blanket kicked away and the jacket wet with a breaking temperature. Holding her breath and with a gentle care that she had never imagined she possessed, she managed to peel the jacket off without pulling him up out of his sorrowful dreams, and pat it neat in the light of the moon. Then she laid it across the bed in case the boy should need it later, undressed herself, and got ready to lie back down beside him. A few last tucks, then she had to retrieve his bare left arm where it had escaped from under the covers, and then she could go to sleep, too, and not have to think anymore about what in the world might happen to them next.

It was when she came around the bed that she saw in the gray light the ink brand on the inside of his arm. She knelt to squint and see, but all she could make out was a smear of characters.

'33 . . .'

Those damned DP camps, she thought as she hugged his arm to his body. Have they no shame at all?

When Evelyn got up with the cold dawn, she found Herr Heuter just outside her door, fidgeting from side to side like a wary cat.

'*Guten Morgen, Fräulein Winter*. I was only now coming to see you. All is still well, I hope?'

He gestured significantly at her closed door, and she told him that everything was as well as could be expected.

'I have some good news for you,' he went on, his voice low. 'I've been able to arrange an interview for you with the Piñas in Libro Verde Street. You remember, the family that took in—'

'I remember.'

'It's the best I could do, I'm afraid. The whole town is fairly hopping with rumors and searches and paranoia. You'd think they were looking for one of those escaped Nazis who are running around Spain now instead of just some common refugee.'

'Maybe,' Evelyn suggested, 'in their minds they are.'

'Perhaps. At any rate,' he said as he slipped a paper out of his pocket, 'if you could be alone at this address by eleven this morning, I'm sure you and the family should be able to find some legal solution to this terrible dilemma.' He had added stress to the word 'legal,' but then left it hanging in mid-air.

The woman took the paper and asked, 'But I thought you were going to help me track down his sister?'

Herr Heuter sputtered an apology as he backed away from her.

'Oh, I tried, I did try. But there was really no way that I, a stranger here in Spain, could ever persuade the authorities to tell me anything that they don't want generally known. That's why I thought this family might be able to do more for you than I ever could.

'Another thing,' the diplomat concluded, 'you should be sure not to take the boy out with you, especially back to the family. I'm certain the police have the apartment building under watch. I doubt if you'd want to endanger him now after all your good efforts.'

'But I can get in without any trouble?' Evelyn asked. 'Past the police, I mean?'

'You are an American.' Herr Heuter bowed and spread his arms ironically wide. 'You are the victors. You can do what you will.'

'But what if we do manage to get the brother and sister back together again?' she added, holding him beside her a moment or so longer. 'What's going to happen to them then? I don't suppose it would be wise for them to stay in Escorial. So where can they go now?'

'Who knows?' His oval body hovered.

'I thought you used to work with refugees in Switzerland. If you know someone in an agency . . .' She was losing him. 'Please. Give me a name or a number, anything, and you wouldn't even have to be there. I'll do all the rest. I promise.'

'I really can't say,' he said. 'But I will tell you this. If I were you, I'd worry more about your English friend who seems to be so sweet on you. I've heard some of his opinions on what might happen down in Palestine, how his country's Mandate has to endure for as long as possible and how any new colonists would only have a negative effect on the region. Believe me,' he added gloomily, 'he's the last person in the world whom you should let know about your little orphan in there.'

He turned then, and the round shadow of a dead bulb clapped over his head and face like a visor, leaving him a stoical knight with all his duty done. Then the door closed, and the woman stood alone at the end of a long hallway that would not stop growing.

Before leaving the hotel, she ducked back into her room for a second to check on Herschel and almost fainted. He seemed to be gone. The bed was empty and the window open to the chilled air. She panicked, then she found him standing in a corner, paper and pencil in hand, the formless wallpaper merging with him as if he were a chameleon in a brown thicket. Even as she watched, she saw his outline flicker with every motion of his hand, until she knew somehow that she wouldn't have to worry any longer about the maid flushing him out. Herschel was far too clever to be caught. When she led him back into bed, murmuring in his dreams, she felt his body melting in her hands like the moon in water, until under the covers he all but disappeared.

The old apartment building in Libro Verde Street was a vertical European oblong of three or four stories with two dormer windows on top beneath the debris of terracotta tiles. There was nothing to distinguish it from its neighbors, except for the stone statue of the Madonna that graced the right edge of the door, leaning an anxious face out over the troubled streams of people passing by, the toe of one foot burnished smooth by repeated kisses and caresses. Evelyn couldn't help touching it herself once as she greeted the *portero* and asked her way upstairs, petitioning on behalf of the children an unlikely power that she doubted had ever done anyone very much good.

The Piña family lived in a gloomy apartment on the uppermost floor, just where the lower marble faded away into a more modern, colorless stucco. There were in the hallway the impersonal smells of dust and onions that linger in all old buildings, but in front of the Piña door these were replaced by sweeter odors, sugar and tea perhaps, or the mingling of flowers and fresh linen. Tapping on the door brought out a slow blossoming of sounds as of someone climbing out of a distant barrel filled with silk fans. A couple of voices swung back and forth, a child mewed, and then the door was opened by a short woman about ten years younger than Evelyn. She was sleepy or sad, and she stared numbly at the American as she washed her hands in a towel she wore looped over her belt.

'Buenos Días.'

'Guten Tag.'

Evelyn hadn't meant to answer in German, but her nights with the boy and a few tête-à-têtes with Herr Heuter had switched her signals. The reaction of the woman in the door was extraordinary.

'Come in! Quickly!' she whispered and pulled her through the door and locked it behind her in one smooth gesture.

'I really shouldn't have barged in like this . . .'

'Keep your voice down. Do you speak any Spanish?'

Evelyn found herself in a wide sitting room, neat with dark woods and clouded fabrics and brightened by a range of windows on the street. She had time to notice friezes of books and a cabinet of glass candleholders and figurines before the younger woman was joined by an older, less excitable housewife.

'What is it, Elisa?'

The older woman's Spanish was perfect, but the one with the towel answered her in a language that might have been German, but wasn't. Evelyn understood little of what was going on, but stayed near the door and kept her unfocused eyes moving, so no one would think she was searching for dust or reading the mail on the sofa table.

'You are Miss Winter?' the older woman asked, coming closer. Evelyn inhaled the starchy smell of peeled potatoes.

'Yes. Herr Heuter told me that you people might be able to help me with the children.'

'You have them?' Elisa cried hopefully. 'Coca, did you hear that?'

'Why shouldn't I hear it? Am I out in the street?' The older woman's face was stern, but more from worry than anger. 'Wouldn't they have to be somewhere? So why can't they be with her just as well as with anyone else?

'Please,' she added to Evelyn, fluffing a cushion, 'sit down and have some tea with us. Elisa?'

While the younger woman hastened out into the kitchen, eager not to miss any news, the other two sat and regarded each other. The woman Evelyn saw was big and solid, her frame wider than some men's, but with a surprising gracefulness in the way she sat and moved her hands. Her round face was made for smiling, and the traceries of wrinkles about the eyes proved that; but now there were shadows under the lids, and some red was still hiding there and on the edges of the nose.

'Herr Heuter,' Coca Piña began, 'only told us to expect some woman who might have some information about Herschel or Rifka. We were afraid to trust him, and we thought the police must be up to something tricky. These last few days have been a nightmare, and at first Herr Heuter seemed too good to be true. We don't know if we can believe anyone anymore. We always knew something like this might happen, the way they always harass us so, but to lose both of the children at once—'

'I can imagine,' Evelyn said gently.

'No,' the other said. 'No, you can't.'

Evelyn was about to apologize, when the younger woman walked back into the living room carrying one of the oddest teapots the American had ever seen. It was a tall, ceramic samovar of brown earth colors, square turquoise petals, and a clawed base. Heavy as lead, it had to be wrestled onto the table, tipping out water and constantly threatening to crash into their laps. But once it was righted and lit, its brewing action made it almost float over the table, and the bitter air of its steeping perfumed the entire room.

'Did you bring the jam, Elisa?'

'I'm sorry, I forgot,' the girl said, running back.

'What are we? Animals?'

The older woman arranged the cups, muttering, 'The children always loved the jam so. They just couldn't get enough of it. How sweet it will be to have both of them back with us again!'

'Both?' Evelyn gasped. 'Oh, forgive me. I thought you knew. I only have Herschel. I was hoping you could tell me where Rifka is being kept so I could bring them back together again.'

'Only the boy?' cried Coca.

'I'm afraid so.'

'What about the boy?' Elisa asked, returning with a jampot.

'He's still alone,' the older woman told her.

'But what happened?'

'I should know?'

As soon as this disappointment was shared by the two Piñas, Evelyn told them over the jam-sweetened tea about how she and the boy had met, why he was hiding in her room, and what very little she knew about the whole situation. Saying it all aloud like this for the first time, Evelyn felt some relief that at last she had someone else to listen to her. The fact that they were all women helped. Evelyn felt free to tell not only of her meeting with the boy and of her fears for his safety, but also of their games and his magical talents with a pencil, of his nightly fevers and the naughty pranks he had played on her in the street. As they traded stories, the tea softened some of the winter's glare and polished the heavier colors inside, until the only sharp thing left in the room was a pair of eyes hung near the bottom of a curtain leading into a side hallway.

Coca looked, too, then lowered her head and squealed.

'Ruth, Ruth, who sees Ruth?'

'Abuela does!' a shrill voice answered, galloping in.

The older woman was suddenly attacked by a churning toddler who crawled up onto the couch and gave kisses to grandmother and mother, then hid her face from the intruding stranger.

'This is my little treasure,' Elisa said. 'She and Rifka had grown to be like sisters in the few months they had together.'

'Rifka?' The child looked up and around.

'What I still don't understand,' Coca wondered, 'is how you ended up with Herschel at all. You really didn't know him?'

'Like I said,' Evelyn explained, 'it was just plain chance. If he'd been unluckier, he might have wound up with the police or with someone who wouldn't have been so charmed by his ways.'

'That's our Herschel,' the Piñas agreed. 'Always blessed.'

'I take it, then, you don't know where his sister is?'

'If we did—' Elisa began.

'We've done all we can to get her back,' Coca continued. 'As soon as we heard that the police had picked her up, we asked our friends to find out as much as they could, but all they knew was that Rifka had been taken to some place in town where the police thought that Herschel might come looking for her. We were worried sick, of course, but being guilty of keeping undocumented aliens, we couldn't very well make too much noise. My husband,' she ended morosely, 'always said it would come to this sooner or later. How I hate it when he's right!'

'Oh, Mamá.'

'Jaime's a teacher,' Coca told their guest, 'so he's always been respected by most of the town and kept their darkest suspicions turned aside. I don't know what would have happened to any of us if the authorities hadn't always been too wary of his scholarship to do their worst to us.'

'I wonder,' Evelyn thought aloud, 'where that place might be where the children would go looking for each other?'

'Who knows? They were always solitary children together. And with Herschel in the lead, even though he's so much younger, they could have gone anywhere. He's half squirrel.'

'Three-quarters,' Elisa smiled.

'Brother and sister must be very close,' Evelyn suggested.

Both women considered for a moment, then the elder said that she thought they were.

'But it's more than just family or tradition. Their growing up together was so sad, so frightening and hard, that they almost seem more like lifelong friends than just brother and sister. In fact, sometimes it's difficult to tell where one of them ends and the other one begins – like one of Herschel's designs and the real thing itself. But that's what happens when the world tears apart a family and makes the children grow up so much more quickly than any happy children should.'

The ornate samovar bubbled empty, the little girl skittered from lap to lap, and the shared concern hung dark in the glowing room. Occasionally, in the hall outside, footsteps rang out, and then the Piña women tensed and joined eyes until the passerby had gone. The delta of yellow sunlight through the window would shine stained by the red stroke of a flag sailing outside before either of them could shake off the alarm, and it took a few minutes for them to come back to the American woman who now sat puzzling over what they had said.

'Herschel's told me so little of who he is and where he came from,' Evelyn said slowly. 'I've heard all the talk about how he and Rifka are refugees from the war and the DP camps, but I still don't know much about their background. He said he was from some village called Brezh . . . ?'

'Brzez?' the younger woman pronounced more precisely.

'That's it. Where's that? Somewhere in Germany?'

The other two women seemed to disappear.

'No, Poland,' Elisa said, gazing blankly at her daughter.

'The whole name is Brzezinka,' Coca added. 'It must still be too long for Herschel to say all of it. Or too hard.'

'I've never heard of it,' Evelyn said. 'Was it one of those towns destroyed by the Germans?'

'Oh, no,' the grandmother whispered. 'It thrived for years. God must have been sleeping . . .'

'Coca! The child.'

'Well, what would you call it? Either God hates us, or else He means for us to hate Him back. Either way, we're left with nothing but each other, and now even that's being taken away from us.'

'All isn't lost yet, Mamá.'

'Only because we keep things hidden,' the woman said to her daughter with a meaningful stare.

'But was their village broken up eventually?' Evelyn wanted to know. 'From some of the little things Herschel said, I got the impression that he finally left the place in ruins.'

'At the end of it all, yes, after the worst damage had been done,' Elisa said.

'But that only set the poor children off,' Coca mourned, 'on their wanderings across the face of the earth. Separated from all their family, sick and hungry, knowing nothing in this world but Brzezinka . . .'

'They must have traveled quite a bit,' Evelyn said. 'I mean, Herschel said he'd even been to Canada and Mexico. Was that true, or was I only being teased again?'

The older woman frowned at her and said, 'You really haven't understood any of it yet, have you? Brzezinka! Brzezinka was not a village, at least not a living village of families and work and growing children. It was a place of ashes and unhappiness and rot that nothing could ever make clean and white again, not even snow falling down off the moon, as little Herschel likes to say.'

She bent forward with her elbows on her knees and both hands over her ears as if she couldn't bear to hear her own voice. Yet she continued.

'Brzezinka was Birkenau, the darkest part of the camp called Oswiecim, Auschwitz, where—'

The grandmother mumbled on, but all that Evelyn heard was a flurry of refreshing, inhuman voices that suddenly deafened her, crowding the room. There was the shivering of the glass figurines with the traffic passing below that reminded her of how brisk and lively the winter winds back home could be. The child snoring in her mother's dress and the rustling of fabrics in the living room made Evelyn miss her breakfasts with her father in the last dark of a waking farm and baking bread with her mother as the freezing sun turned the lace curtains and doilies into ice. Each of these remembered sounds cost her nothing, while the jangle of December noises that now surrounded her soon took on the same rhythms and tones as those of when she was small and harmless. After a couple of minutes, she settled back and gazed at the silent mouth before her, opening and closing, as patiently as if she were waiting for an icicle to melt outside her own girlish bedroom window.

'So now you can see,' Coca finished, 'why little Herschel and Rifka have nowhere to go. With everything behind them already dead, and who knows what still ahead of them, they might as well still be lost in the mountains.'

'What?' Evelyn asked.

The hallway door opened and woke the child, and she bounded across to the man who entered, and demanded sweets from him.

'Find them first,' the gray man said, crouching down to

let the girl go through his pockets. When he stood and saw Evelyn, he adjusted the kerchief around his neck and waited for his wife or his daughter to introduce him.

'Miss Winter,' Coca said, 'this is my husband, Jaime. Jaime, this is the kind woman who is taking care of little Herschel.'

'Don't tell me!' he cried happily. 'Is he still all right?'

'He's fine,' Evelyn repeated. 'Some fever . . .'

'He just can't seem to shake that,' Elisa commented.

'Give him time,' the older woman advised. 'He's still trying to get back on his feet.'

'What about Rifka?' Jaime asked. 'Has there been any word of the girl?'

'None,' Coca said. 'That's why Miss Winter here came by, to see if there might be something we could do to get both of these poor children back together again.'

Everyone sat, the samovar was replenished, and the talk went over again the few options that were still left open to them.

'I wonder if the police . . .' Jaime began fearfully.

'Here?' Coca objected. 'In Spain? Haven't they bothered us enough with all their questions and their doubts and the way they have turned the whole town against us?'

'Still,' Elisa said, 'there might be some legal way to—'

'I told you this would happen.' Jaime shook his head. 'Don't think for a moment that I begrudge the children a crumb of bread off our table, but . . .'

'Perhaps if you went to see the authorities, Miss Winter.'

'I've already tried,' Evelyn reassured them. 'Nothing. What about foreign relief agencies in Spain, though, like some of the ones that Herr Heuter used to be involved with? The Red Cross or something like that?'

'This is only Escorial,' Elisa said bitterly. 'Not Madrid.'

'If it were,' Jaime told her over his sweetened tea, 'there would have been more help for us, but more attention, too. When one comes, the other usually follows. Even here, in the past few days, there's been talk of someone like Herr Heuter come sneaking into town. That's probably one of the reasons why the police went after the children now, after all this time. Franco may have been gracious enough to welcome many refugees over the years . . .'

'Only because,' his wife reminded him, 'the fool hoped it might bring more money into the country.'

'And,' Elisa put in, 'because he wanted to distance Spain from the side that he finally realized was going to lose.'

Jaime gently battled the two women for the floor.

'But,' he went on in resignation, 'there has never been a place set for them at the table. The men are put into camps, the women are put to work in homes or worse, and the children – if no one has a legal claim to them – are hidden away for months in some orphanage or convent. Don't get me wrong. Being a neutral country during the war, Spain was one of the safest places for many Jews and others to be, and everyone has felt thankful for that. But as soon as the fighting stopped and the refugee problem intensified, the peninsula became just another conduit for the runoff from up north. Now, every survivor who can run, walk, or crawl is making his way out of Europe as fast as he can, either carrying all his family with him or arranging to meet them somewhere else as soon as possible.'

'But where are they all heading?' Evelyn asked.

The whole room shrugged, even the little girl.

'Palestine, usually,' Jaime informed the American. 'Or even Africa. The United States. The Soviet Union. Or

Cuba. Even South America. Anywhere, as long as it is worlds away from Germany and Austria and Poland.'

'And Canada and Mexico?' Evelyn asked Coca pointedly.

The older woman shuddered. 'Those were just camp-names for certain neighborhoods in Birkenau. Herschel and Rifka never went anywhere but farther in.'

'Unfortunately,' Elisa added, 'many borders have been closed to them, or there have been restrictive quotas set. Your country, for example,' she pointed out to Evelyn, 'has hardly been one of the best.'

'Especially now,' Jaime said, 'now that Truman wants to shut the door at the present levels.'

'Those of us who have lived here all our lives,' Coca noted, 'hardly used to notice these things, all the uprooting of people and whole families, living their lives on the run to who knows where. But ever since the children came to us – since that evening when a cousin of ours passed through town with two tired children in tow – we've learned a lot more about it. We blame ourselves for not knowing more sooner, or not trying to find out. But when your life is everything you want it to be,' she said, holding the room in a single glance, 'it's hard to think of anyone whose isn't.'

'And what we've learned,' the younger woman sighed, 'is that there are a lot more lost people than there are places for them.'

'You said something about orphanages,' Evelyn asked Jaime, once she had thought about all she had heard. 'Are Herschel and Rifka really in danger of being put in one of those? I knew some people who had grown up in such awful places, and I wouldn't wish that on my worst enemy.'

The Piña family scholar sadly nodded.

'Lately, the city fathers have started to worry about

every single problem that might get them into trouble with Madrid.'

'Don't forget the Holy Church and their fine works.'

'Coca, Coca, Coca,' Jaime snicked his tongue. 'The fact is, a mayor or a priest alone is never enough to turn a whole group of people either for or against anyone. In the end, it's every man, woman, and child in the village who's to blame for shutting their hearts and doors to others in trouble. It happens every time some child makes fun of another boy different from him, or a woman says she won't give up her place in line to someone hungrier, or a man doesn't want a stranger to make as much money as he does, even if he's making almost nothing. None of this is new. People have been killing one another with cold looks and cold thoughts for as long as anyone can remember. Why should today be any different?

'But, yes,' Jaime said, returning to Evelyn's question, 'if the children are found and detained now, they won't even be sent out of the country where their own parents might be able to come and meet them or at least send them help. They'll be lost in bureaucratic hallways until they're old enough to run away and become criminals or until they forget who they were and turn into ghosts. At this point, I'm no longer sure which one of those two futures might be worse for them . . .'

The room sat silent for a while as the day wore on and every light in the window faded. Evelyn fidgeted with her cup, her mind numb and her heart flickering uncertainly in her chest. She felt as if she had lived decades in the past few days, as if she must have already left for home while someone strange and nameless had stayed behind to cuddle a fever out of an unknown boy and lie to everyone who trusted her. Now she began wondering who was really in trouble and who was only passing from one life to the next, and how displaced any of them might one day find themselves, even in their own hometowns.

'But there must be something we can do,' Evelyn insisted, and she stared hard at each of the others in turn. 'There must be someone who can help us. I can't believe that we've thought of everything yet.'

The Piña family conferred in a pantomime of bowed heads and trembling hands, until finally young Elisa nodded, took Ruth away to bed in her own room, and returned with a courageous look that made her seem even older than Jaime.

'There is someone,' she admitted slowly. 'I'm just afraid he might put himself in danger when he hears of this.'

'Or us,' Jaime agreed, and then he motioned Evelyn to follow them out into the colder, emptier hallway as if they were all one family going to visit their dead.

At the top of the last flight of stairs, the Piña family and the American woman came to a stop in a mask of shadow. Before them was a ladder, leading up to a boarded-over door. Jaime and his wife hung back, while Elisa climbed up to the door and made cat-like clawing sounds on the wooden stairs. These she continued for a while, then she tapped a complicated code on the bottom of the door and stood back, as if framing herself in a viewfinder. Just as Evelyn was beginning to tire of this dumbshow, the door with its boards quietly separated itself from the frame and swung open a crack. An elongated, anemic face ending in a triangular goatee of burnt red squeezed out and regarded the gathered family with a comical glance.

'Hullo. Elisa! Is it Thursday again already, my love?'

'No, Efraín, it's only Monday. Let us in.'

'All of you?'

The man retreated, and the Piñas and their guest filed into the garret that had been forgotten by everyone else living in the apartment building. Once they were inside, the man shut and sealed the door again, then groped for a shaded bulb that threw the one room into a dizzying well of light. The dormer windows had been painted and caulked so that no light could escape, as the door had been fixed into its frame with added braces to prevent anyone from breaking it open by mistake. Inside, the furnishings were simple – a chair, a bed, a folding table, a covered chamber pot, and an electric ring for heating water. All the rest of the room had been taken over by books, leaning or stacked; their cardboard and leather gave the hideout the rich smell of unhurried study.

Under the low ceiling, the tenant stood with his goatee down on his chest as he motioned his guests to the best seats he had.

'I see you've brought me a new friend,' he said to Elisa.

'I'm sorry.'

'But why should you be?' he said happily. 'Your judgment is good. And yours, too, of course,' he quickly said to his parents-in-law. 'I was only wondering why I haven't heard anything lately from any of you. Is there something wrong downstairs?'

As he spoke, he made himself at home on the floor and tugged at his beard as if he wanted to make it grow even faster. Evelyn watched the pale man closely, not quite sure what to make of someone who apparently lived his daily life alone in a cubbyhole, yet didn't seem to mind. Except for the unavoidable pallor, he was as steady and unflappable as a man on a park bench, even though the air in the garret was cold enough to fog their breath. He didn't even seem to mind the close quarters around him, now drastically reduced by company, but squatted where he was and smiled up at the creaking rafters that drooped so low over everyone's head.

'Just remember to keep your head bowed,' he said to his new visitor after they had been introduced. 'It cost me many a raised bump to learn that it's easier to get through life with your head held low.'

'I'll try to remember that,' Evelyn said.

He grinned at her and mischievously hugged his knees.

'I suppose you're thinking I'm the mad relation the

family's been keeping hidden away since childhood.'

'You don't look that mad.'

'Oh, just a little, I thank you.' He laughed in a curiously choking way, but Evelyn assumed that after long hiding the hermit must have developed the habit of doing everything as silently as he could.

'My husband,' Elisa began, interposing herself between them, 'is hardly a lunatic. In his day, he was one of the most greatly respected lawyers in all of central Spain.'

'In my day,' the tenant echoed wryly.

'Until,' the wife went on, 'until Franco and the Civil War made it impossible for a free man to live and work according to his own principles. Then Efraín was hounded from his practice and made to hide up here for the past six years, praying that someday the country will return to its senses enough to forgive a younger man for his philosophical mistakes and let him come back into his family and the work he loves. No man should have to pay for ever,' she finished heatedly, 'for taking the wrong road only once.'

'In other words,' the husband informed Evelyn, 'I'm a damned Communist.'

The whole family twisted their noses delicately aside.

'Tzah!' Jaime wailed. 'There's no call for such language. I see women in the room.'

'Efraín,' Coca reasoned, 'how many times do we have to tell you? We were all Communists when we were young, but then we grew out of it. You will, too.'

The man with the goatee snickered to himself and raised his straw eyebrows at the American.

'Do you see what I'm up against? Not only do I have to hide out from Franco's vengeance, but I also have to stop acting like a spoiled child. I wonder which one I'll end up doing first? What do you think?' he teased her.

'The way you've settled in here,' she said, glancing around the garret, 'I'd say you were doing fine just as you are.'

In spite of her bewilderment and distrust, Evelyn found the puckish renegade lawyer intriguing and comforting. By now, she'd had enough wartime despair and Spanish earnestness to last her a lifetime, and for the first time in years she could feel a wicked tension inside her beginning to unravel. She stared at the man in the workman's shirt, with his red hair, and realized that this was how little Herschel might have turned out, had life only let him be. In the frowning attic, the man on the floor had made quite an unlikely home for himself by simply always knowing where and who he was.

Slowly, the happy reunion turned darker as the guests tried not to think of why they had come.

'Efraín,' the wife began reluctantly, 'we've come with some bad news—'

The colorless man looked up. 'Not Ruth!'

'No, no, she's fine. It's little Herschel.'

'They caught him?' he guessed.

'Not yet,' answered Jaime. 'But he's been missing for a few days.'

Coca cut in. 'We've only just found out where he is. He's been staying at Lorenzo's hotel with Miss Winter here, and he's doing just fine.'

The defrocked lawyer looked up at Evelyn in surprise.

'How did that come about?' he asked her. 'I suppose he chose you, too?'

'Chose me?' she repeated.

'Our little Herschel is wiser than his years,' Efraín said, 'and which of us even knows how many those are? In the short time he and his sister have been in Escorial, he's been up here almost as much as I have. Sometimes I think that he came up to roust me out of my hole on purpose. He's sneaky that way. He can get you to do the most outlandish things merely by wishing it.'

'Or drawing it,' Evelyn mused aloud.

The lawyer reared his head back and remembered. 'Of course! How could I have forgotten all those times that he sat where you are now, doodling away on the inside flap of one of these books, drawing every corner of this room or this building, but without a sign of me, so that no one would ever catch a glimpse of me? Come to think of it,' he marveled, 'no one ever did. Except for him.'

'You told him that your husband was hiding up here?' Evelyn asked the wife. 'A total stranger?'

'He found me out,' Efraín replied for her. 'He was able to accomplish in a week what no one else in town has managed in six years. But we got on wonderfully together, and I knew he'd never tell anyone, not even his sister. And he didn't, not even when he had to lie to her to keep me hidden. And he never lies to Rifka. Eventually, of course, I told him that it would be all right for him to tell her, and then I enjoyed the company of both of them.

'But what's going on?' Efraín demanded irritably. 'Why does this woman have him? And what about the girl? Is she all right or isn't she? Why have I been kept in the dark for so long? Isn't it bad enough,' he cried out in anguish, 'that I've had to waste my life up here where I can't change anything, where I can't make a difference in the outside world? How much more will be taken away from me, now that I don't even have the chance to save the little part of the world that's left worth saving?'

The Piña family dithered and chewed their lips, but finally Elisa told her husband everything. As Evelyn watched, the reddish man on the floor grew whiter, flatter, as he sorted out the many consequences of what had happened over the past few days.

'So Rifka is with the police,' he stated, 'and poor Herschel is sick and staying in a hotel. Is there anything else?'

'It's not really as bad as it sounds,' his wife said.

'Of course it is,' Evelyn put in. 'Aside from the fact that I can't take care of him for ever – I do have a life of my own back home, such as it is – the girl has to be rescued before they place her in an orphanage and separate the two of them for good. No one wants that, do they?'

For the first time since they had come up, the visitors saw the lawyer lose his composure. He glared hard at Elisa and her parents.

'And how is it that no one thought to tell me any of this, as soon as it happened?'

'Well,' Jaime started, 'we were so busy looking for them on our own . . .'

'And,' Coca added, 'it's not as if the boy has never stayed out by himself for hours on end. He's as independent as a Hasid, most of the time.'

As if she were lowering herself into a bath or down onto a more respectful level, Elisa crouched next to her husband with a look of excessive patience, the same look she wore when explaining the workings of a toy to her daughter.

'Besides,' she said, 'we all knew how you would react. You'd blow up the way you always do, imagine the worst, run around here until your head ached, then probably escape and go screaming from one street to the next trying to find the girl and save Herschel. And in the end, even though the rest of us could have taken care of the children just fine, you would have exposed yourself to the authorities after all the hard work we've done to keep you hidden and well. You'd put all of us at risk of prison or death, just to keep two children out of some orphanage where they could eat more anyway and meet other children just like them. I suppose that we should have told you right away, but you have to admit that what we did was a lot more reasonable, don't you think? Efraín?'

Beneath the scowl of the ceiling, the lawyer slowly rose to his feet, stronger now and less flippant, moving alone for the first time, peering down at his wife in sorrow.

'Escape?' he whispered.

'What? What did I say?'

Husband and wife regarded each other from a great distance, as if the attic room had suddenly swelled in proportions.

'Now, Efraín,' Jaime Piña cautioned, 'there's no reason for any of us to go off in a blind panic. What can you hope to do tonight, with every policeman in Escorial out on the streets?'

'He's right,' Coca said. 'It might even snow some more. And you wouldn't want to risk catching a chill after all this time up here.'

Efraín began fiddling about his attic, laying his hands on a scarf here, some gloves there, and a striped coat.

'Well,' he said, dressing, but looking only at Evelyn, 'you said that the police were probably keeping Rifka in a place where they thought little Herschel might come looking for her.'

'So?'

'So where else would the nephew of a rabbi go,' he said with the door in his hand, 'but to a priest?'

On their way through the darkest streets in Escorial, the lawyer told Evelyn that the boy had always been naturally curious about spiritual matters and that the friendship between him and Father Fermín had been better for Herschel than any school.

'He was able to ask all the questions and talk about all the ideas he had with a grown-up who really cared about such things,' the lawyer said with the smallest hint of jealousy.

'Someone to take the place of his father?' Evelyn said.

'Exactly,' Efraín nodded as they slipped through twisting cobbled lanes with the moon nearing its first quarter overhead.

'What about you? It sounded as if you two were just as close as most fathers and sons are.'

'Ah, but I've never had a head for religious subjects. I've always found man's laws baffling enough. I leave God's laws to others more inspired. I was never able to teach Herschel what he wanted to know, and he always wanted to know so much.'

'And your wife and her parents? What did they think of it?'

'What – of Herschel and the priest getting together as they used to?'

'What else?' asked Evelyn.

Trotting along beside the lawyer who seemed to be stretching his legs like a colt in spring, Evelyn tried to make sense of all that was happening around her tonight. She had no idea where she was going or what she was doing, except that she was alone in the dead of winter with a wanted fugitive on his way to confront one of the most important people in town. She would have felt better with the whole Piña family beside her, but she sensed that Efraín had deliberately excluded them from his impetuous foray out into the suspicious night. And now she wanted to know why.

'It's just that,' the man finally admitted, 'for them, it's

a bit different, harder and less natural. I think that's probably normal for people in their situation. They're *Marranos*, you know. Are you familiar with that word?'

'Not entirely.'

'It's just a little bit further,' he promised, as he saw her hugging her coat and reaching for breath. 'That's a terribly ugly word, but I suppose somebody must have thought it fitting at one time. *Marranos* are Spanish Jews who, when the Christians made them decide between leaving in 1492 and converting, chose to stay in the only country that most of them had ever called home. After all these years, families like my wife's that are Jewish on the inside, but sort of Christian outside, tend to shy away from any discussion about religion. They know there's a lot to be said from all sides, but they'd rather not bother and just get on with their everyday lives. I don't mean to say that they've changed in any real way. It's just that it's always been less painful for them not to argue than to be actively abused.

'And,' Efraín added as he led them around a final corner, 'that's why they all looked so shocked when I told them where the boy used to go, and why they didn't even offer to come along. The whole thing has nothing to do with them. Talking about God to my wife or her parents would be like chattering away at a Norwegian in Chinese.'

Looking up at the dark half of the moon's face, Evelyn told the lawyer that she had never had much faith in faith anyway.

'Me neither,' he agreed. 'But I respect those who do.'

'You're one hell of a Communist,' the woman observed.

'Oh, I didn't say that I believed, only that man's relations with God are surely the most significant relations he can have in his life, even beyond those with his family. What else is there?'

'After the German war,' Evelyn said bitterly, her head thick with a growing ache, 'why should we even bother to ask?'

They suddenly came upon a modest door set into a stone wall with another Madonna in relief carved into its side. When Efraín had finally stepped out of the apartment building in Libro Verde Street for the first time in six years, he had stopped to moisten the tips of his fingers and then touch the statue's foot with all the reverence of a sinner in a church. Here, however, the lawyer ignored the Virgin entirely and started rapping on the thick door as quietly as he could in the ringing street. The two waited for minutes in a wind that seemed to turn into crystals and flakes on their eyelashes, until the door groaned open and a voice blessed them hoarsely and ordered them to return in the morning.

'Six years,' Efraín whispered back, 'is a long time to wait for absolution, Mario. Even for a Red.'

The priest's breath caught on the door as he opened it wider and the light inside showed him who was there.

'Mother of God! Efraín Cota, still alive? But it can't be.'

'I'm afraid it can.'

'But—'

'Let us in,' the lawyer pushed ahead. 'It's about the girl.'

The door resisted a moment longer, but then Evelyn followed her fugitive into a hallway of stone with leather on the walls, past a locked sacristy and the smell of dribbling water, and finally into a tall study overgrown with bookshelves and the warm light of healthy flames. The priest sat them in the fire's glare, served them tumblers of mahogany brandy, then perched himself on a corner of his desk to view the renegade who had so miraculously returned from the dead or the missing.

'I can't believe my own eyes,' he said with wonder. 'You

were supposed to have fled into France or have been killed trying to get across the border. The whole town knew the story. And now here you are, returned like the Prodigal Son from his harlots and his swine, with nothing to show for all these six years. Have you been here in Escorial all the while?'

'More or less,' Efraín answered. 'This *is* my home.'

'And now I suppose you're expecting us to welcome you with a fatted calf, just as if nothing had happened?'

'Well, I do thank you for this fine brandy, Mario.'

The lawyer's casual courtesy, perfectly natural in him, only seemed to goad the other man.

'And you're to be forgiven,' the priest persisted, 'for the time when you almost drove your country toward the doors of hell itself?'

Rocking unhappily on the edge of his desk, Father Fermín with his reddened eyes and sour mouth contemplated his enemy as if six harsh years had been but a single day.

'We fought for justice,' Efraín said, 'and a society where a man might share what he has with all.'

'And where he would live only for today and not give a damn about what might happen to his soul in the future – is that it?'

'Man makes his own future,' the fugitive concluded, 'as well as his own justice and morality. Any adult should know that.'

The other man snorted at him rudely.

'Was it justice and morality you had in mind when you robbed God's holy churches of their gold?' the priest asked. 'Or when I had to stop you from clogging our courts with senseless cases, so many that even traitors couldn't be tried in time? I suppose such legal shenanigans were for the welfare of Spain.'

'If we're going to talk about the welfare of Spain,' Efraín fumed, 'why don't you tell us how *you* saved Spain by helping a torturer massacre his own people with hired Moors and maniac Germans?'

The two men squared off now, ignoring Evelyn completely.

'You confused people with strange ideas,' Father Fermín said sorrowfully. 'You gave them impossible hopes.'

'You lied to them.'

'You turned them against their one, true God.'

'You turned them against each other.'

The churchman bent down a face swollen black with pain.

'You killed priests,' he said in a broken whisper.

The lawyer shrugged Herschel's innocent shrug.

'You killed children,' he whispered back.

Both men fell silent, giving Evelyn a chance to rise from her chair slightly and remind them of why they were all here.

'I think what matters most here tonight is what we should do for the brother and sister, not what you two should or shouldn't have done years ago. Agreed? I mean, none of us has made all that many right choices, or we wouldn't be here in this room tonight, sitting here distrusting each other – and ourselves.'

The priest looked at her for the first time since his two visitors had interrupted his reading.

'You're an American?' he asked.

'I am.'

'How is it—'

'I have Herschel.'

Father Fermín smiled at her almost jealously.

'So where is my little scholar now?'

'Where's Rifka?'

'Why should you think she's here?' cried the priest.

'Save it for your parishioners, Mario,' the lawyer said, and then he lied, 'Both this woman and Herschel saw her being brought in here. We don't want you to get into any trouble with the Civil Guards or the police. We just want to see these two *niños* brought back together again. Is that so very evil of us?'

'No,' Father Fermín admitted. 'No, I suppose it isn't.'

The priest moved around his wide desk and sat himself with a weary sigh behind it. He reached into a drawer, pulled out a pair of cigars, and in a moment the two men were filling the air with contemplative clouds of silver-blue smoke. The fire coughed with the winter cold outside, and Evelyn watched as the old rivals let some of the rancor between them drain away with their brandies. A rich, wooden tone colored the room's air, and Evelyn sat back and watched the little boy scampering up the ladder that was hidden in a bookshelf frame and then saw him up on the balcony of books that encircled the entire room with a dark halo. Looking up made her dizzy, though, so she closed her eyes and rested.

'Damn it all, Efraín,' Father Fermín said with a slow shake of his head. 'I don't know why they brought the poor girl here to me. I know that she used to bring her brother over here and pick him up again, and I think once in a while she even stepped in to listen to us finishing one of our talks. She was never as curious about such things as Herschel was, but she liked to sit here and run her eyes over some of my titles. I even caught her reading a page or two behind my back a couple of times, though I can't seem to recall what kind of book it was. History, perhaps, or science. Never theology.'

'So they brought her here,' Efraín asked, 'just because they thought her brother might come looking for her?'

'Oh, who knows why any of those officious fools do what they do. Since you've been gone – or rather since we *thought* you've been gone – the city authorities have taken leave of their senses, not to mention their Christianity. Homes broken into, people made to look suspicious or weak, a man's most private thoughts exposed to the dirty fingers of clerks who can barely read one word after another.' He rattled his coxcomb of white hair in the firelight. 'Do you remember Luis Ochoa, Efraín? A little man with eyes like emeralds who lived across from the monastery?'

'The artist who used to paint those wonderful pictures of peasants and artisans building the palace way back when?'

'That's him,' Father Fermín answered gravely. 'He's gone.'

'What do you mean, gone?'

The priest flashed his hand through the air, and the mirror reflection of it became lost in the permanent shadows above them.

'What I say – gone. One day he's working on a new painting of farmers on their land, and the next he's disappeared into an office downtown and then into a detention center somewhere in the depths of Segovia Province. After that, who knows when any of us will meet him again? Not this side of heaven, I'll wager. It happens all the time,' Father Fermín mourned. 'Hardly a day goes by that someone doesn't vanish without even the formality of an explanation. When everything in Spain is untrue, why should anyone even bother to lie anymore?'

'My God,' the lawyer murmured. 'How much have I missed? None of the newspapers they smuggled in to me mentioned any of these nightmares.'

'It's not only that . . .'

A sudden falling sound from an adjacent room stopped Father Fermín and brought him up around the desk again. Without saying a word, he took his guest's cigar and glass and pulled him roughly to his feet.

'Quick, Efraín, up on the balcony.'

'What?'

'Hurry, use the ladder.' The priest trundled him over to the bottom rungs. 'Hide up there in that far corner. It's darker.'

'But what are you doing?' the lawyer protested.

'Get going, will you?'

Evelyn sat stunned as the flustered attorney clawed his way up the ladder, through the hole in the hanging balcony, and over to the end of the walkway where the mustiest shadows had fallen. As soon as he was crouched there and the priest had disposed of the extra cigar and brandy, a second door opened to let in a large man dressed in a long, woolen nightshirt.

'Did I hear a knock, Father? Oh,' he stammered when he saw a woman in the chair, 'excuse me, Miss.'

'That's all right,' Evelyn said in her best Spanish, looking down into her lap.

'It's just one of my congregation,' the priest said quickly, 'come for a little late-night reassurance. These December nights leave all of us feeling a bit unsure of ourselves.'

'I thought it might be the girl . . .' The intruder in the nightshirt clumsily retreated. 'I mean, I thought it might have been someone who was having trouble sleeping tonight and who wanted to come into your office without your permission.'

'No, Paco, you don't have to worry about that. If anyone did have trouble sleeping,' Father Fermín said, spreading his shaking hands over his desk, 'I'm sure she would probably just come down here for a book and then go back to her room where she belongs.'

The guard puzzled over this for a while, then he nodded at the priest, wished him a good night, and waddled back through the rear door to his makeshift bed.

As soon as the lawyer had slithered down again, he said, 'I never thought I'd live to see Paco Gomez inside a church again.'

'The police wanted one of their own on hand,' Father Fermín said ironically, 'just in case I couldn't be completely trusted.'

'I don't blame them. I've just been reading over some of the titles up there.' Efraín winked at Evelyn and lifted his eyes to the far balcony corner. 'I see you were young once, too, Mario.'

'I beg your pardon?' The priest frowned at the fugitive, then allowed a weak smile to relax his features. 'You two come with me,' he finally decided. 'We'll go around the other way to the girl's room – but only to see her, if she's awake. I'm making no other promises, Efraín. You do understand that?'

'I wouldn't have it any other way – comrade.'

The two visitors were taken through a courtyard full of snowdrifts into a rear section of the building. In the dark and freezing air, Evelyn felt as if she were touring the monastery again, lost in its solitude and cold age. She stumbled along, unsure of where she was and totally ignorant of where she might be headed, caught between one door closed invisibly behind her and another flashing open ahead. She knew that this was not her, that Evelyn Winter of Madison, Wisconsin, could not commit such uncharacteristic acts. But for the first time in her life, she felt herself standing on some fatal edge and daring herself over for no other reason than that she knew she shouldn't dare it. And as they arrived at the innermost door in the church, she thought with a thrill: Yes, at last, it's about time. Now it really is too late to ever turn back again. It really is too late to stop anything now . . .

'*Mädchen*,' the priest called out in a German that betrayed his past sympathies. 'Are you still awake, my dear?'

From behind a wicker partition at the rear of the cell came a questioning hum, followed by a girl in a tall dress of severe corners and dull black. Up close, the boy's sister was even more angular and hard than she had appeared across the morning street. Evelyn saw that she was pretty, but mostly in an inward, meditative way that might seem unhealthy outside of this hidden room. Rifka could not have been older than seventeen, but as she looked from the priest to the visitors, tired and wary, she might have been a widow at a wake, welcoming strangers. Evelyn looked at the girl's dark eyes beneath the darker, squinting brows and wondered if she had been crying. But the shadows there were too deep for tears alone.

'Where's Herschel?' Rifka demanded immediately.

'Oh, he's still quite safe,' Father Fermín answered. 'Don't you worry about that. He's being cared for by this nice woman and our friend here. They've just come tonight to see how you've been getting along on your own, as it were.'

'As a matter of fact,' Evelyn spoke up, 'Herschel wanted us to tell you he was well and to see if we could do something about getting you two back together again. Wouldn't you like that?'

The lawyer, left out of the German conversation, walked from wall to wall of the nun's retreat, comparing it to his own. While the others talked, he made his way to an end of the wicker screen and gazed idly around it.

'I hope we didn't wake you,' Evelyn began again.

'It doesn't matter.'

'I just thought you might want to know about Herschel.'

'Why is my brother staying with this woman?' the girl asked the priest.

'It's a long, long story.'

'We just happened to meet,' the woman added. 'He was in the monastery courtyard, drawing in the snow, and I came by to watch. It was pure chance, really.'

'God's work,' Fermín muttered to himself.

'Is the policeman still here?' The dark girl advanced toward the door.

'He's asleep, I believe. But, yes, I'm afraid he is.'

'Then there's no sense in bringing Herschel here to me.'

'He's still having trouble with his nightly fevers,' Evelyn reported. 'And it's so cold outside tonight.'

'That's normal for him,' Rifka dismissed the news. Then she turned to face the priest. 'Am I still being kept prisoner here, Father, or am I free to go whenever I want?'

'My child, you never were, as far as I was concerned. I was only trying to keep you away from that awful police station. I've heard too many stories,' he said, shaking his head in sorrow.

'Because,' the girl said forcefully, 'I want you to help me get out of here. Now. Tonight.'

'What did she say?' the lawyer asked from across the room as he heard her raise her voice.

Evelyn translated for him, then said to the girl, 'But there are police all over town looking for Herschel. He can't walk out into that. I was thinking that if we could just wait a little bit longer, then maybe after things have settled down, you could both move back in with the Piña family or with someone somewhere else who could take care of you. At least then you wouldn't have to be in some orphanage until your parents finally came to get you.'

At the mention of her parents, the girl suddenly became more animated. Her face flushed, and her cropped hair bristled as if a current of electricity had passed through her.

'But that's just it!' she cried. 'That's why Herschel and I have to leave town now. We have to be in Barcelona in a week, by the eighteenth of December at the latest. That's when our parents are passing through with some others on their way to Palestine, and that will be the only time they'll be able to pick us up. If we don't meet them then, who knows when we'll be able to catch up with them, or where?'

'My Lord!' the priest breathed out.

'Tell me, tell me,' Efraín demanded. Evelyn did, and then he faced the girl, held up a fold of paper, and said in Spanish, 'Is this how you found out about it?'

'What's that?' asked the priest.

'That's mine. Give it back!' The girl answered Efraín in his own language, distrustful of both men now and the unknown woman.

'I found it behind the partition,' the lawyer said. 'It's a letter from somewhere called Bergen-Belsen, but I can't read much of it.'

He surrendered it to the girl, and she backed away from the others toward her lonely partition.

'It's from my mother,' she finally admitted. 'I got it only last week.'

'However did it find you?' the priest wondered.

'A man brought it to me, a man I'd never seen before who was working for some relief agency. He said that he'd been given the directions by my mother herself. That's how the police caught me. I was so excited by the news that I went running out to find my brother right after that man had met me in our street. The police must have seen us together and got suspicious.'

Evelyn slowly reached out a hand. 'May we read it – please?'

The two women stared at each other, the older one less sure but full of trust, the younger one stronger and trusting no one, until at last Rifka put it in Evelyn's hands and stood back.

Evelyn bent over the letter and translated it aloud for the benefit of the lawyer.

'The gist of it, then,' she finished, 'is that their parents are being held in this transit camp until they can make some new arrangements for transport south and then abroad. Because no one seems to have any proper papers, legitimate or not, all they can do is pass through Barcelona as quickly as possible, then out by way of the harbor. Evidently, that's the best place in Spain for them to get through without calling too much attention to themselves.'

'Barcelona and its seaport,' Efraín commented, 'has always been a central escape route for many who want to leave Europe behind them. What with its location and the three or four different languages spoken there, it's a perfect place to hide and transfer through. And its Jewish community has always been strong, too, so that can only help.'

'But this is terrible,' Father Fermín pronounced after they had all mulled over the contents of the letter.

'What – that they might get to see their parents again? Isn't it enough of a wonder that any of them are still alive?'

'No, Efraín,' the priest shook his head. 'What I mean is, I

don't see how the children could ever get to Barcelona in time.'

'Not on their own, no,' he conceded. 'I suppose not.'

'Then what about with some help?' Evelyn suggested.

The priest asked Rifka, 'This relief worker who found you – is he still around? Do you think he could do something for you?'

'I haven't seen him since,' she said. 'And the only thing he said about getting to Barcelona was for us to be careful.'

'How hard could it be for a grown-up girl and her brother to get there?' Evelyn asked. 'How far is it, anyway?'

'Almost seven hundred kilometers,' said the priest.

'Over four hundred miles,' Efraín calculated.

'But that's nothing,' Evelyn said. 'Only a little more than from Madison to Duluth. Someone could drive them there in four or five hours.'

'Not over Spanish roads. Not these days.'

'I have a car,' the priest said, 'but I'm afraid it wouldn't make it even halfway.'

'What about by air?' the American went on.

'Impossible.'

'Impossibly expensive,' Father Fermín shivered.

'By train, then?'

The two men looked at one another and saw a dim light, while the girl stood gazing anxiously at everyone as though she were a mute statue waiting for the dawn.

'That might work,' the lawyer agreed. 'The train is cheaper, no one polices it all that much, and it's easier to get lost on it. They could get there in a day or two by way of Madrid.'

'And there's a train to Madrid,' the priest added, checking his pocket watch, 'stopping at Escorial station in a few hours.'

'Do you think they could?' Evelyn said quietly.

'Oh, anything is possible, sometimes even the impossible.'

'Still . . .'

The priest took a quick turn around the cell as if he were a retired lion testing its cage. He clasped his mouth, mumbled into his sleeve, and gazed for inspiration at a wall, a bare bulb, and at the toe of a wall-mounted Madonna. Then he stopped in the center of the room and laid a hand on the fugitive lawyer's shoulder.

'I think we can do it, my friend,' he said, 'but it's going to take all of us working together.'

'All of us?' Efraín repeated skeptically.

'What do you mean by that?' Evelyn asked.

'Well,' the priest waved cobwebs of reservations aside, 'I'd have to help at this end—'

'But the policeman?' Evelyn worried.

'Oh, he sleeps like the dead. Thinks that way, too.'

'But what about all the rest of our good citizens?' Efraín's face hardened above its red goatee. 'Won't they be on the lookout for any late-night sins against the State?'

Father Fermín gave a familiar shrug. 'It's late and cold and threatening more snow. Who's going to be out? Besides, I've been seen driving out at night often enough to administer last rites, so why should tonight be any different? I'm a trusted citizen of Escorial,' he said with a mischievous gleam at the lawyer, 'not a radical Communist sympathizer.'

'Do you mean they're not the same?' Efraín wondered.

'I can drive you over to your hotel to get the boy,' he went on, turning to Evelyn, 'and then out to the station before anyone even notices I'm gone. As soon as you and the children are on the train, whatever anyone suspects here in Escorial will just be left far behind you.'

'Me?' Evelyn echoed, then swallowed. 'Did you say me?'

'Well, someone has to accompany the children. I can't,' the priest insisted. 'I'm too well known. I'd only draw attention to them. But I doubt if they could make it on their own, not without papers or at least an adult to bribe a policeman into looking the other way at just the right moment.'

Evelyn shook herself and tried to stand alone, but the room was too small and her feet too unsteady to hold her up.

'But how could I take them all the way to Barcelona? I don't even know the way myself. I'm not even Spanish. If anybody would stick out in a night train, it would be me,' she concluded.

'She's right,' Efraín agreed after a long silence. 'It will have to be me.'

'But you're already wanted,' Rifka cried out from a corner.

The lawyer passed off the objection as casually as he could, a grim purpose smoothing the crook of six years out of his neck.

'So I've got less to lose. I'll cut off my beard, wear a hat and scarf, and no one will ever recognize me. Who's expecting to see a dead man, anyway, in the middle of a crowded train?'

The four in the dark cell stood calculating the odds as out in the courtyard a new storm began to tumble down off a whiter moon. Anchored to the iron earth, the church stood in the circle of the town with the monastery brooding on its edge and the dead winter countryside spreading out to an unseeable horizon. Somewhere out in the darkness, a pair of tracks coiled and unwound across Spain toward a harbor where illegal boats might be waiting for men and women and their children on the run. But further than that no one in the cloistered room could see.

The priest took his deepest breath of the night and suddenly decided.

'Then you'll have to go together,' he said to the lawyer and to the woman who was swaying on her feet. 'Whatever could be more natural than a family traveling as a single unit?'

Efraín slowly nodded, and the girl's pale face cleared, but Evelyn seemed not to have heard him very clearly.

'I'm sorry. I didn't quite get that.'

'He said we should all go as one family,' the lawyer said.

'As one what?'

Everyone looked at her, and the priest suddenly stepped over to take her arm in his.

'What is it, Miss Winter? You don't look at all well.'

'No, I'm fine. Really, I am.'

Father Fermín held the back of his hand to her forehead and then to his own and then back to hers.

'Lord,' he said to the others as he tried to keep the woman from buckling to her knees, 'I think she's gone and got the boy's fever.'

Years later, Evelyn still remembered her last night in Escorial only as one blurred roll of unwinding images. First had come the shoeless sneaking out of the church, the floor like a skating rink and the levitating escapees like figures in a cartoon. Then the drive in the priest's car to the hotel, churning through the woolen roads without headlights and the priest navigating by enthusiasm alone. Then, finally back in her room, Evelyn had scooped the boy up out of a tossing sleep, the lawyer had stuffed her most intimate underclothes into her suitcase, and like an immigrant family making for the border they had scurried down the hallway and out to the car and the station in a wet, blinding blizzard. Even then, the flurry of sights and sounds had not stilled: the pretending, the tickets, the ignored policemen, the farewell telephone calls, the waiting, the waiting, the sudden appearance of the Piñas and their grief, and at last the sickening lurch of the train and the refreshing window pressed against her forehead. Nothing about her last night in the mountains would ever make much sense, and after several years even the fear and the feverish uproar blended into a harmless nightmare that meant nothing more than a good story told to her children at bedtime.

But out of that night, unforgettable as childhood, the

woman would always keep two memories alive. The first was of the hotel. In the light from the first-quarter moon, she had found Herschel lying rumpled among the bedclothes and picked him up while Efraín went ahead down to the waiting car. The boy had weighed so little that she might have been lifting fog. Silent and motionless as a stack of linen, he had not stirred as she carried him out of the room. And even when she was stopped in the hallway by the sudden appearance of the Englishman coming out of the bathroom, the boy had only slowed his breathing. Even in his sleep he thought of escaping by pretending to be dead.

'Shooting the moon, Eve?' the man asked unhappily, his robe slumped open to reveal a white chest. That frail whiteness seemed to blind Evelyn, until she had to squint in the dull light of the hallway bulb, and her eyelids burned. Even when he shortened her name to try to move closer to her, all she could hear was an echo of a typewriter in a military office and a window lined with gray and white stripes of rain.

'I have to go, Martin. Really, I do. I'm sorry for any hurt this might cause you, but—'

'So who's your new friend?'

'He's – sick,' Evelyn said. 'I'm taking him to a doctor.'

She tried to carry Herschel past, but the hall was narrow, and the Englishman too miserable to let her go.

'He looks like a prisoner with that short hair and all.'

'He just has a little fever. He'll get better soon.'

'Or a refugee,' Dearing went on. 'Does he have a sister, by any chance?'

'Martin—'

The Englishman advanced a step and reached out a hand toward the boy who was dozing warmly like bread. Confused, Evelyn wanted nothing more than to disappear into the brown shadows at the end of the hall. Now she wished that she had never spoken to Dearing in the first place – or perhaps she should have given him something more lasting than just talk . . .

'Are those your clothes, too, Eve, there under your arms?'

'Some of them,' Evelyn answered. 'Some of them are for him.'

'I see.'

The two adults faced each other, the man impatient with such sentimental foolishness, the woman only weary and feeling nothing. Try as she might, Evelyn could not seem to form a single, lucid thought in her mind, much less connect two or more. All she could do was feel the horrible stillness of the boy in her arms, growing more leaden the closer he came to the waiting train.

'You're never coming back again, are you, Eve? Here or home or even to England?'

'I don't know,' she replied uncertainly. 'I suppose—'

'You're not.' He wagged his head. 'Where will you go, then? What will you do now?'

'I really can't say.'

'Have you thought enough about what you're doing? I mean,' he stressed, 'have you really thought this whole thing through?'

'I can't think right now, Martin,' Evelyn stammered and blew some hairs off her face. 'I'm not feeling very well. I haven't eaten, I need some sleep, and I'm late at getting downstairs. To tell you the truth, I have absolutely no idea what I'm doing, and I'm sure that it's probably the worst thing for me to do, anyway. But I can't think of all that just now, not if I'm going to get this boy to safety. And I am,' she added, her voice breaking, but stronger. 'I'm going to take him and his sister to their parents even if I have to go through every person in Spain to do it. I have to. Do you understand?'

Martin Dearing was impressed by her newfound determination, but he still knew what was best.

'You're about to change your whole life in a single night, you know. Don't you think that requires – deserves – more thought than you've obviously given this?'

'I don't think I have much choice, Martin. Please, please, try to see this my way, just this once.'

'We all have choice,' he said, stepping helpfully forward. 'You, me, even the boy. We all make our own choices every day.'

'But—'

'Whether we like to admit it to ourselves or not,' he added, 'we all choose everything we do, even when we tell ourselves that we're not choosing anything. Even doing nothing is a choice, Eve, even when you let others do your choosing for you. Isn't that the case here?' Dearing whispered, desperate to reach her. 'Violating the law, harboring fugitives, smuggling refugees, helping people to break into a country that's already filled with its own native population, inflaming all those ancient passions that my country has been working so hard for so long to keep in check – are these things you want to do, or are they only what someone else wants you to do for them?'

Evelyn still resisted. 'Sometimes,' she said, 'we don't have the choice to choose or not to choose . . .'

'Think about it,' he urged her, blocking her way with both elbows angled outward like a gate. 'For God's sake, before it's too late! You know better than this. You know that this can never work, either for these children or for you. They'll be hounded from country to country. That's what you're starting when you take this first step, Eve.

You're not being heroic, and being a martyr doesn't do anyone any good. If you think this will make up for your not doing much during the war,' Dearing implored her, 'you're sadly mistaken. Once you get involved, this will strand you so far out to sea that you'll never be able to swim back to land again.

'You're going to fall, Eve,' he said, 'doing this. And then you'll never be able to get back up again. Not in a world that's as unfair as this one.'

For a moment, Evelyn seemed to consider what he said, moving back a step in the direction of her old room. But then the child in her arms moaned and stirred, pulling her toward the steps that led down to the street below.

'Would it matter so much,' Evelyn said to him, 'as long as I keep on falling forward?'

'Some people will hate you,' the Englishman said quietly. 'I think a lot of people will hate you for what you're doing.'

'Will you hate us, too, Martin?' Evelyn asked as she held her burden between them. 'Do you hate us now? Have you really gone that far already?'

The man in the robe wavered, caught the combined scent of a feverish woman and a napping child, and exhaled very slowly.

'Excuse me,' he murmured politely, sidling past. 'It's late, and we working men have to get up early.'

'Thank you, Martin,' she said, brushing her arm against his. 'Thank you, from both of us.'

He smiled then. 'Do you need any help going down?'

'No, I don't think so.'

'Watch the stairs,' he pointed. 'There's not enough light.'

'I will,' she promised him and moved away, the boy

suddenly weightless in her arms.

'You have my best wishes, Evelyn. All of you. I mean that.'

'And you ours, Martin. I know you do.'

The final leavetaking on the Escorial platform was a second memory that would never grow fainter. When the Piñas had arrived to say goodbye, Jaime had stepped forward to place something wrapped in a rag in the boy's weak hands, telling him to keep it for his next home and his next family. Evelyn had not recognized it until the train started moving out into the long dark; then she had seen the broken toe of the stone Madonna off the apartment building in Libro Verde Street lying in the boy's lap, along with powdered masonry and flaked-off paint, and a miniature roll of parchment. Efraín told her that it was a hidden *mezuzah*, containing Biblical verses which spoke of the houses to come full of all good things, of wells and olive trees and vineyards, and of eating and being filled. But in her fever, all that Evelyn had been able to imagine was drawings of houses, designs of fields, and dining tables yellowed by time until their grains became the fibers of paper, shredding under a broken lead and a worn eraser.

Evelyn's final glimpse of Escorial was of its gray roofs and the lonely monastery holding up its skeleton's face to the moon. As the train ran away, the town settled back into the earth, the fogs piling over it until only the monastery's towers emerged like wintered and blasted trees. And even they had soon become invisible, swallowed by the drifting sand that under the imperfect moonlight might have been mistaken by anyone for a canvas of snow.

During the first leg of her journey, Evelyn was too blurred with fever to know anything for sure. They were leaving Escorial behind, with its bone palace and its palace of bones, its curious hotels and its interchangeable men . . . that was all she knew. She felt too ill to care what she was doing or why, while the hammock swaying of the train seemed to suspend her pleasantly between the life she had left and the life that was waiting for her somewhere ahead. All she wanted was to feel a cool pillow under her head, the frost-cool window shining on her face, the landscape of cool snow or sand that was unscrolling on the outside of the train like a speeding tapestry running past stationary carriages.

Even their route seemed vague to her. They might have been anywhere. The night of the countryside was complete, without the blur of a distant farmlight. But the stations were daytime, as the train shunted slowly past pumpkin-colored lamps and travelers who were also sleepwalking between stages, some of them clear and clipped in their walk, but most of them staggering. At times, she thought she was riding through Wisconsin again, its flat fields, on her way from aunt to aunt, or following her mother's advice to find a new home away from home. Evelyn must have slept, although later she could never say which was the nightmare and which was the dream of a foreign woman sailing through darkness and winter. She woke occasionally to find the carriage beginning to fill with others: an ancient woman alone with a string bag, a man turned away wearing strange clogs smeared with machine grease, the leather uppers knotted with twists of wire, another family like theirs on the dark side of the window, riding transparent in mid-air. Across from her sat Herschel, scribbling sleepily in the moisture on the glass. Efraín rocked next to him, half-asleep, watching out for a prowling conductor, the lawyer's face carefully blank, shaved now, and with a peasant's *boina* on his head. Rifka sat beside Evelyn, a clattering of sharp angles folded into a wedge, her black eyes seeing nothing in the unseeing night. Evelyn's eyes, too, could see little, although sometimes she awoke and surveyed the rest of the coach with its passengers huddled against one another, all of them melted together in the hanging, reddish light. And then she awoke again, this time opening her eyes, to find the scene around her the same, only herself shifting from the hard wooden bench to somewhere just outside the window, looking fondly at the warmth within.

Finally, the railway junction of Villalba appeared. There, they had to crawl out of the train and wait for ever on a long platform amidst café tables and a few curious passersby. The station was surrounded by a desolation of blood-red clay houses, some new of brick, a dead gasworks, and a dump. Every idling face watched them, knew them, and was eager to inform on them. Finally, they hurried back onto the train again and started moving anxiously away from the cars and telephones pursuing them through the mercury night. The ride down the mountainside to Madrid took longer than they had expected. The moon helped a little, flying alongside, carrying the whole train across bridges of dark, from one island of lonely light to the next. The carriages swept past hills with their shoulders guarding their ears, past inexplicably glowing strings far off in the distance, through deafening tunnels and over trestles where the earth would drop fearfully away from beneath them and leave them hovering like a linear cloud between silence and sound. After Villalba, they did not stop again until Madrid, except for a few transfers from one track to another, out in the middle of nowhere, the iron wheels slowing to a stop, then squealing backward, knuckling over points, then starting to stop, stopping, stopping the stop, then starting and going. These three or four dances in the night shifted the passengers from dream to dream and left Evelyn feeling slightly queasy, at sea, as if she were riding on the Thames or motorboating over Lake Mendota or following the course of the Guadarrama Sierras as they fell crumbling down onto their knees northwest of Madrid. As they neared the end of their first stage of traveling, Evelyn lay back in a continuing haze, so disorientated that she no longer knew if she were a living American woman rushing into unknown exile, or a lost German mother returning from barren years of torture.

When the conductor finally came by for their tickets, Evelyn and Efraín were the only ones still sitting. Rifka had gone off, looking for a water closet, while Herschel had wandered away in search of whatever discarded pieces of paper he could find. Asleep on his feet, the conductor barely glanced at the bouquet of fabricated documents that Efraín offered him, as he hardly noticed the boy across the aisle who Evelyn pretended was their own, or the girl over there whom Efraín claimed as his daughter. As easily as storms form, the lawyer became

Ruy Sánchez, a descendant of a poet even the conductor had heard of, and Evelyn was transformed into Eva Thompson, the sister of an internationally famous writer and columnist whom no wise man would ever wish to offend. After a bundle of pesetas was exchanged for a pass that might carry them all the way through to Barcelona, the danger continued strolling down the train and let Evelyn go back to pretending that the roll of the tracks beneath them was only her father's monotone in the front seat as he drove them back home from a Christmas dinner.

She sat up suddenly at another halt in the journey. Mysterious figures at the windows were walking in thick boots and with bars in their hands to the front and back of the train. Unfamiliar families were being loaded off and on. Voices massed. Bodies formed choruses in the airless carriage until she could not hear or breathe. Outside, there was no station to be seen, only trucklights and smoke and loose dogs trotting back and forth through the beams as in a movie. The cold night winds off the foothills shook the train on its moorings. In the middle distance, through the distortions of the spongy glass, Evelyn thought she saw an arch of branches or iron, and lanes that receded parallel to a vanishing point of smoke and brick. It must be a private garden, she thought, or a public park that could once have been a prince's playground. There would be winding paths in there, leaf-blanketed walkways and promenading waters, benches of stone, and shrubbery shaped like zoo animals, sundials and swings. The maze would be neverending, like a journey through absolute darkness. She would be able to hide in there, hide even from herself, wander for ever in one place and never have to face again anyone else's looks of disappointment or inattention. For the rest of her life, feverish and solitary, she could continue to go further and further in, to the bottom of the garden where its great library shelves and locked Bibles would be arching overhead in canopies of frescoed galleries and its tombs of the granite dead would shimmer like toys on the surface of an exquisite illustration in the colorful snow. But then Evelyn saw, as her eyes grew moist against the window, that this garden would never reach an end anywhere in this world . . .

A brutal jolt of doors and couplings, and they were on their way again. As the night wore on, it bore them through moods of expectation and escape, and Evelyn began to notice more of her fellow travelers. The old woman with the string bag was now working on a rosary fashioned out of spit and bread, while the family of three or four generations gathered all together as though to warm themselves around a brazier between their feet. They were hatted, kerchiefed, jacketed, coated, and as they turned, they turned into the bigoted woman from Barcelona and the stupid maid Lulú, the kind proprietor from Escorial and the studious historian from the museum city of Toledo, the Englishman in love and the couple from Bern who had finally decided to run after the Andalusian sun. As Evelyn watched them staring at her, she understood their vicious conspiracy at last, their plans to change her name and her home, their schemes to transfer all the orphans in the world into her care and send her out abandoned and hopelessly lost into another country where her only choices would be to disappear or die. Then they became a family of strangers again, turning back to the soup that the grandmother was heating over a small stove. From now on, Evelyn decided, she would have to be more careful about what she saw or who she looked at. From now on, anyone could be anyone.

But the man in the clogs is never anyone but himself. As he twines his wire shoelaces, he finds in the slatted floor at his feet an infinite loneliness. And past that, separate but connected, a flickering of railway ties like the pages in his calendar of sorrows.

'Where are we now?' Herschel asked again when he came back.

'Aren't we coming into Madrid?' Evelyn asked the lawyer, but Efraín was still asleep, his naked chin tucked protectively down into his collar.

'How much longer, Eva?' Herschel wanted to know.

'I don't know. A lot longer, probably.'

'Are you tired, too?'

'We're all tired.' Evelyn tried to comfort him where he sat across from her. 'You should try to get some more sleep.'

Herschel thought about it as he breathed fresh canvas onto the window, but then he changed his mind.

'Have you ever been so tired,' he said, shaking his legs to keep himself awake, 'that you were too tired to go to sleep?'

'Who, me?' Evelyn answered. 'I haven't slept for years.'

So far, the train ride seemed to have made Herschel feel the best he had felt in months. He was everywhere at once. As the carriage grew more and more swollen with seated and standing passengers, he was in his element, taking possession of the entire coach as if he had never known another home. Everyone became a new friend. Additional cargoes of salesmen and couples and families only appeared to inspire him to learn more, and he clambered over knees and bags to reach a cough that sounded interesting or a whimper from a child who he thought might need some extra attention. The pace thickened and the air dimmed with the weight of cigarette smoke and human heat, but nothing seemed to slow Herschel down. He moved more quickly than the conductor and reached more people. And when Evelyn was finally able to catch him rushing by and force him to sit down, she was relieved to find that last night's fever had not broken out in him again. Instead, he seemed to have handed over most of his illness to Evelyn.

'Aren't you feeling well, Eva?' Herschel said, studying her carefully.

'Why?' she wondered. 'Do I look so poorly?'

He nodded and bent over to stroke her overcoat, then touch his innocent forehead to hers.

'Is there anything I can do to help?'

Evelyn shook her head. 'With a little more rest, I should be fine. Don't you think so?'

Herschel turned toward the night, but the only answer it could give him was the semaphore of lighted windows flashing past.

'Do you think Rifka will be all right?' he asked Evelyn.

'Why shouldn't she be?'

'I don't know. Does she look all right to you?'

They both glanced at the sleeping girl. Her mouth lay slightly open like a baby's, and a feminine snore came out from between her lips. Although she wasn't feverish, Rifka still looked prostrate and dulled, her fine corners blunted by months of taking care of her brother, detention by the police and the priest, and an insomniac train that would not let her rest well. Herschel had been fussing over her ever since they had left Escorial, and now he obviously wondered if there might be something he had left undone.

'Don't you think she looks pale?' he whispered to Evelyn.

'Don't you think we all do, in this light?' she said.

Herschel shrugged and went on, 'Why do they stop so much out here where there isn't even a station?'

'They must have their reasons.'

'But what reasons, Eva? What possible reasons could they have?'

'How should I know?' she asked, too impatiently. Then she said, more kindly, 'But don't you think they probably know as much about their trains as you do about your drawings?'

'I suppose so . . .'

'And you know your drawings, don't you, both inside and out?'

He frowned up at her. 'Which is which?'

As they drew nearer to the lights of Madrid, Evelyn's fever began to ebb, and she felt a little stronger. Even with the men and women and children crowding all about them, with the wine sacks slung around pillars and the coachlights wheezing from the congealed odors, she now sat taller on their wooden bench. Always watchful of Herschel and his restlessness, she craned above most of the other benches and gauged the dangers from the front door and the back. The conductor had apparently gone for good. There were no soldiers on this train, few police at the stations, and only a deep December silence filled the black surrounding fields. Evelyn was still profoundly frightened. For the first time since the worst days of the war, she found herself in a situation that would have been impossible back home. Here tonight, anything might happen – even her own violent death – and she wouldn't be able to stop it. She wouldn't even be able to understand why.

Now Herschel was squinting at something distant that he could not quite see.

'What do you think is going to happen to us, Eva?' he asked her after some thought.

'You'll be fine, you and Rifka. You'll find your mother

and father waiting for you in Barcelona, and then you'll probably go down to Palestine or someplace else that's nice and warm.'

'Tell me about it.'

'What?'

Herschel sat eagerly forward, his crow's knees pointed and his legs dangling.

'Are we going to find new friends down there?'

'New friends? Well,' Evelyn said, 'why not? A couple of great kids like you shouldn't have any trouble finding a lot of new friends. Besides,' she added, dropping her voice away from the other two who might be only half-asleep, 'down there you'll be able to live alongside a whole country full of your own people. I'm sure you'd like that better, wouldn't you?'

'Really?' Herschel puzzled. 'What kind of people are those?'

'What? Well, you know,' Evelyn retreated a step, 'people who are a little more like you and Rifka than I am, for instance.'

'What are you?'

'I'm – well, I'm a little bit different, I suppose.'

'Do you mean,' Herschel questioned her, 'that you're kinder and better and happier and that you know how to play football and adventures with your hands better?'

He gazed up at her proudly, as if she were his best student at the only games that mattered.

'I mean,' she said slowly, 'that I'm not Jewish like all you folks are.'

He considered this, apparently for the first time.

'How do you know for sure?' he asked.

'Excuse me?'

Herschel explained. 'Where we come from, a lot of people and their families just aren't sure. My uncle used to tell me that no one should call himself or anyone else anything until he can find out if it's true or not in his own heart. He said that all of us have the same kinds of memories and dreams and that made it hard to call any one of us one thing without calling us all the same. He was a wise man, my uncle,' Herschel said, grieving. 'He always thought that only God had the right to decide who was what, and usually even He kept His decisions to Himself. He said that God didn't want us to know who we were because then we might decide who was like us and who wasn't, and then we might not act nicely to them. He said we'd find out all that on the day we died, so why should any of us worry about it until then?'

At the mention of his uncle and death, Herschel's face grew clouded, and for the first time since Evelyn had met him, he seemed near to tears. But then he thought of something else and brightened up again.

'Do you know what?' he shouted.

'No,' Evelyn replied, lowering his voice with hers. 'What?'

'My uncle used to say the same thing about my drawings. When I said that just now, I all of a sudden remembered.'

'What do you mean?'

Herschel went on, 'Well, he said that my drawings are always changing the way they do because they never want to be one thing, because that would mean they'd have to stop being all the other things they weren't. He said that as long as I leave gaps in all my drawings – you know, like the places I left to hide myself back in your room – then they'll never be finished and then I'll never have to watch them turn all yellow and shrivel up and die. And he was right. All my pencil sketches, all my drawings in the earth or the snow, stay nice and fresh as long as I leave something undone in them – a corner of a background or the leg of a bridge or even a single window in a palace. That way, there's always some room for the drawing to breathe and grow, the same as children do, and then I don't have to worry about it becoming something that it was never meant to be. Do you understand, Eva?' he said to her.

'I think so,' she replied.

'I did have one picture once,' Herschel admitted, staring at the scene on the bare floor between them. 'A picture of a man and trees and a road that disappeared into nowhere. That one I really finished. But now I know that I should have left some empty gaps in that one, too. I should have left hundreds of them, thousands of them. Millions. Then maybe,' he faltered, 'then maybe I could have taken a lot more of my old friends with me when I left to be with my new ones. That would have been nicer.'

To divert him from his suddenly bleak mood, Evelyn told him that the new land where he and his sister were going with their parents would have plenty of people who would love his artwork, whether it was finished or not.

'Really?' he said hopefully. 'Do you really think so?'

'Why not?'

Herschel still had his doubts.

'It's just that a lot of the time, some people don't like my drawings very much. They don't trust them.'

'They don't trust them?' Evelyn repeated. Then she glanced at the other passengers around them to see if their quiet German were being overheard by the wrong people. It was not.

'Well,' Herschel continued, 'they seem to think my drawings should do more than they do – or less – even after I tell them that they never do anything that isn't already being done anyway, only out of sight. I never draw ghosts or evil spirits or God. I'd be too scared to. I just draw people when they act like evil spirits or God. Or ghosts . . .'

'I thought you told me in Escorial,' Evelyn reminded him as gently as she could, 'that you never draw people, only places.'

'I know,' he conceded. 'But how can you tell the difference between people and where they live and work and die? They're all so close together.'

'If it troubles you so much,' she suggested, 'maybe in your new home you should put away your pencils and paper for good.'

'Oh,' Herschel breathed out in horror. 'But I could never do anything like that. Never!'

'Why?' Evelyn asked. 'Is drawing that important to you?'

The question seemed to bewilder him, as if Evelyn had asked him if breathing or dancing were important to him.

'How could anyone live,' he said honestly, 'without knowing where the page ends?'

As they were talking, the train fell down a long slope, slogging through its brakes with a harsh, soprano screech. Madrid gradually appeared outside both sets of windows, a warmer glow of lights and shadows rising from the ground. The conductor had told them that they would be arriving on the north side of Madrid and departing from the south and that the connection would be rushed. Now, as the jellied crowd surged forward around a final bend, the woman woke Efraín and Rifka, and they all started fumbling over tickets and schedules as if their lives would be lost if any of them fell behind. Efraín fussed about like a crazy woman, while Rifka tried to calm him down and Herschel stared at the changing shades of the gathering lights outside. Their fellow passengers seemed less afraid. The other families piled their possessions on their laps like cousins, while the old woman tightened the knots in her bag, and the clogs scraped out into the aisle to hurry away before anyone else. The train's frame shuddered as it glided through the sidings, passing between beveled stone walls and beneath the mountain of a black barracks, then tripping as it walked beneath the crystal and iron shell of the station. It seemed that it took for ever to stop, creaking up to the platform where two or three people were waiting, no, more, everyone walking or standing still in a dream. When the tottering finally subsided, they stood up and carried their bags toward the door at the front end, the children out ahead behind their father with their mother behind, shuffling sideways to pass by a pair of wooden shoes. Stepping down, they looked from side to side, as if they could ever recognize anyone from Escorial or do anything to change anything now, and made their way toward the taxis waiting in a half-circle just outside. One final look back, and all the others had gone down the platform in the opposite direction, and on the train window the circular drawing of a family that the boy had left behind drained away as the carriage emptied. Rifka took her brother's hand. They were suddenly very tired. Both parents seemed sad. It was past midnight, cold and clear. To Madrid, all these travelers must have seemed as dazed as cattle on their way to market.

Except for the clogs, now complemented by a pair of striped trousers with ragged cuffs, that stumble doggedly off the train and out of the station and vanish into the park across the street like paper fog drifting through barbed wire.

★ ★ ★

Little Herschel chose the taxi and climbed in before either adult could object. He drew a quick picture on the misty window, then promptly fell asleep behind the lawyer, who rode stiff and brittle beside the rounded hulk of the driver. Rifka had to take the middle, and Evelyn was against the opposite door which rattled loose after only a minute's drive through the city. Behind the condensation that had built up on the glass, she watched the orange night-city flowing past, flashing all the noises and outlines of streets that never seemed to sleep.

From the first, Evelyn had been worried about Rifka. The girl had never really accepted this new woman who had inserted herself in the life she shared with her younger brother. In Father Fermín's cell, she had been moody and suspicious, glaring at both Evelyn and Efraín as if they were partly responsible for the events that had ruined their childhood. And in the train, dipping and rising out of sleep with the rhythm of the wires outside, the girl had remained distant, aloof, jealous of anyone who tried to take away from her the duty of caring for Herschel. She was old enough and mature enough for both of them. Had everyone simply left them to themselves, she made it clear, she would have undoubtedly been able to make her way across Spain on her own and keep the rendezvous with their mother and father that she and Herschel had been looking forward to for so long.

But now in the taxi, Evelyn could feel a change come over the girl. She was more wary now, trembling softly with the sudden weakness that afflicts those who have been woken up too roughly. She stared out at the moving city, mistrusting every street of it, and folded herself small in the center until there was hardly any of her to see in the uncertain sheen from outside. It was clear to Evelyn that the girl could not bear to sit next to her. Rifka's left shoulder shrank into her body as the uneven road jumbled them accidentally together. She would not look at the woman or talk or acknowledge her presence in any way, but only continued to ride in the middle of the cushion, musing and bitter and twisting their mother's last letter between her hands.

At the same time, Evelyn sensed at once that Rifka was now thoroughly frightened. Evelyn would have liked to whisper words of encouragement, but she didn't want the driver to wonder at her German. She had earlier noticed that Rifka's command of Spanish was not equal to her brother's. He was younger and more flexible, while she was too contemptuous of the land that hated them so to let even its words take root in her. Never able to speak or hear well, she seemed to understand only a fraction of what was being said to anyone else near her. Even the most harmless phrases and verbs seemed to take on overtones that no one else would hear, and she hid her face from sentences that Herschel knew were little more than general observations.

The grim driver began gossiping at once, swiveling his head to talk to the lawyer and the back seat about all his late hours, the weather, the war. The back seat sat back, trying to give him less to see and talk about, while the girl in the middle vanished from his sight altogether.

'You folks from Segovia, then?' the driver asked.

'Segovia?' the lawyer said. 'No. Near there.'

'Got ghosts around there, too, though, I suppose?'

'Ghosts?'

The driver snorted rudely against the windshield. His jowls shook with reawakened anger.

'Can't have years and years of words and hate without

a few ghosts left over. Screaming horses, moans behind barricades, mad Republicans, mad dogs. Thank God most of it's over. At least the world's back to normal. We won it back. Bastards. Communists. All those goddamned refugees—'

Rifka's breathing froze in mid-air.

'Excuse me?' Efraín said carefully.

'—refuse to believe any of the lies the Reds are spreading from their camps, saying that Franco did this and Hitler did that and Mussolini did the other. What the hell did they expect? Law and order means nothing to them. We were fighting for our futures and for the futures of our families. Values make a difference, I say. A man will do anything he can for them. Worse and worse.'

The driver changed into a higher gear, and from the back seat Evelyn saw the hard bulk of his shoulders. Her Spanish wasn't much better than Rifka's in a dark, clanging car, but the panting rage of the man was the worst she had ever heard. It flooded the interior of the taxi, hurt her ears, and smoldered in the trapped air. Evelyn was thankful that Herschel, at least, was asleep. And she would have liked to take one of Rifka's white hands to hold in hers, but they were nowhere to be found.

The driver said to Efraín, 'Do you know what it is, what's gone so wrong with everything in the world today, friend?'

'No,' the other man said, 'I'm afraid I don't.'

But the driver did, grinding gears as he spoke.

'Goddamned Jewish Marxists. Ideas and fads and books that no normal, honest working man could make head or tail of. What's that? Sometimes I wonder if they know how much harm there can be in trying to change everything a man's known since he was a boy. If you change what a man is, then you change what he was. And no one wants to lose the first and last good years he's ever going to have in his life. No one. Would you?'

The lawyer spoke quietly. 'There's nothing worse than years when a man didn't have the chance to do what he knew in his heart needed to be done. You can't get those back. You can't even hope to borrow them from your children. That would be unfair even if you could.'

'That's right,' the driver cried. 'Those two darlings you've got back there should be kept as innocent as they are now for as long as possible. Your wife, too. What are their names again?'

Evelyn heard the lawyer murmur something vague enough to be safe and to satisfy the curious driver. But the girl beside her continued to grow smaller and smaller.

'No,' the driver resumed, 'I say there's nothing better than goodness in this world. Nothing better. Nothing easier, either.'

'Goodness easy?' Efraín argued. 'In this world?'

The clutch dropped and carried them wildly through the dark.

'Why not? You listen to your leader and your priest and the one true God, and it's all open road from there on out. Don't see how anyone could see it any different. Just because other people have other ideas,' he declared, 'doesn't mean they're right or that we have to listen to them or let them say them out loud. That's how we got into all the troubles we've had during the past ten years or more. We listened too much and didn't do enough. If we had started cracking a few more heads – stomping a few more sick bastards into the dust when we had the chance back in the days of the Semana Trágica in Barcelona, before Azaña lost his faith over in Escorial—'

'Where?' the lawyer said.

'—then we wouldn't find ourselves at the broken end of

the stick right now. We'd have won, not only in Spain, but throughout the rest of Europe, too. And now we wouldn't have to sit back and listen to all those people bellyaching about how bad they've had it all these years and how they deserve some special help in the future. As if the rest of us haven't suffered just as much! As if we didn't lose everything when we lost our own neighbors!'

The streets outside were burnt with a ghostly light made of lamps and winter. Traffic had cleared for them, except for flags and shadows furtive as cripples. The ride across Madrid was not long, but the darker neighborhoods beyond the centre never seemed to end.

'It's all their fault, of course,' the driver resumed. 'They have only themselves to blame if it all came out bad for them in the end. That's what I say.'

'Who?' Efraín asked him as he accelerated on.

'Running, ruining our streets, their children in our schools and their men pressed up against our women at market. Niggers and faggots and gypsies and Protestants. All the rest. Lawyers. We all know who we're talking about here, don't we? It's not as if it's any secret, is it? Not here in Spain, at least. Never has been. Never will be. Wickedness without end.'

'What do they do? These lawyers, I mean.'

The driver sprayed his disgust across the glass.

'Oh, you know. Pettifogging, shylocking, shystering. All the little tricks they have to trick you. Money, money, money. That's all it is with them and their banks and the greasy way they stick together. God has always hated them, so why shouldn't we? If they weren't cursed, then there wouldn't have been a reason for Christ to come and save them. Never change. Each and every one of them, always the same. Can't tell them apart. Stick together like flies in shit. Displaced—'

Evelyn sat upright and listened harder. Rifka stirred at her side, now so alarmed that not even her brother's gentle snoozing could calm her back down. She jumped and jumped where she sat.

The driver turned down darker, more private ways.

'—disgrace us all with their freethinking unionism and who knows what else. Keep us away from the Ten Commandments and every other standard that a Christian has to keep beside him through the long nights behind the wheel. You wouldn't want that to happen to us, would you? You being a husband and a family man and all, just the same as the rest of us, right?'

The renegade father muttered something, but his words melted in a rain of tires along pavement, and the driver took his sighs as signs of approval.

'I didn't think. Jews are clever that way. Once you let one of them get into the government or the universities, you might as well give yourselves up for dead. Didn't used to be that way. Used to be simpler. When you had only one way, you didn't ever have to wonder about anything or get lost. Things were so much easier then. You had maps then, and routes, and roads that everyone knew and took. None of this gallivanting around with anyone you wanted to be with. There were standards then,' he said woefully. 'Meanings. Morals. Virgins. Not Christ-killers, Communists, and Republicans. Sons-of-bitches. Well, am I right, or am I right?'

'You're right,' said Efraín, and looked helplessly at his own motionless hands in the glow of the streetlights.

The cold taxi rode through winter rain and fog that made the outside world seem more circular than the driver's thoughts. The lawyer let him ramble, and the taxi ran past buildings and across bridges and past trees stood in squares that would remain unknown for ever, only a thin visual memory to be used years later to help enrich a sleeping life. The mother in the back seat had shut her eyes to slits as if she meant to find something in the dark, some man in a kitchen perhaps listening for a phone call from overseas or some woman in a hall wondering whatever had happened to the friend she had brought from England and why no one could ever be trusted to do what they had always done before.

'Stinking Jews!' the driver joked. 'Not worth the beans they're made of!'

Desperate to find something that might make Rifka relax and not endanger them all with her growing panic, Evelyn's eye alighted on the dribble of mountains and shoreline that Herschel had drawn on his window when he first got into the taxi. Lifting a fingernail to her own damp glass, Evelyn began tracing a pair of figures in dresses, holding hands. Her work was shamefully crude compared with the boy's, but at least they were recognizable in the alternating backlighting of browns and grays and hazels and darks. She hoped to show Rifka that she was not alone, that another woman stood at her side through her family's troubles and would not let her go. But after a first curious glance at the amateur handiwork, Rifka merely retreated again behind her own stubborn misery. Even when Evelyn added the smallest profile of Herschel to her picture, the sister would not notice her message, but leaned even further away and held herself upright with her brother's help alone.

The driver told them that he had all the proof he needed of the evil pitted against him and his.

'You can see what they're like in the cathedral in Toledo. A painting of a dead Christian boy-child, all his blood drained out of his body so that it can be used by the Jews to spray over the Passover bread. People think that's all in the past, but it's the same now. I've been around enough. I've seen it. Happening still. Barcelona, mainly. Libro, Verde—'

Rifka whined out loud.

'What?' the lawyer said, louder.

'—Lugo, Vigo, Montjuïc, all their old strongholds. I can see that only a few years of lessons won't be enough to teach them. Well, we've got more. Listen to me, friend. We've got lots more, ready and waiting to be used again. You can trust me on that one.'

The glitter of the train station appeared in the near distance, but for his own reasons the driver slowed down.

'Our next train leaves soon,' the lawyer reminded him.

The driver crawled, then draped a strong arm across the seat to have his final say as he steered toward the kerb.

'I'm so tired of your Rothschilds. They say that he was here in Spain for a while recently, trying to save himself from a cold winter. What galls me is his wife. I can just see her with a leather money belt filled with gold coins or her furs or her odd, foreign ways. Comes flying on a friend's airplane into a land she knows nothing about, staying at the best hotels in the mountains, sightseeing the sights, the monasteries and the palaces, meeting men, buying sweets and hot chocolate for kiddies until they love her even more than they love their own mothers and fathers, then turning other men's eyes toward her wherever she goes, strangers and professors and even priests, I don't doubt, and then all of a sudden having to hide and expecting everyone else to risk life and limb to protect her, telling people that she's not who she seems to be, but something new, and then the rest of us are supposed to work day and night to try to be like her, hide like her, keep quiet like her, sit back in the shadows like her, steal another mother's children like her . . .

'But it's your children who are the worst!' the driver spat. 'All your Sendels and Esters and Evas and Herschels and Efraíns and all your godforsaken Rifkas—'

The girl tensed horribly, but now Evelyn held her back with her right hand and with her left erased their portraits from the window, leaving nothing behind but a smear of three invisible and unidentifiable gaps.

And then Rifka finally turned to look at her. And nodded.

Now little Herschel was awake and grouchy, but they were out of time for panic. Now it was time for the arguing over the fare, for the echoing rush into the station, the fears over finding the right train, the last minute, the final glance down the platforms for police or prying onlookers, the hurry to make a place for the four of them in the surprising crowd, the press, the thankful breath at leaving. Before they knew it, the family had settled down into a nook that separated them from the other travelers where they could all relax at least for the rest of the night. The train started out through yards and gypsy camps, its hard heart laboring under a night sky that was fresher now with a dew-washed moon, and the mother turned away from the windows to stop her mind from racing after every suspect thought and shape of voice in the darkness.

They are halfway to Guadalajara before they spot the wooden clogs, the striped trousers, and now a long striped jacket appearing and disappearing in the shifting crowd, and another fever begins to steal over Evelyn like an illegal dream.

This second train was different – longer, heavier, crammed with so many more people that even its walls could not inhale. Only a few slats of windows let in any night air or any gray light, once the winter dawn and day came. Although there were more passengers, there were fewer benches, and many had to stand, and before long their groans were mistaken for the moans of the metal wheels below or the wheezing of the plank sides. Both Evelyn and Rifka were lucky enough and seemed ill enough to claim a bench, while Efraín was banished to the end of the coach where he tried to balance himself on his attic legs and look as if he were not there. On this train, a conductor would have been only another lost traveler, so most of the riders simply clutched their papers or their bribes in case the train were boarded later by officials or soldiers. No one could ever be misplaced here. They had nowhere else to go.

But even in the smother that encased them all, Herschel had no intention of resting. He dove among the others, striking out first in one direction, then in another. Small and slippery, he insinuated himself between coats and over suitcases and sometimes even under legs, nosing out everything in the coach that had the slightest suggestion of interest or unhappiness. An even greater kindliness came over him even when he was scolded for scuffing a shoe or jostling a cup containing a precious sip of broth. Still, he proved to be a godsend to the packed car. From a distance, or every time Herschel orbited past their bench, Evelyn learned of what he was accomplishing as he played. She heard that, in various locations, helpful miniatures had suddenly appeared to charm the lonely and the frightened or silence the angry before they could make more noise than was allowed. Paper was in scant supply, and the pencil in Herschel's pocket had by now grown shorter than his thumb. But he found no lack of dust to fingerpaint in, and even the dullest of the crowd could imagine a scene picked away in the grains of the wood or scribbled in a palm. Eventually, strangers became friends and offered the backs of their birth certificates, marriage licenses, and death registers to the little artist, and Herschel beguiled them with memories and promises of life outside the train. Evelyn soon lost him to the others altogether and only glimpsed him as if he were a photograph in a closing album. His sudden absence made her fever worse and her mouth even drier than it had been before.

As hours and hours rolled by, an inward change spread throughout the carriage. One family gathered its last belongings together according to an arrangement outlined in a corner, while another learned how to shield an infant from a draft by consulting an engineer's blueprint drawn in a cake. Old women, their final breaths approaching, fell into healthy dreams beneath kerchiefs folded out of cardboard. Baby girls, whimpering for water, were satisfied with princesses fashioned out of shaped threads, and louder boys were hushed by polar bears of lint that they could hunt through the mountains of their folded jackets. As Herschel trotted lightly from bench to bench, he administered to the claustrophobic and the bored, to the screeching and the dumb, forgetting no one. Whether it was a child's rattle made out of an odd glove or a portrait of a lost child in a mother's rouge, what was easy for him soon became indispensable for the others, almost more necessary and yearned-for than a full breath. And as Evelyn sat and watched him flash his bright wings through the thicket of the train, she began to feel – for the first time since they had met – the awful longing of what it really meant to miss him.

On one of Herschel's circuits through the rocking carriage, Evelyn reached out to steer him back to where he belonged. Then she tried to keep him with her.

'So who are all your new friends, Herschel? Anyone I know?'

'Which ones?' he said brightly. 'There are so many.'

'It might not be such a good idea,' she cautioned him in a low voice. 'Talking to all kinds of strangers, I mean. Especially not since the authorities will be on the lookout for us all now, not to mention poor Efraín's situation. None of us wants anything to happen to him now, do we?'

She nodded down toward the lawyer where he stood resting his chin on the beard that was no longer there.

'They're just people, Eva,' Herschel told her. 'You should try not to be so afraid of everyone. It's not good for you.'

'Well, that could be said about the worst of them,' she said logically. 'That they're just people.'

'Or the best of them.'

She closed her warm eyes, then opened them.

'Herschel, I don't want to argue with you. After all, I know I'm not your mother—'

'Yes, you are.'

She looked down, startled, at the playful face. 'But I'm not, you know. Not really. You're old enough to know better.'

'In here you are,' he noted. 'At least until Barcelona.'

Evelyn could feel the silence of the sleeping Rifka beside her as she looked uncomfortably about, honored and shamed by his simple trust in her.

'That's kind of a funny thing to say. Wouldn't it hurt your real mother's feelings to hear you say that?' Evelyn asked him.

'No, not really. Look at all these people in here.'

'What about them?' she said, looking around with him.

'Well, some are families, and some are just traveling as if they were a family. You know, together for a day or two, like us. And just look at how hard it is now to tell any of them apart.'

'But, Herschel, that's not really the same thing . . .'

'Yes, it is,' he proclaimed. 'If I had enough paper to draw a picture of the whole train, you'd be able to see. The people on the train and the pictures of the people on the paper would seem the same. You wouldn't be able to tell one from the other – if one was good or one was bad, if one was a family or just strangers in a bunch, who was who or what was what. That's the way it is in a crowd, Eva. Always. People leak into each other like water leaks into the ground and disappears.

'Except,' he corrected himself, 'if I were to leave someone out of my picture on purpose – then he wouldn't be here anymore. But then, of course, that would be the same in both places, too, wouldn't it?'

'I suppose . . .'

Confused by his complicated rationale, Evelyn drew him down onto the bench beside her and tried to get him to rest. But the seat was cramped, and she almost had to hold him on her lap not to disturb the girl on her other side.

'Still,' she repeated as she tucked him in, 'you should be more careful.'

'But they need help,' he implored her. 'A lot of them do.'

'Do you like to help people so much? I thought you liked to draw pictures more.'

His usual shrug, only more solemn.

'What's the difference? When you draw a picture, whether on a piece of paper or in a puddle of rain, you make something look like you want it to be, if only for a moment. When you try to do something for someone, it's the same thing. The world looks just a little bit more right. Is that so wrong of me, Eva?'

'No, Herschel,' Evelyn said wearily. 'No, I don't think so.'

Still too worked up to sleep, the boy started fiddling with a splinter on the arm of the bench, picking at it until it stuck up like a signal on a platform. Although most of the carriage was now asleep, a few people remained restless, smoking or whispering or reading the endless countryside as it floated by. These unsettled ones seemed to concern Herschel, keeping him leaning out into the aisle as though some fresh game or project were being started without him and he could not bear to miss out. Finally, Evelyn had to beg him to sit back and go to sleep, but that only made him sulk, and she soon had to tell him he could go, but only for one more pass through the coach.

'And keep to yourself more, will you? We still have a long way to go.'

'I'll try,' he said, melting away.

'And Herschel—' she called after him.

'Oh, let him go.'

The first murmur from the girl made Evelyn gasp. Since the taxi-ride through Madrid, Rifka had been more relaxed and almost friendly, although she still held Evelyn and even Efraín at arm's length. She had sunk down into a half-sleep as into a cloak that she could pull up around herself and forget where she was. But now the coach was too stifling and Evelyn's nagging clearly too irritating to allow her to sleep.

'You're awake?' Evelyn asked her unnecessarily. 'How are you feeling?'

The boy's sister, her night hair muddled by sleep, her cheek blushed by the pressure of the bench, sat up and washed her face in her dry hands.

'Herschel can take care of himself,' she informed Evelyn.

'He's still just a boy, Rifka, and we are on a strange train filled with who knows what kinds of people. After all—'

'He's been in worse places. We all have.'

Evelyn looked down into her lap.

'I heard a little from the family you were staying with. The place where you came from—'

'Which one?' Rifka asked. 'We grew up in so many places that even we still hardly know what to call ourselves.'

'But you both had to have been born somewhere. What can you remember first?' Evelyn said.

The girl grew more thoughtful and began to soften around the edges, looking back over past years and letting down her guard as she finally began to trust someone again.

'Well, I do remember a little village – a real village – over in eastern Poland or western Russia, depending on who was telling the story. But that was before Herschel was born, so he probably doesn't remember any of it, even from family gossip.'

'He wasn't born there?' Evelyn wanted to know.

'Actually,' Rifka said, 'he was born in Hanover, Germany.'

'Oh, really? In what year?'

'In nineteen thirty-five, I think. I forget exactly.'

Evelyn glanced sadly down the length of the coach.

'I knew he looked so young . . .'

'Almost as soon as he was born,' the girl said, 'our father enrolled him in the Zionist Misrachi in Hanover in the hopes that he'd be sent to the Yeshiva Seminary in Frankfurt when he got older, but that was before everything went bad, before that silly business about the candle and all the rest of it happening around us. Since then, I think it's been hard for him to grow up at all anymore. I just wish he wouldn't let it bother him, being so short and all.'

'Excuse me,' Evelyn interrupted, 'but what is your father's name? His full name, I mean.'

'Sendel Silberberg. Why?'

'Well, Herschel never told me.'

Turning her face away, almost as if she had let out a family secret, Rifka said that they had been taught not to repeat it to strangers.

'What was this silly business about a candle?' Evelyn asked quickly to help put the girl more at ease.

'Well, it was just before those dark nights in thirty-eight when all the stormtroopers of the SA went crazy because of that Jewish boy who killed that German embassy official in Paris. They arrested every Jew they could find, burned synagogues everywhere, and broke as many glass windows of Jewish shops as they could. In Leipzig, where we were living at the time and where my father had a tailor's shop, they smashed in the door, stole everything they could lay their hands on, and then set fire to the shop and made Father sign a confession that he had committed the arson himself. Then they carried his mannequins out to the Altermarkt and burned them in a ceremony next to the bodies of some Nazi heroes they'd dug up and put in coffins. I didn't get to see any of it myself, but Herschel did, and he blamed himself for everything.'

'But why, in heaven's name?' Evelyn said.

'You see,' the girl went on, shaking her head, 'a day or two before, he'd accidentally broken the Yahrzeit candle that we used to burn once a year to remember the death of our uncle, the rabbi back in Radomsko. It was nothing, really, just a cheap glass base that we were able to replace without too much trouble. But little Herschel took it to heart, and when all the troubles started soon after – all the broken windows and the fires and arrests – well, I suppose he just thought it was his fault. He never seemed to get over it, and that's when he started to get so wrapped up in drawing pictures and sketching in the snow. His way of making amends, perhaps, or of hanging onto things. He's hard to understand, sometimes. I think it's because he's still just a child. But I only hope he gets better as he grows older. He'll have to.'

Flustered by these nightmares that she was hearing for the first time, Evelyn settled a hand sympathetically on the girl's arm. Her touch was as gentle as a snowflake, but Rifka still shrank away.

'Where were you when all this was happening?' she asked the girl.

'Oh, I was out of town, up at a farm near Gräfenheinichen to learn how to work at a kibbutz in Palestine. I'd registered with the Palestinian Service in Berlin, and I was all ready to go, when the trucks filled with SS and SA men showed up on that night in November. After a few days of scaring us to death, the Gestapo drove all the boys off to the camp at Sachsenhausen, and we girls were left behind to clean up. I helped them bury the bread dough out in the garden myself,' she said proudly.

'You did what?' cried Evelyn.

Rifka smiled grimly and went on.

'Don't ask. It was all insane. Anyway, that's when we first started to lose contact with one another, our parents and myself and little Herschel. Back in Leipzig, they took Father off to the camp at Buchenwald, and Mother and my brother were left alone to fend for themselves. Fortunately, we had some family and friends in the city, so I was able to meet up with them as soon as I came back from the countryside. Still, with the family business ruined and all the lunacy that was still going on in the streets, we were wondering what to do to keep us all alive until Sendel could get out and back to us again. Ester, our mother, was at her wit's end trying to decide what to do, but I was able to help her to some extent. By then, I'd grown up quite a bit, so I could do more to help Ester and Sendel, even if little Herschel couldn't.'

Occasionally referring to her parents by their given names, Rifka seemed to grow older in the walking shadows of the train, and her voice became that of a wise housewife recounting all the adventures of her wandering brood.

'Whatever did you do next?' Evelyn whispered.

'Well, we were lucky. We knew some people in the little town of Tiefenort, so we made our way there and hid out until the last window in Germany was broken. In the villages, most of the people were too backward or too tired to get too worked up about much of anything. The three of us just stayed there until Father was let out. After all, what did we have left for us back in Leipzig?'

'Until he was let out?' the woman echoed. 'But I thought the camps—'

Rifka blanked out for a moment, then reappeared.

'Not then. Not yet. In thirty-eight, they were mostly being used as detention camps. They didn't turn really ugly until some years later. Father wasn't old or sick enough to get released at once, though. Even in January, when the Germans let go anyone who had a visa for another country or a quota number for America, he couldn't get out. None of us had the right papers, and he didn't have anything left to bribe anyone with. It wasn't until late in the spring that he came back, and by then it was almost too late for us to go anywhere.'

'What was it like for Herschel?' Evelyn asked as Rifka paused.

The girl only shook her head in wonder.

'I remember Herschel used to paint a miniature of our father walking toward us on the window of the house where we were hiding out. Even when the warmer weather took away the frost, he traced the same image in his breath or in smoke. And when Father finally did come to get us, he really did fit himself into the picture on the window as he approached the house. He even looked the same, a good man turned old by typhus and beatings just like Herschel had imagined him. That's when my brother knew what he could do, when we all knew what he could do.'

'What do you mean by that?'

'Well,' Rifka said uncomfortably, 'he changes things. He can make things become the way he wants them to be by drawing them in that way. I know it sounds crazy, but—'

Suddenly shaken, Evelyn leaned out to see what the boy was up to and saw him bent over a piece of paper with another child, the two of them concocting miracles together.

'But what happened then?' she asked the girl. 'How did you children and your parents end up in . . . you know . . .'

Rifka told her. It was a long story. As the girl droned on, the train continued on its way into the dark, ticking along with a rhythm that soon matched the girl's weary voice and the regular flashing outside of villages and signals and stars. Though Evelyn heard every word, the story gradually became as subtle as a sheet of moonlight in a meadow or a necklace of jewels or fireflies on a stream. Rifka might have been describing one of Herschel's own drawings, or a vast series of them that had been strung together into a continuous film that both re-enacted and took the place of the actual lives they had lived. Even the girl's narration of it seemed fictional and real at one and the same time, as her level voice modulated with the cough of the distant pulling engine and with the echo of every storyteller who had ever finally been made to tell the truth.

The family lingered in Tiefenort, Rifka explained, unsure whether they should stay or try to return to eastern Poland, through a waiting summer and into an autumn of early cold. When news came of the invasion of Poland, and even through into the following winter and spring, the father hesitated, suspended, standing all day long at door or window, one foot out and his back still leaning against the cabin for rest. There was no hurry because there was nowhere to go, as the countryside emptied, smoke arose, children cried, and the boy and his sister fell behind in their studies. Gradually, so gently that no one even noticed, the family began spending more time in neighboring villages, scouting around for more reliable information or a sign of what others like themselves were doing. Nothing moved. At chance moments, letters or messengers arrived from family or old acquaintances in Poland or even further away, carrying impossible tales and assumptions that no one in his right mind would believe. Still as undecided as stormclouds, the family kept weighing their options, letting them run through their fingers like tears, as the spring went by and they kept foraging further and further southward. Denmark, Norway, Holland, Belgium, France fell. Months passed. Months. The children grew, but slowly, as imperceptibly as grass. The visible seasons changed, but not as swiftly or as viciously as the people around them, and the family never wondered how all this might end because they had begun to forget how it had all started. Brother and sister held their parents' hands, and found themselves standing in front of the British consulate in Frankfurt with thousands of others. A few months later, they flirted with Switzerland, but they found a brace of efficient guards at the border, one of whom had the name of Winter. Even later, the father opened up a tailor's stand down in Toulouse, and the children read Victor Hugo for the first time in French. Before their journeys ended, just as the worst of the distant thunder could be heard in the night, the family landed at a Vichy French camp at Gurs in Navarrenx near Pau with no logical memory of how they had come there, but with friends beckoning to them from across the border into neutral Spain. And that was when the train to Auschwitz-Birkenau passed by to pick them up.

'After that,' Rifka concluded with a wave of her hand, her face turned out into the night, 'well, you already know the rest. Why should I bother telling you what you already know? How could repeating something over and over ever make it go away for good?'

And then Evelyn remembered some of what Coca Piña had tried to tell her in the apartment in Escorial, but Evelyn had been too distracted by the furnishings to pay enough attention. And then a new drowsiness stole over her as she tried to respond fully to the girl, and failed. And the coach with its helpful Herschel ricocheting from sorrow to sorrow carried them all forward into the first gray of morning where the earth hung still between a dream and a dream.

The train stopped to take on more and more passengers,

more and more of them forced to keep standing. Still asleep, they had to shift ever closer to each other, their shoulders crushed until their lungs had the fresh air pinched out of them. If Evelyn had been awake, she would have seen families tightened together into sheaves like straw and the lonely old growing lonelier among the crowd. Talking was harder, thirst consumed them, until some found pomegranates stashed in their shirts and others spread toothpaste on their lips to taste the watery smell of mint. The children had it worse. To breathe at all in the wintry vacuum, they had to do whatever they could – find holes in the floor, cracks beneath the vents, bowed legs, yearn upward with mouths shaped into spires of flame, befriend couples who could lift them higher, or fashion an opening in the coach's walls out of ink and imagination. Because the ride had been designed to last for ever, the passengers began to continue their lives where they stood or slept. The old crone with the string bag opened it to count and recount the teeth, the lenses from stolen spectacles, the locks of hair, the dried clots of blood. The man in the wooden clogs and cap reviewed his family property in Escorial, imagined the Giralda in Sevilla, wept again for his fallen daughter, made a note about E1 Greco, tucked away a receipt for a sold tractor, and decided he would not survive in any train without a toilet. Across from him, paler but prepared for the worst, a dedicated mountaineer helped to make prisoners from France and Italy and Poland feel less alone. Throughout the coach, children tried to get on with their schooling by listening to strangers discover moments of shelter in others' bodies and by watching the hopeless die on their feet and be buried between the breasts of women who turned their faces as far away as they could to sniff at life. Couples twisted like fires, boys scribbled out masterpieces in the window fog of a final breath, while bloodied partisans and homosexuals were pressed into the sleeping lap of an American woman who had no business being there. Yet the train still went on, the lives and deaths and dreams of the human herds went on, and the only things that could still breathe as they had before were the sunlight through the wired window and the morning moon that was always the same between one stop and any other stop except the last. And no one, not even the mothers or the fathers, knew which of the stops would be the last.

Then the train lugged forward as if it had struck a snowbank and began a long, slow descent into a depression filled with warm brown bricks between two cathedral spires and the aromas of sugar and new cloth. The people in the carriage moved sluggishly as mud as some made their way toward the exits and others stood aside to let them go. Some caught sight of a sign that read 'Zaragoza' and lay back to rest their eyes and thank God how little they had yet to go before they reached Barcelona.

But before anyone could climb down from the train, a trio of military guards bullied their way in, bringing with them guns and batons and headgear that in the waking light shone like triangles of sick green.

'Eva,' the boy shook her. 'Wake up, Eva. They're here.'

She opened her eyes and saw his dark, serious face staring at something.

'Who's here?'

'They are.' And he pointed toward the front of the train.

Evelyn woke Rifka, and with Herschel they saw two soldiers marching harshly through the crowd, checking documents.

'Where are we?' Evelyn asked.

'Zaragoza,' Rifka replied.

Evelyn looked around. 'Where's that?'

'Here they come,' the girl said. 'Get ready.'

Even from a distance, they could feel the tarpaulin uniforms and the close shaves, the smell of cold off the helmets and hard metal. As they watched, the two young men passed by the clogs and the string bag to concentrate on weaker families. They picked some, plucking at their edges until grandmothers betrayed their in-laws and cousins said they had never seen their own cousins before. As the train rocked as silently as a cradle, shoulders were steered between gloved hands as the guilty were trundled away, and pleas for mercy were ignored in favor of jackets that could be proffered to superiors, and curls that would bounce more softly when stuffed inside mattresses. Wives were turned against husbands. One by one, half the crowd flaked apart and faded away toward the steps that led down to the station platform. The remainder shrank back to see how inconspicuous they could be and yet not disappear for ever. Everyone tried to avoid being seen by not looking at all, and in places hungry babies were left alone on laps that felt harder than the flat benches beneath them.

Evelyn pulled her two children closer and looked frantically toward Efraín, but the lawyer had already escaped the soldiers by pretending dysentery, and he dared not change his story now. For a moment, Evelyn took heart and glanced back toward the rear of the carriage, but there she only saw a third soldier advancing on them with the same kind of leaden stride as the other two. There was no escaping now.

'We have to do something,' Evelyn whispered. 'On our own. I don't think it would look very good if we suddenly joined up as a family right under the eyes of the soldiers. They'd wonder why we weren't sitting together, why

Efraín was up there and we were all the way back here.'

'They might not ask us for anything,' Rifka hoped. 'Hasn't that happened before?'

'The conductor did,' Evelyn reminded her. 'But I don't think I could manage these men the way Efraín did the other. My Spanish isn't that good, and I don't have nearly enough money. Or papers, for that matter.'

'What about your American passport?' the girl asked.

'That might help me. Might. But as for the rest of you, how are you going to explain an American tourist accompanying a pair of foreign children? You'd be lucky not to be hauled off and locked up,' Evelyn decided. 'They'd probably throw me in there along with you for good measure, and we'd never be heard of again.

'No,' she went on vaguely, 'we'll have to think of something else, some dodge that these soldiers have never seen before. If we only had a little more time . . .'

Now the thick dough of passengers was spreading itself open, and machine smells began to invade their section of the car.

'There is no time,' Rifka said. 'They're almost here.'

'I know,' said Evelyn.

'Let's run,' the girl whispered hoarsely, starting up.

'No,' Evelyn said and held her down.

The uniforms were growing larger from both sides now.

'Eva,' the boy finally spoke up.

'What is it?'

'Ich hab' etwas.'

'For God's sake, Herschel!' Evelyn said. 'Whatever you do, don't speak German.'

'Why not?' Rifka muttered. 'It might work on some of these *civilones*.'

Herschel switched to Spanish. 'But I think I can help us.'

'You can help most,' Evelyn told him, 'by keeping quiet.'

An odor of khaki flowed over them. They sat perfectly still, like animals on their guard. The three soldiers met not far from their bench, conferring over a parallel family of four. But that family had papers, papers that rustled and fluttered like banners or cards across a felt table. After a long moment of arguing and nodding, the other family suddenly was taken away anyway, neatly packaged by brutal gestures and complaining uselessly until their last whining could be heard draining away down toward the bottom of the station.

Evelyn could not seem to stop squirming where she sat.

'Stop making so much noise,' she finally commanded Herschel. Then she looked down at him and said, 'What's that?'

He held up a limp piece of brown paper.

'It's a drawing.'

'Oh, Herschel. Not now. Please.'

She tried to make him put it away.

'But it might help us,' he pleaded with her. 'It might.'

'It couldn't hurt,' his sister put in hopelessly.

'Oh!' Evelyn moaned.

She took it from his hands. It was a quick vignette of their train carriage, complete with all the fixtures and almost all the passengers. Even the puppet figures of the soldiers seemed to be moving as the soldiers moved, and a shadow of the morning station flickered all around them. The only blank sections, the only gaps in the scene, floated just where they sat and where Efraín stood, watching their predicament. The blind spots were gray, ambiguous, settled on the surface of the paper like breathing scum.

'Here, Eva,' the boy cried brightly. 'If you hold onto it, it will probably work even better.'

'What?'

'Here.' He forced it into her lap. 'Take it now before they get here.'

'Herschel—'

'Take it, Eva!'

She stared down into her lap and saw nothing but soldiers in uniforms and unattainable platforms where free men and women were streaming through the station. Evelyn could feel the shadows of the guards. Their breath was colder than triggers. And all she had to defend herself and her family with was a scrap of paper and the meaningless scrawlings of a child.

Suddenly, she seized the paper, raised it to her face, and shredded it into dozens of pieces, scattering them with disgust onto the floor at her feet.

'Grow up, Herschel,' she hissed at the startled face. 'Leave all this goddamned silliness behind. Aren't we in enough trouble already because of you?'

Little Herschel looked up at her and said nothing at all.

'They're coming,' Rifka interrupted them.

'No,' Evelyn said, raising her head. 'No, they're here.'

What happened next would never be clear in Evelyn's mind, no matter how many times she thought and dreamed of it during all the years to come. She remembered smiling for the coming soldiers and opening her blouse a button or two, and she was sure she heard a sharp gasp from the girl as one of the soldiers bent down toward her bare legs. But the rest of it was vague, at least the moments between the danger and the escape. Evelyn knew that Herschel had fallen to his knees, fumbling for the ruins of his masterpiece on the floor and trying to piece it all together again. And she knew that he could never do it, never paste the paper carriage into the way it used to look. Too many of the bits were fractioned and creased beyond repair. All he could find was an edge where Rifka's hands might have been and a spot where Evelyn's elbow would have grazed against the wood of the bench. But all the rest was gone, his own safe hole in the floor and Efraín's sanctuary near the door. None of the picture's magic remained.

But then, just as the soldiers' helmets were hovering above them like feeding bats, Evelyn had felt him jotting down a brand-new detail, filling in a blank that should have been left vacant. Without looking, she sensed that Herschel had added the figure of the lawyer where he stood in full view of the single soldier from the rear. And as the boy gave the lawyer away to the uniforms and the leather boots, Evelyn saw Herschel staring across at the man from the attic for the last time, the boy sobbing uncontrollably and the fugitive nodding with satisfaction as he saw approaching him the first signs of a supreme accomplishment that he had been waiting six selfish years to finish. And then Efraín Cota and all three soldiers were gone.

After the train had climbed out of Zaragoza and past the cemetery where four thousand Italian soldiers slept unmourned among aisles of mourned Spaniards, it passed by gardens and fortifications and stopped briefly at another station where chimney sweeps and dirty shoemakers worked their brooms and awls in perfect, choreographed unison. When the train finally arrived in Barcelona in the light of a humpbacked moon, a woman in a gray suit stepped down with a girl in a black dress and a smaller boy in a torn jacket. A young woman on the platform with a white rose in her heavy hair trailed them to the taxis where she offered to help them find their hotel in Barcelona. Once they were all together, she took them instead to the apartment of a friend of hers, where the woman in the gray suit was finally able to wash, the girl in the black dress combed her short black hair, and the boy in the torn jacket found sheets and sheets of blank paper. By midnight, no one back in the train station remembered anything about the gray suit, the black dress, or the torn jacket that had been riding in the carriage with the outdated trousers, smelling of attic. Or the wooden clogs on the journey that will never ever end.

Antonio Liot looked down at the American woman who was seated in his mother's favorite chair and smiled in apology.

'I didn't mean to frighten you all by sending Sophie to the station to look out for you,' he said quietly. 'It was only that I couldn't be sure if I would make it back to Barcelona in time, and I wanted someone trustworthy to take you in hand before you got in too much trouble on your own. Sophie's German, one of the few survivors of the anti-Nazi White Rose movement in Munich. She was the one who helped us get the children out, so I thought she would be the best contact I could find for you.

'But from reports I've heard about your ride on the train,' he added, wagging his head, 'I'm aware that we were too late to help you avoid everything. It's always hard, isn't it, when we lose a good man at the last moment like that.'

Evelyn looked up at him from the overstuffed leather chair where she was sinking deeper and deeper.

'And you really don't think there's much chance of finding out what happened to Efraín?' she asked. 'It's only been a day or two. Maybe he'll still turn up here, alive and well.'

'When people disappear in Franco's Spain,' Antonio told her, 'they're always gone for good. Even their Christ would never have come back from the dead here.'

Unable to bear the thought of the missing lawyer, Evelyn asked about the young man's fierce mother and what Señora Liot would say if she could see Evelyn sitting in this chair, as well as two unwashed refugees sleeping in her bedrooms.

The young man blushed, his delicate features disappearing in a delta of pink shadow, as he tried to find excuses for the woman who was still inspecting family property back in Escorial.

'She's not as much of a general as she sometimes appears. In the past half-dozen years, she's welcomed quite a few people who were on the run and put them up here for days on end. Of course,' he conceded sheepishly, 'she did think they were all members of a climbing club . . .'

'Even the children?'

'Well,' he maintained, 'we start them young, don't we?'

The Catalán maid interrupted them with more marzipan and fresh coffee, and the dark sitting room took on an even thicker feeling of contentment and safety. The sounds of a vast city going about its business just outside the window seemed to shut them in, and the casual rain hissing against the glass might have been the tender snoring of the children in adjoining rooms. A fire burned, surrounded by old paneling, and the smell of leather reminded Evelyn of well-kept stables and barns. But suddenly it didn't matter how long she had been away from home, or what she had gone through, or even what she might have to do to find her home again. The silent wood and the rain in the night were just enough for now.

Still pacing the room, the young man glanced down at Evelyn and then away. How much she had changed in only a few days! Even after one or two days of rest here in the apartment, she had not yet regained the innocence he had first noticed in her in the hotel back in Escorial. Her hair looked weary, the skin of her face had grown more granular in texture and more gray, while her mouth had begun to set itself in a grim pucker that he was seeing in almost everyone nowadays. Yet, for all that, there was a hard steadiness in her gestures and in her voice, and an energy about her that he would never have predicted. Now, Evelyn seemed to be ready to do absolutely anything – even if it meant doing less or nothing for herself. And that was new.

Fortified by the coffee, Evelyn sat forward and made Antonio stop moving and tell her more of what was going on.

'I mean,' she said, 'I've been here a few days now, and you and your friends have walked me around the neighborhood a little, so now I have some idea of what your set-up is like. And I recall your telling me that you brought the letter to Rifka because you were going to Escorial anyway, and you wanted to be sure that the children would have some way of getting to Barcelona in time for their parents to pick them up.

'But,' Evelyn went on, 'what I still don't understand is how you're involved in all this refugee mess and why you didn't just come out and take the kids home on your own. Why did you have to let me get caught up in it, not to mention poor Efraín? It's not as if I have any particular talent for this kind of spying. And,' she said mournfully, 'it surely would have been much better for Efraín if he had stayed hidden another six years in his attic.'

'I don't know,' Antonio disagreed. 'He might have had to be up there for another thirty years, if not more. I don't see much hope of Spain coming out of this nightmare for a long time, not even after the fall of Germany and Italy, not with all the powers that Madrid has in its hands right now. None of us does.'

'Us?' Evelyn repeated. 'You and Sophie?'

'And all the rest. I've been working for a private refugee relief agency for almost ten years now, and I really think we've been able to do a lot of good, even though I have to keep it mum at home to maintain the peace. That's why I couldn't bring Herschel and Rifka here myself. Even traveling with my mother to Escorial drew too much attention to them. Evil, it seems, never sleeps.

'Sometimes,' he sighed, 'we can't find much hope in what we do, but we don't want to give up now. This is our country, even if it doesn't usually want to acknowledge its Jews and Cataláns and others. But it's still our country, and we would still like to make it into something we could be proud of, someday. We all want that.'

Evelyn gazed with admiration at this new kind of patriotism, a less shrill type that believed it was better for a nation to do good than to think it was always right.

'Which relief agency is yours?' Evelyn asked. 'I've heard of a few of them by name.'

'That's right,' Antonio said. 'You fought in the war, didn't you?'

'I typed in the war. But I did try to learn as much as they let me know. Evidently,' she faltered, showing every mile of the train journey, 'I still have quite a lot to learn.'

Speaking in guarded tones, Antonio Liot gave her an outline of the People's Relief Agency and its work in Barcelona. Whenever a Displaced Person in what was left of Europe needed to discover a way back home, or invent a home to go back to, the agency tried to do as much as it could to ease the transition back and support the returned refugee wherever he might come to rest. This aid had in the past included everything from gifts of money and reuniting families to false papers and illegal transport to and into closed lands. Without being too specific, the young man admitted that he and his companions were prepared to do anything they could to see as much of the world returned to normal as was possible.

'Obviously,' he concluded, 'none of this is the kind of work a good Barcelona Jew should be devoting his life to, according to my mother. This is why it's always seemed so much easier to leave her out of it altogether.'

'And she really doesn't suspect anything?'

'I don't think so. She's always too busy.'

'Working?' Evelyn asked.

'No,' Antonio said sadly. 'Complaining. Fearing. Hating.'

They both fell silent in the room, so uselessly luxurious, until Evelyn asked for more details.

'So this agency of yours helps Jews to get to Palestine?'

Antonio nodded eagerly and took a seat on the arm of another chair.

'Well, because of our location, most of our work does point in that direction. But we're active everywhere, and we're helping as many people get to as many places as we can. It really doesn't matter who you are, where you came from, or where you want to go. We could even help get you back to Wisconsin,' he said cheerily, then added in a lower voice, 'if you're still thinking of going home, that is.'

'Why in the world wouldn't I?' asked Evelyn.

'It's just that you've been through so much these past days and weeks . . .'

'And?' she said as he hesitated.

'And,' he mumbled, 'I just thought that you might have had a change of heart.'

'I don't know what you're getting at,' she said stiffly.

Antonio searched her face for something, but he did not find it yet, so he let the conversation hang.

'Well, the children—' he began.

'What about the children?'

A distant clamor sounded and brought the young man to a halt as he listened to the maid's diminishing footsteps. The soft rain grew suddenly harder against the window, and somewhere in the wet night could be heard the heavy body of the sea turning in its bed under the hidden moon.

After a breathless wait, the maid's steps came nearer again until they reached the closed door.

'What is it?' Antonio asked as she entered.

'The gentleman from up north. He's here. With Antoni and his friend Joan.'

The young man was still serious.

'You've checked his papers?'

'Of course,' the maid answered. 'Besides, do you think Joan wouldn't have? You know he's more careful than that.'

'Oh, the children will be beside themselves,' Evelyn began. Then she added more quietly, 'But what about the mother?'

The maid didn't know, but both she and Antonio assumed that the parents had traveled separately to arouse less suspicion.

'Matilde,' the young man decided, 'why don't you send Antoni and Joan on their way with our thanks and take our guest straight up to his children. As long as he's checked out all right, we can wait to see him ourselves until after he's spent some time alone with them. But leave the entrance lighted, for when their mother comes. That might be at any time now.'

Antonio turned to Evelyn as the maid left them and said, 'We can't be too careful these days. A lot of times, we'll get people coming by who aren't who they say they are or who have been paid to snoop around and find proof of what we're doing. This isn't in Spain alone, either, but almost everywhere we operate, including your own New York City, I'm afraid.'

'But who wouldn't want to help people who have lost all that they had through no fault of their own?' Evelyn asked him.

'Well, for some it's a matter of economics. Most people who have been born and raised in a country will resent being asked to share any of it with newcomers. And then there's always religious and cultural differences, though you would have thought that most of that inhumanity would have been taken out of us by the war. We all suffered, in our different ways. Some of us suffered for being who we were, while others suffered for making their own mistakes. It all came to pretty much the same in the end, unfortunately.

'But,' he went on, 'that only explains the kind of distrust that my mother and her friends feel. It doesn't tell us very much about those people who are simply uncaring, uninvolved. I myself think that's more a matter of the heart or spirit, the way people naturally turn aside from anything that doesn't directly concern them. That's just human, though not a part of ourselves we should be particularly proud of. But most of us can't help it. We always assume that there must be a definite border between you and me. We can't see how we all run together like pavement paintings in the rain. Children don't have that problem, and that explains why their happiness is usually so much purer than ours.'

'And their *un*happiness?' Evelyn said.

'I don't know . . .'

Even though the young man was obviously more at ease dealing with such practical matters as arriving refugees and comrades-in-arms, he seemed to be hungry to explain his feelings and thoughts to anyone who would listen. He gazed across the rich rug lying on the floor as if he wanted to make Evelyn see what his mother had never cared to see and what his father would have understood, had he survived the Republican excesses of the Civil War.

'And,' he finished, 'if we could only make nations feel what people usually feel when they work with each other, then maybe we wouldn't have to sneak people across borders and oceans to settle them in safer homes. Anywhere anyone lived would be their home.'

'As with Herschel and Rifka and their parents.'

'That's right. I love this work, but I can't wait for it to come to an end. That's the greatest paradox about goodness. Once you've started it, you want nothing more than to make it totally unnecessary. Yet it takes you for ever to reach that point . . .'

The room remained perfectly motionless, though outside, rain and winds ran and fought one another in the darkness, and clouds spun the planet beneath them.

'I seem to remember Rifka's letter saying something about a date. The eighteenth of this month. What happens then?' she asked him.

'That's when we have a boat leaving for Palestine with just as many refugees on board as we can fit. The Silberbergs have to be all together to get places on it, or others will step forward to shut them out. We never have a shortage of people ready to get away, I'm sorry to say.'

'But why the eighteenth?' Evelyn persisted. 'Why not earlier or later?'

'That's the night of the full moon,' Antonio told her.

'Ah, so they'll be able to find their way better, and their crossing will be safer.'

The kind eyes across from her looked suddenly worried.

'Actually, it will be more dangerous, because then they can be seen that much more easily out on the open sea.'

'Then why—'

'I know it sounds crazy,' the young man explained, 'but many times we've found that the ships in the Mediterranean that are on guard against illegal vessels don't watch out for them as closely under a full moon. I suppose they think that only a madman would go under those conditions, so they relax their grip just enough for a boat or two to slip through. We're hoping it will work for us on the eighteenth. Lately, we've lost far too many vessels.'

'Lost them? Where?'

'Eventually to detention camps on Cyprus or elsewhere. After that, it's hard to keep tabs on what happens to so many refugees from so many different countries.'

'But who stops them from crossing?' Evelyn said.

The young man's face soured and grew narrow.

'Oh, the British mostly. Don't you remember your friend Mr Dearing back at the hotel in Escorial? He didn't seem to be very happy about the possibility of hundreds of thousands of Jews down in Palestine, fighting the Arabs for land and turning the entire British Mandate into even more of a pretense than it already is. He and his kind would rather that all the refugees, and the Jews in particular, would just disappear back into Germany and Poland as if nothing had happened, like rain into the earth. It would be so much easier that way for everyone – except, of course, for the Jews themselves. But who has ever cared that much about them?'

Remembering her last meeting with the Englishman and knowing him better now than Antonio did, Evelyn waited before she asked, 'But is that the only place they could go? There must be others. It's an awfully wide world, isn't it?'

'Where?' Antonio wanted to know. 'During the past decade and more, we've tried everywhere. There are Jews who have run as far away as China, and even that doesn't seem to be far enough. Most of the other nations have turned them away by the boatload, the United States included, and those like Cuba that have taken some of them in seem to do it mainly for the money and belongings they can squeeze out of the deal. Before the war, during the war, and even up to today, no one has helped anyone, except for a few relief agencies here and there, and apparently everyone has been in agreement to help the Jews last, if at all. At this point,' he said angrily, 'the only place left open for them is the moon.'

'And now that,' Evelyn remembered, 'is buried in snow.'

'Excuse me?'

Sitting back in her chair before the man's sudden intensity, Evelyn swallowed any other questions she might have had and tried to murmur her sympathy.

'Nothing will change,' Antonio concluded, 'until the British and the rest of the world decide to cancel the Mandate and throw open Palestine to free immigration and to Jewish statehood. And, I'm afraid, right now that seems to be just about impossible.'

'Why do you say that?'

'Why? Well, why should anyone ever want to change any policy that has worked well enough for decades, if not for centuries? No one wants to change the way he's always felt and the way that his father and grandfather have always felt. Jews and non-Jews alike, gypsies and Jehovah's Witnesses and Communists, anyone who isn't welcomed anywhere, have always been left to search for a home for themselves. And those who already have a hot fire and a room have never been that eager to share them with complete strangers. It's so much easier just to keep on thinking that someone else will be there to take care of them. Why should anyone want to give up the illusion now, now that everything is over and it's time for us all to go back home?'

As he spoke, the young man had glanced about the comfortable room as bitterly as if he were sitting in a cell. The rich wood seemed to darken his features, and the warmth inside flushed his cheeks with embarrassment or fever. If his mother had been sitting across from him, he would probably have named every humiliation that his eyes had witnessed. But Evelyn seemed more gentle, or more touched by recent events, and he relaxed a bit and shared with her a part of his deepest feelings.

'It's the same with everything, isn't it?' he said vaguely. 'I – have a friend, a young man about my age whom I've known for years and with whom I like to spend a lot of my time. He's a kind and decent man, and he knows without thinking that every gun and piece of money in the world is wrong and that nothing is more important than a child or a poem or a faithful gesture. Still, we could never tell my mother who we are together, or anyone else in this world for that matter, without finding ourselves thrown into prison or chased out of our home country or branded as unnatural for the rest of our lives. That's something that makes you wonder who you are, doesn't it? When someone who doesn't even know what you're feeling tells you that you're not supposed to feel it?'

Reminded of something, Evelyn said, 'I don't know . . .'

'What I want to know,' Antonio concluded mostly to himself, 'is why so few people can see themselves in everyone else. Don't they understand that, once they lock up even one person who is different from them, they make it possible for someone someday to lock them up, too? Don't they understand that you can never be safe unless you make everyone else safe at the same time? You can't just have it one way. You can't. No one can.'

They finished their coffee in silence, and Antonio got to his feet and walked over to the raining window where he talked to his guest without looking around.

'I suppose, then, you'll want to make immediate arrangements to get back to the States. Now that the children are safe here in Barcelona and their father has come, there's no reason for you to be inconvenienced any longer. You have your own life waiting for you in Wisconsin, don't you? All your family and friends.'

Behind his back and reflected in the glass, he heard Evelyn muffle her voice in her hands and speak from a great distance.

'No, I think I'll wait around to see them off. It's the very least I can do, don't you think?' she asked him.

'Yes,' Antonio said. 'The very least.'

'Did I tell you,' Evelyn continued, 'how Herschel seemed to save the day for us when the train stopped at Zaragoza?'

'I don't think so.' Antonio turned from the window with some relief. 'So what happened?'

She told him as much as she could before the maid returned. Matilde's hands and voice were shaking, her eyes in a storm of tears.

'What is it?' Antonio asked the maid. 'What's wrong now?'

The woman in the faded dress held out a slip of paper. 'The children are gone, Toño,' she wailed. 'Both of them!'

Evelyn and Antonio were suddenly on their feet.

'What do you mean – gone?' Antonio asked.

'What I say!' the maid cried. 'Their rooms are empty,

and no one else has seen them in the entrance, or in the bathrooms, or—'

'But where could they have gone?' Antonio demanded.

'And why?' Evelyn said.

As if she had forgotten it until now, the maid noticed the piece of paper that she was holding out in front of her as if to defend herself.

'What's that?' Antonio asked.

'It's a note,' she said. 'From the girl.'

Antonio Liot started to reach for it, but the maid swept her hand toward the American woman.

'It's for her.'

Uncertainly, Evelyn came forward to read it. Part of the message was in Spanish, directing the maid to carry the note to 'Eva,' but the rest was in perfect English.

'What's it say?' the young man asked her.

Evelyn looked from the paper to the maid and her master and then out into the squalling night.

'It just says, "We're going back." Then she sends us all of her and Herschel's love.'

Her hand fell, dropping the note, and the young man tried to catch it as it wafted downward. But his eagerness drifted it like a winter cloud into the clutches of the fire, where the paper was instantly turned into gray ash and lifted up the square chimney.

The next few days were crowded with enquiries and searches, fears for the children and idleness for Evelyn in the stuffy apartment. As Antonio's organization set to work, she paced in her room or through the surrounding streets, not wanting to think about what might be happening to Herschel and Rifka or about what she should do now. There was nothing holding her there, no family now that they were off the train, no real purpose she could serve by standing and waiting. It had been more than a month since she had written to anyone in Wisconsin, and she knew that such an agonizing silence would be exactly what she would dread most from a child of her own. But still she dawdled, too agitated to run away and still too undecided to stay too near. As 18 December came closer, the search extended beyond the Jewish neighborhoods with operatives being contacted or sent to Escorial, the Pyrenees, and even back into liberated France and Germany. In such maneuvers, a woman from America could not be of much help, so before long the Liot apartment became more of a prison for Evelyn than a shelter, yet it was a prison that she could not seem to leave on her own.

During these troubled hours, she found that she did not know her own feelings very well. She was angry with the children, the boy especially, for abandoning her after all she had done to help them. She missed Herschel and his peculiar ways, his drawings and the impossible faith he had in them, and she missed the girl with her darker wisdom and the odor of rain that for some reason clung to her black dress. Worrying at the window, Evelyn would find her shoulders shrugged stiffly up to her ears without her knowing it, and her fingers would be scribbling on the fogged glass senseless figures that melted away before she was done. She tried to read, tried to listen to the radio for news she might understand, but a white film seemed to have formed between her and the outer world, and more often than not she simply sat in a chair before the fire and felt her heartbeat gently pounding in her chest. It had never occurred to her that a heart, any heart, could be suddenly halted in its rhythm, but now she could think of nothing else. And this new thought – of someday not even being able to think of not being able to think about Herschel and Rifka – frightened Evelyn almost as much as if she had been suddenly struck both deaf and blind.

Given her selfish yearning after the children, she could not bring herself to share her grief with their isolated father. She could hear him sometimes venturing softly out to use the bathroom or to take a tray of food from the maid's hands. Knowing nothing at all about Barcelona or Spain, Sendel had been reduced to weeping alone in his room or singing a low dirge in an accent she could not quite catch. Evelyn had yet to meet him, though she had caught a reflection of him once in a hallway mirror and felt glad that he had apparently regained his health after his experiences in the camps. It must have made the children happy to find him so heavy and looking so strong, even if there was still in his face the wintry pallor of too little light, and if he too often covered his eyes with his hands. Why they should have left as soon as he had come was a mystery to her, unless they were both so impatient for their mother to join up with them that they had gone out to meet her on her journey down. But then why not take their father with them, wondered Evelyn, now more confused than ever as she watched slipping away from her the two children who had once been almost hers.

Came and passed dull days of rain, rain, and sleeplessness.

A day or two before the boat for Palestine was scheduled to leave, Evelyn was getting ready to go out to find presents for the children in the superstitious hope that it might bring them back. The knock that she heard should have been the maid, coming with fresh linen, but on the outside of her door stood a man in faded clothes that once might have been gaily striped, but now hung gray and limp. He was in his forties, she thought, not tall but not short, heavy in the face but with a frank, open expression that startled her as soon as she saw it. His hair was short and light, but graying now, and his eyes were mild and focused, though drooping in exhaustion and bloodshot with worry. He looked straight at her as if he expected to recognize her somehow through his odd spectacles – gray lead rims around the lenses, gray bands fixed around the ears, a gray band across the nose – that made him look more like a robot or a man in a soldier's gas mask than a fleeing refugee.

Evelyn stepped back and might have shut the door in his face if he hadn't spoken first.

'I heard you curse in German outside my door yesterday—'

He said it in a German that put her own to shame, completely free of accent, and Evelyn apologized and said, 'Not very well, I suppose.'

'No,' he replied, 'you were quite accomplished. I could tell that you miss little Herschel and Rifka very much. You're the one who Sophie said rescued the children, aren't you?'

Embarrassed by the praise, Evelyn murmured that she had done only what anyone might have done under the same circumstances. No one, she said, could have left such children alone and helpless.

'In this world,' the man whispered, 'more children than you could count have to die with nothing but their last toys in their hands. And the rest of us can't even keep the toys with us after they're gone.'

He stood perfectly still, until he shook himself and asked, 'Do you think we could talk for a few moments? Together, maybe we could work out where the children might have gone. I have to do something . . .'

Evelyn backed away, but she left the door to her room open.

'I'll try to find us some places to sit.'

The room was over-furnished with chairs and cabinets, mostly for show. She finally thought that the ebony stool might hold the father's weight, so she set him down there as she took the bottom edge of the bed. The two strangers regarded one another silently for a while, the man studying the shocking luxury of the bedroom and the woman studying the man. Outside, even the rain waited.

The man on the stool stopped her from beginning by politely asking for her name.

'Herschel didn't tell you? It's Evelyn Winter.' She said it in her father's careful German. 'Eva, to some people.'

The ebony stool tottered dangerously beneath him.

'But that can't be!' he cried out.

'Why not?'

'There can't be two of you.'

'What are you talking about?' Evelyn asked him in alarm.

In answer, the man reached into a pocket and took out a tiny patch of pink fabric that must have once belonged to a petticoat. The swatch lay as delicately as a butterfly's wing in his hard palm.

'This is the last thing I have left of my sister Evelyn. She gave it to me as a keepsake when I – had to go away. It's kept me alive for years now. If only she had kept it for herself.'

'Is she—?' Evelyn said quietly.

He nodded and reverently tucked the piece of cloth back into his pocket, a soft groan escaping from between his lips.

'She'd been living in Dresden. She disappeared, evaporated, in the firestorm there right at the end of the war. In that awful temperature of goodness,' he finished bitterly.

'What was she like?'

Herschel's father shrugged his son's shrug.

'She was you,' he said simply. 'She was good and natural and eager to start her life again after the long nightmare of so many years. She could do things in the kitchen that were impossible to believe, and she could sing and dance like an angel even when the world had no more song in it. She would have been married by now, probably, maybe even a mother-to-be. In time, she could have told her own children about her brother and that square of pink cloth, a bedtime story whose goodness would have kept their dreams pure for years and years to come.

'But,' he mourned, 'none of that was ever allowed to happen, and now all that I have left is a worthless bit of cloth to help me pretend that I still have her near me.'

'Did Ester ever get to know her?' Evelyn said to chase

away the quiet that was filling the room.

'Who?' the man said.

Evelyn swayed on the edge of the bed.

'Ester,' she repeated. 'The children's mother. Your wife.'

Quickly, he corrected himself. 'Of course. It's just that I used to call her "Berta." It was her favorite pet name when she was a little girl.'

'What was yours?' Evelyn asked him.

'Ernst,' he answered, and changed the subject. 'Where do you think the children have run away to? You don't really think they would have tried to go all the way back to the border, do you, as Señor Liot imagines? I can't see why they would have wanted to go off to find their mother,' he went on. 'As I understand it, the boat is supposed to leave in only a few days, and if we miss this one, there's no telling how long it will be before the next. All the people here have been very kind, but the children should know better than anyone that whoever stops moving these days is lost.'

'I don't know,' Evelyn disagreed. 'Herschel and Rifka strike me as knowing exactly what they want and how to get it. I have no idea what they're up to, but for some reason I think they do, and I guess we'll just have to trust them to take care of themselves. I don't know why I feel this, but I do. I'm sure everything will come out all right in the end, Herr Silberberg. I know it will.'

Hoping to encourage herself as well as their father, Evelyn was startled to see him stiffen uncomfortably, then squint at her suspiciously through his goggle spectacles. It took her a minute to realize that it was her using his name that had unsettled him so, as if he still shared some of Herschel's caution about saying it out loud. Even the way he accepted her reassurances seemed to be guarded. He muttered wordlessly and chewed his lips, uncertain whether he should answer her or simply pretend that he had failed to hear clearly. He glanced about for help, then eventually gazed down at nothing, hoping to disappear in the red fabric wallpaper hanging behind him.

Very carefully, Evelyn went on in her most casual voice.

'I know that Herschel, at least, is smart enough to take care of them both,' she commented. 'From what I've heard, he learned a lot from that old uncle of his back home.'

'I told you,' the man said shortly, 'that my sister died in Dresden. She never married, and she was the only family I had left. Who is this uncle you're talking about now?'

'Well,' Evelyn said, 'the one with the candle.'

The father clutched his head in total bewilderment.

'Candle? What candle? What do you mean, Miss Winter? Why are you talking nonsense when our children might be gone for ever?'

'The candle,' Evelyn said as she rose slowly to her feet to stand above him, 'that you used to mark the death anniversary of Herschel's rabbi uncle. The same candle Herschel broke, and which made him think everything that happened afterward was his fault. His sister told me all about it. I wonder why she didn't remember to tell you.'

Moving toward the door, Evelyn suddenly swung it shut, trapping them both in the thick, airless room.

'Before we decide to go out and help the others search for the children,' she said firmly, 'we should first decide who you want to be. Now,' Evelyn added, 'that we both know you're not the children's father.'

'If you're not Sendel Silberberg,' Evelyn said, 'then who in the world are you? And why are you here pretending to be what you're not? Are you the reason the children have run off? May God help you if you are,' she whispered.

They had both taken their places again, but the man sitting on the stool could not bear her hard look, so he dropped his eyes to the hands clasped between his knees.

'My name is Ernst Rampp,' he said slowly. 'I'm a soldier out of Hamburg originally, born and raised on the banks of that same Elbe River that my Evelyn was probably standing next to when she died. They say that even the river burned that day.'

'Then you really aren't the father of Herschel and Rifka?'

'I'm afraid I'm not. Although,' he added in a voice as heavy as stone, 'many times I tried hard to act as if I were.'

'That's what I thought,' Evelyn said. 'Rifka said that their father is Polish or Russian. But your German is just too good.'

'And you,' he said, raising knowing eyes to her, 'you aren't their mother.'

'No,' she admitted.

'So we two are the same then, yes? Not the right people, but maybe the right people for a wrong place and time.'

The two strangers glared hatefully at one another until the German soldier pressed his advantage.

'So who are *you*, and what are you doing here with these two children who don't belong to you? I've come here for help and to help the children,' he said, 'but I'd like to know who I'm dealing with. What about you?' He looked at the woman through his war glasses, and his eyes seemed to be inside a fishbowl, swollen to twice their normal size. 'Don't you think we should find out a little more about each other before we judge the worst? Don't you think Herschel and Rifka deserve at least that much from us?'

As cautiously as a guilty prisoner, Evelyn told him all

that had happened to her in the past week or so, leaving out only some of the more private intimacies between her and Herschel. When she was done, she sat back and waited for him to speak, but he didn't appear to be ready to tell her anything.

Finally, Evelyn mentioned that Antonio Liot and his refugee organization would have to be warned of his presence. She started for the door, but the man held up his hand to stop her.

'If you do that,' he said, 'then you'll be endangering the very work that I was sent here to do.'

'Which is?'

'To save the children. To carry them out of this awful land, once and for all.'

'You said you were sent,' Evelyn went on. 'Who sent you?'

Rampp lifted his arms. 'Who else? Why do you think Herschel and Rifka didn't tell anyone who I really was? They thought their mother might have sent me for reasons of her own, and they wanted to wait and see. If they ran off, it was probably because by now they don't trust anyone. But why shouldn't they believe me? What else could I possibly have come here for?'

'But why should they trust you? Why should their mother have sent you, of all people? Aren't you one of those monsters who—'

'No man is a monster,' he observed unhappily, 'unless all of them could be. And then God help us all. Both me and you.'

'But—'

She stopped, and they both heard dozens of words and phrases ringing among the furnishings like bees in a closet. Evelyn stood and walked from one side of the bed to the other, her hands held together in front of her, and then she returned to the crease she had made on the edge. At no time did she pass close to the man on the stool, but she could still smell the clean, wholesome aroma of fields and work, and that helped her to calm herself down.

'I think, Herr Rampp, you'd better tell me your story. Your whole story.'

'Why should I tell you instead of just telling the children, when the right time comes? Why should I trust you?'

'Why?' She waited, but there was no one to help her now, so she said, 'Because Herschel and Rifka love me, that's why.'

The surfaces of things in the room in Barcelona softened now as the two strangers leaned toward each other and the silver light outside carried the noises of the city out to sea. Across Balmes Street, other windows in other apartments winked with the arms of maids flapping dusters, like rags of surrender, and with children's faces, round with curiosity and play. Occasionally, the baritone of the harbor sent waves of longing through the streets, reminding everyone of urgency and open waters and safety in flight. But as the turn of noon came and went, the day grew longer and the light became more curdled than cream, and the only evidence of passing time was the shadow of the window frame and the hollowness growing in the eyes of the German soldier on the stool.

'At Stalingrad,' the man began, speaking to the floor at his feet, 'I took a bullet in the belly that should have got me sent straight back home. I thought I was lucky, and in a way I was. If I hadn't left the Eastern Front when I did, I would probably have ended up in Siberia with the rest of my mates, if not worse. But at the time, I was expecting to be invalided to Hamburg or maybe even Dresden, but this was in forty-two, and I wasn't hurt badly enough to get out, and they needed whoever couldn't fight anymore for some new, different work. I didn't know what, pushing papers across a desk maybe or driving a truck, but I didn't really care. Almost anything, I thought, had to be better than freezing my old heart out in a campaign that was going nowhere. Almost anything.'

Taking a deeper breath, Rampp searched the room from side to side and then found Evelyn still sitting on the bed, overwhelmed by his sudden confidences.

'Have you ever been a soldier, Miss?' he asked her, and then went on, 'I tell you, it's got to be one of the worst things that could ever happen to a person. You women are lucky, in a way. You have a lot of burdens, don't get me wrong. Childbirth, being weak and in danger a lot of the time, having to put up with us men and our silly pride and strength. But nothing could ever be harder or colder than being a soldier. It's not even the bullets or the bad food or the loneliness, not even having to watch your best friend empty his blood out all over your hands or see a man you just met the day before leave half of his body on the ground and the other half up in the branches of a tree. Those are nightmares that you can almost get used to over time – almost – though once you do, of course, you're no longer as much of a man as you are a suffering animal. Still, you get numb after a while, and then it's just the same as dying in the snow. You see and then you rest and then you don't see anymore and then you sleep and then you don't ever have to wake up again. It's fitting in its own sad way, though I can't see any sane man ever wanting to see his son go off and do any of it. Yet some fathers do. I know mine did.

'But that's still not the worst.' The German soldier pulled off his lead glasses, wiped them on his sleeve, and put them back on. 'No, the worst is how your life ceases to be your own, how it becomes something you never expected or wanted it to be. You know that your life is still your life, but it seems so far away from you, so far out of your control that you might just as well have read about it in a book about someone else. Do you know what it's like, then, never being able to surprise anyone? Never being able to do or be something no one expects, go where you shouldn't have gone or do what no one thinks you should be allowed to try, just because someone else has the idea that he has more rights to your life than you do? That's what being a soldier is all about. Oh, I suppose there's always a little bit of patriotism still in it, a feeling you have for saving your own and preserving the best that you can remember from your own childhood, like the kinds of foods that you grew up with. And I know that some of the men like to go into it to impress the ladies or their fathers or themselves. But when you put all that aside – and you do that as soon as some man on the other side actually tries to take your life away from you or cripple you, and he doesn't even know you! – when all the music and the flags are gone, all that a man is left with is a dream of running and crawling and crying that he can't wake up from or see an end to. He might just as well not be himself anymore, like the dreams he used to have when he was still a civilian, when he could watch something happening to himself from the outside. That's it, I think,' he nodded to himself. 'A soldier's the man outside, no matter who he is or what circumstances he finds himself stuck in. He's the man outside the man who used to be who he really was.'

Evelyn held her breath. She didn't want to disturb him now as he dragged his head from side to side, like a cow, trying to pull up memories from deeper and deeper roots.

Finally, when he remained silent, Evelyn felt that if she didn't say something, the man might never speak again.

'Though, of course,' she replied, 'that is never any excuse for—'

'No, of course not,' the man admitted. 'Excuses are only for the living.'

'Where did they send you after Stalingrad?' Evelyn asked him gently.

'Well, at first I thought I was just going to do some simple office work at a field station. There I was, coming back from the hospital outside Berlin, heading to what I thought was just some advance position in occupied territory, the same thing so many of my buddies had disappeared to over the years. How was I supposed to know any different, being stuck on the Eastern Front and up to my chest in muck for so long? I might as well have been living on the moon. Even when we got there, at first the place looked like nothing more than a run-of-the-mill Polish village with the usual peasant houses, mules, and rickety streets. It wasn't until we'd gone past the town limits that we had our first glimpse of what was waiting for us on the other side. And then it still took most of us quite a while to realize where we were. It was just so hard to believe at first, that any of us should wind up somewhere that we thought had always been nothing more than a wartime rumor or a Hades to frighten unruly children.'

'It was a camp?' Evelyn prompted him as he paused.

'Oh,' he faltered, 'it was so much more than a camp. It was like a whole city, a whole world, a galaxy of planets with fibers of roads and wires connecting it all together. I never saw all of it myself. Who could have? There must have been forty of them all told, from Auschwitz itself to Birkenau about two kilometers away and Monowitz-Buna with its rubber factory, all the way to a camp called Brno that was supposed to be a hundred kilometers distant. There were still others that I heard talked about – strange names like Janin and Jaworzyn – but I was never sent too far abroad. As soon as I got there, I was assigned to the main camp, and it took a few months for them to start shifting me about. Like I told you before, a soldier's life isn't his own. It's as if he has two of them, one at work that has to move and function like a machine or a trained dog, and one in the barracks that does whatever it can to forget that the other life even exists. The trouble is, before long, his work life gets to feel more and more like a dream, and his private hours become the only ones that are real. It's scary, but you actually start to feel as if you're falling asleep as you head out to work in the morning and starting your real work only when you go to bed at night. You're so tired all the time, and no amount of bed sleep ever seems to be enough for you to catch up. And when you're that tired,' Rampp said, looking across at Evelyn for some understanding, 'then you hardly know what you're doing, even when you're doing it. Do you know what I mean?'

'I suppose I do, in my own smaller way,' she said. 'I myself was a secretary all my life, both as a civilian and then later in the Army. Eventually, you start to wonder who that person is who spends all her time shuffling papers and running errands for some world she doesn't seem to have much to do with. It gets to where it could be almost anyone. Anyone but you.'

The man nodded eagerly in agreement. 'That's right. I was on a typewriter for a while, before my belly healed and they decided they could put me out in the cold weather without killing me too soon. Then they found different work for me, or for that man who kept on calling himself me during the day and who didn't seem to have much say left about what was happening to him in the only life he was ever going to have. He learned soon enough that there's always something worse that they can find for you to do.'

'What was it they had you do?'

The soldier looked through his blind goggles at the window's smear of light and shadow. But he was not looking at the window.

'That's when they put the man called Ernst Rampp in Birkenau as a guard and placed his rifle back in his hands for the first time since Russia. And that's when he started forgetting who he was.'

'Forgetting? Do you mean like in amnesia?'

'No,' he said. 'No, nothing as clear as that.'

'Or,' the woman thought, 'like when someone in the same room calls out your name and you look around, too, just for a moment, trying to find out who it is they want?'

'That's it exactly!' the man cried. 'I swear to you, I would be watching myself standing post, hefting my gun in my arms like a child, ankle-deep in mud and freezing, looking like some stone eagle on top of a buried column or a dead tree in the woods. And then someone would tell me to do something or one of the captives would start a fight over bread or soup or there would be a child wailing where there shouldn't even have been a child alive, and I would see myself taking care of it, doing my duty, doing whatever had to be done, and at the same time I'd be wondering, "What's he doing? What does he think he's doing? Don't do that, don't shout like that, don't raise your rifle over your head like that. What is that man doing, running that woman into the ground like that, until she lies back and goes to sleep with a smile on her face as if she really means to wake up sometime later?

Why's he so angry, why is he slapping everyone around him, why is he laying a shovel across that man's throat and standing his feet on its two ends as if he were a little boy rocking on a seesaw?" I sometimes even used to say such things out loud, talking to that other man outside as though we were both crazy, but I never got a good answer from him. Not even once. Not until—'

'Until?' Evelyn heard herself saying in the silence.

The man on the stool went white.

'Until they put me on permanent watch in the F.K.L. The last and first place every one of us wanted to be.'

'I don't understand.'

'The Frauen Konzentration Lager,' he said slowly, 'is where the women were housed in Birkenau. They were kept away from their men, separated right on the ramp as soon as they stepped off the train or truck. That was never my job, but I watched it sometimes and marveled at how efficiently everything was handled, like when a shepherd steers his flock or a tram-driver counts his fares. As the men were taken off to their own barracks and work, the women and children were led away to another area and assigned to blocks and bunks. That was where I came in. I had to help herd them all together, get them where they were supposed to go, and keep them from panicking or fighting back. It wasn't hard. After nights and days on the transports, the women were happy just to breathe and find their children by their sides. And the children, like all children, were tired and curious and a little bit wary. Never afraid, though, never afraid. We were very good about that. That sounds like awful work, but I preferred it to having to stay back on the platform and help clean out the trains. I don't think that I could have stood that for very long.'

'Were they that dirty?' Evelyn wondered.

'There – there were always some who didn't make it. And they had to be brought out. Old men, the sick, swollen babies that you had to carry out by the legs like dead chickens. I knew some men who had to do that all the time, who finally couldn't do anything in their lives but that . . .'

The American woman glanced into a corner of the room and then she asked, 'Is that where you first met the children's mother? In that part of the camp?'

Rampp's face brightened momentarily, or it might have been only a quick blinking behind the glinting lenses that made every part of his features cleaner and more transparent.

'Yes, I met Berta – Ester – the first or second week after I started in the women's camp. I began using that pet name for her whenever we saw each other. I suppose it was a code so the other women would get the idea that we had known each other from before and would leave us alone and not think that we were just another couple of pathetic *kochani*, part-time lovers.'

'Do you mean you two . . .' Evelyn frowned, then moved on. 'But how could you ever be alone together in there?'

'Oh, you'd be surprised at how many nooks you can find when you set your mind to it. Remember, the camp was a city or bigger. There were streets like H-Strasse where the stores were, separate houses or barracks for different functions, neighborhoods like up in the northeast corner for the black market, Number Ten Block for doctoring—'

'But why,' she interrupted him, 'why would Ester want to be alone with you? Why you and not her own husband, if she could?'

If the soldier was offended by her tone, he didn't show

it. He only adjusted his glasses a little to see better into the past and overlook nothing.

'Because,' he said calmly, 'I helped her save her children.'

Evelyn wondered if she had heard him correctly, the way his flashing eyes were distracting her so, and she shifted around to find a different view of his face.

'What kind of glasses are those?' she asked him suddenly and pointed a trembling finger at her reflection in their lenses.

'These?' He pulled them slightly away from his face to look. 'Oh, these are called respirator's glasses. They're only meant to be worn under a respirator, but now they're the only pair I have. Even seeing poorly is better than not seeing at all, isn't it?'

Nodding, Evelyn got up and pulled a straight-backed chair to a place right beside the soldier. Then she sat down and watched a stray thread on the hem of the blanket dance in a random current of air.

'I want,' she said carefully, 'to hear all of it. Even what you don't think I should hear. I have to hear everything now.'

And so he told her everything.

The story that the soldier told in Evelyn's bedroom as the end of the afternoon gave way to the evening was of a miracle that came true in a place where miracles were forbidden. It had more to do with blind chance than with anything else, unearned good fortune that for years just missed the mouse of a tiny hand disappearing beneath a cot or a rooster's comb of mussed hair pecking at some food on the other side of a window. But there was also some human goodness at work there. There was sacrifice, as honest as it was accidental, and a perfect kindness in the face of an offense that was simply too impossible to be believed. By the time the soldier finished, Evelyn had even learned of an artistry she would never have suspected in the suffering of one small boy who had refused to learn how to die.

Yet even as he described his former life for the first time, Private Rampp seemed to be trying hardest to picture the soldier who had worked, eaten, and slept at the camp. Sitting upright, as if perched upon an unstable point, he leaned slightly off to one side with a mystified air, approaching as gingerly as anyone could the difficult enigma of another man's inward world. For her part, Evelyn, too, sat unnaturally as she listened. Tottering on the edge of her chair, she peered forward for any shadow or outline of the children's parents, especially their mother.

She agonized over every revelation and wept over the worst details, but at the same time her eyes squinted feverishly for some sign of what Ester Silberberg had been. But for most of the story, she was to be disappointed. Except to the uninvolved, nothing could ever be less interesting than pain.

The train from the south of France had taken the Silberberg family directly to the ramp, where they were instantly separated, the father shuffling off to work and the mother and children sent in the other direction to wait, only wait. From then on, for more years than could be counted, the father kept in touch by letters carried in the shoe of a thin electrician with a serial number on his arm so old that it had barely passed one thousand. From what the rest of the family could learn, Sendel Silberberg was kept at work with a shovel until someone discovered how quickly his hands could move and transferred him to the Krankenbau, where he was of more use in stitching up wounds and measuring dosages. There, his luck came and went with the day's weather, as he swam through his own illnesses and those of others, and fevers took hold of him or let go almost as regularly as the arrival of new trains. Shielded from the darkest nightmares of the camp, he lived by always being useful, by working as a *Schreiber* who handled the records for the patients and the clerical papers for the Germans. According to an exterminated confidant, it was Herr Silberberg who first invented a scheme whereby names selected for the chimneys would often turn up counterfeit or multiplied, or moved ahead from page to page for so long that they finally just dropped off altogether. In such a way, many still went up as smoke, but some who did would be later found occupying a bunk in a corner of the infirmary with diseases no one but the *Schreiber* could pronounce. Eventually, his talents sent him to other camps in the system, and his letters grew more erratic and his news about himself less specific, until his wife and children lost sight of him in the twisted storm of their own endurance and only heard of him again toward the very end.

Ester had been sent left toward the women's area in Birkenau where no one was expected to last even as long as haze in warming sunlight. By some mistake, she was able to keep her two children beside her longer than most, and the family began to study every trick and inflection that might teach them how to survive longer. They were all children again, toddlers, finding new ways to walk and eat and sleep, and showing each other how to work without any hope at all. They learned how to make themselves as useful as the father. Sendel had shown the mother how to stitch, and now Ester taught herself and her daughter how to sew for some of the female *Kapos*, using scrounged eyelashes of threads or copper wires. They made their way to the area called 'Canada' with its mountain ranges of suitcases and shoes and blankets and gloves and dolls. Because they were Jews and by definition had nowhere to go after this, it was relatively easy for Ester and Rifka to organize objects from a pile to a pocket, walk back to the barracks in another's shoes, and smuggle missed treasures to weaker women who looked out from their bunks as if from a deepening well. They sorted whole worlds of clothing, stumbled across frozen courtyards with pots of weed-and-thistle soup, and helped tend the blossoming fruit trees near the cottages at the rear of the camp. They even primped the girls who had been forced to choose life over honor in the *Puffkommando* brothel, dabbing on their faces as makeup as much tarry margarine as could be spared from the starving. Gradually, both Ester and Rifka grew older and wiser in the cold village of stone and wire, though their years were cruel, and their wisdom consisted mainly in learning how not to fall down.

As the youngest male child in the women's camp, Herschel was a chick hidden by sisters from a stern father. He should not have lasted a day, but early on he was chosen as a runner – a messenger scurrying orders between *Kapos* and guards or carrying pipefuls of Mahorca tobacco to an administrator behind a desk. The job rushed him through the camp like a winter wind, and soon the gray colors surrounding him broke apart into blue and white striped uniforms, the blue caps of the Union factory workers, the scarlet berets of the work organizers, and the muscular red armbands of the foremen and their assistants. The boy grew stronger as he ranged further and further afield to the Persian Market and the *Waldsee* that his eyes alone could see, and to the new area called 'Mexico' that a Red from Barcelona told him meant the navel of the moon. As he became something of a favorite, he still made himself invisible by being everywhere at once, helping to brew the acorn tea or polishing an instrument for the orchestra that marched the work details in and out of the gates. He flew past latrines and fanged dogs and walls of eyes pinned like butterflies, until he finally ducked under the red and white light bulbs on top of the fence and reached all the way to the main camp with its model neatness and its solid green window-boxes sagging with sick flowers. There, Herschel found out that most of the messengers were expected to become *Piepels*, the boyfriends of the loneliest guards and prisoners, and he quickly volunteered for the bricklaying school where he might find asylum from the worst of the inhuman winters drifting up all around him.

Snow on the Moon

It was as he was learning to work the mortar with his hands that the boy first discovered what magic his fingers could do. In the grainy flesh of the paste he found the models of pyramids and houses and the miniature roads that connected brick neighborhoods into the puzzle of a single wall. He would spend days staring at a trapped bubble in the cement or at a stubble of straws that had no chance to escape, and he wondered at the paradox of creativity and loss that stonework represented. Of all the boys in the brick school, he soon became the most fanciful and innovative. He would regularly crown his work with festoons of trees and valleys with minuscule houses dribbling down their slopes and on some rounded corner insert a profile of a door hung with a strip of grass like a folded note. While all the other boys were content with writing their own names and short messages into the mortar to be found in later years by historians and tourists and moviemakers, Herschel preferred to reproduce models of the camps no bigger than one of his own hands, models so exact and condensed that – like a mirror within a mirror within a mirror – the original would be fixed deep in the earth for the rest of time. The artist was careful to keep his talents out of sight, but even then his shrunken landscapings inspired some of the other boys to dream away a few painful hours, and his reproductions of cities that never were helped the lonely to recall the streets and crowds that used to surround them with so much warmth. Even though most of the bricklayers periodically faded away into the distance like moonlight, Herschel managed to keep on building and destroying and rebuilding as steadily as any boy could in such a place, while he watched the moon whiten with a snowfall that, unlike his, was as soft and as regular as grief.

One morning no different from any other, Herschel and others were rounded up and herded back toward Birkenau for some special assignment. The boy fairly skipped most of the way, gazing in all directions for a sight of his mother or father or sister. But as the work squad passed through the barren countryside and through the moonscape of the camp itself, he saw that they were meant to reach the rear perimeter where a new project was under way beyond a grove of birches and across a road from a cottage with a tower of red bricks, barred windows, and flowerbeds at the entrance. On top of an underground chamber, the boy and his fellows were made to lay a concrete floor and then begin raising a bakery of stout walls around massive iron ovens. Weeks of hopeless work followed. Herschel tried to contact his family as he built walls whose heat might someday comfort a rheumatic joint or a pregnant back, but a long silence seemed to separate the work detail from the rest of the camp, and he had to be satisfied with stolen glances through fog and barbed wire. As the new building rose and the anguish of the bricklayers awakened, the boy bent over his work more focused than ever and hurried to finish his map of the moon in the mortar around the main oven. When he was done, he sat back and rested on his heels with a sleepy smile that not even the foreman pretended to understand. And when he joined the rest of the group to return to their barracks, it was noticed that of all the boys, only their little artist held his face up to the dark sky, as if he had sent a dispatch into space that would take centuries to be answered.

No more than a day or two passed before the bricklayers were marched back to the work site, only this time not to build. When Ester and her daughter heard that

Herschel had been chosen in the next *selekcja* – selection – they hoped that the woman from Salonika might be right when she thought it must have something to do with the moon. But they had already seen too many shadows pass in that direction and had heard old women being bullied through the trees by armed guards who looked more embarrassed than angry. At times like these, there were always jokes – 'Rudolf's run off for a last smoke' or 'Granny always was nothing but a puff of hot air' – but the nervous banter lasted only until the stinging ashes began to descend like dusk onto hair and lips, and then each of the living women went off by herself for a while. When Ester's only son was scheduled to walk into the far, gray forest, the Silberberg women turned within themselves like two flames melted together, and the rest of the barracks joined in keeping them sheltered from every window until the end of their family's future should be past. As another black-and-white afternoon came and went, Ester and Rifka returned to their sewing and waited with the others for the daily arrival of the soup that might or might not contain white turnips and yellow potatoes and maybe even the memory of an onion.

By chance, the only time Herr Rampp ever drew oven duty was when the Silberberg boy trotted at the tail of the line, scanning the freshly fallen ash for the footnotes of animals or the waving signatures of artistic winds. The soldier looked ahead and up at the endless mesh of trees, searching for that part of himself in the distance that might survive this winter's evening and return with a face that could still feel cold and a mouth that might be able to taste something more than salt. Of the murmuring of cries and questions all about him, of the tickling of fingers and pleas that tapped at his legs like so many rodents or bites of frost, a soldier would do better not to be aware – or to remember it as only the scars of fleas and weariness. As the troop neared the glowing bricks, the children began to hurry forward, eager to hug some of the warmth out of the walls and into their own hands, their small cheeks, their chests and bellies. Once they felt the heat, it was easier to persuade them to undress and go down to the saunas for a hot shower and a delousing, and then it was just as easy to do the rest as it was to operate machinery or tighten the screws or light a cigarette at a flame. Even Herr Rampp found it extremely restful to be able to turn away from the peephole, from the sharp smell of almonds and the insect gesticulations inside, and stare out through the Christmas air that was as clean and narrow as his razor and wonder if the new storm might start tonight or wait for tomorrow. The other guards joined him – Tesch and Stabenow and at last Topf and his boys – though none of them talked much, and they all looked off toward the western horizon and thought about when their exile in the east might finally come to an end.

No one, therefore, witnessed the miracle that could not have happened anywhere else but here.

Little Herschel was always short for his age, whatever that age might be, so in any crowd of taller children and lofty adults he naturally settled to the bottom, stretching upon tiptoes with his neck craning upward like a heron's. He usually didn't mind it too much. The view of arms and shoulders was enough for him, and the greater warmth of being smothered by swelling bodies was more than he could have hoped for on a cold, dark night. He remembered a time in Frankfurt when his family had been on the move and they had been caught up in a multitude of other uprooted people before a building on a side street, the tidepool of coats and parcels in lazy motion as outside currents pulled at it from one side, then the other. It had been a pleasant enough experience, that feeling of becoming blended with a mass larger than himself, and when he felt the same sensation in the chamber, he welcomed it as if the pressure within the walls were as comforting as an embrace. Just as the children's panic started, Herschel even let himself relax, lowering himself closer to the floor to share its heat as another child might crouch around a glowing brazier on a homeless street. It was that squatting that saved him at the start, as the sudden boost onto the shoulders of a tall stranger helped save him later right at the end when the gas mushroomed upward like a dry cloud.

As if he were caught in a fire and wisely breathing the cool air at the bottom, the boy stood low at the side of the tight gel of bodies and near a loose vent, and the gas never reached him. A short time later, no longer able to see any heads standing, Rampp led the other guards in, opening the doors for the hooks of the waiting *Sonderkommando*, and they all stepped back. There, at the leading edge of a mountain of dead hands and skin, frail eyes and curled bodies, stood Herschel with a simple smile on his face and a smuggled pencil and paper in his hands. Later, it was said that the paper contained nothing more than a tiny stick figure, a few skeletal trees, and a road that seemed to disappear into the fibers of the paper. (The paper itself vanished from sight until Rampp placed it in Evelyn's lap as they sat together on the bed, and then its mustiness made her sniff for gas from the kitchen at the far end of the apartment.) As soon as Herschel had left, two or three soldiers hurried to beat him to death as they had had to do to the odd survivors before, but Rampp and the boy's perfectly weightless appearance persuaded them to look the other way. As an icy night buried the surrounding hills in a dense mist that would linger over the marshes until morning, the men turned blindly to their next chore, and the boy was reabsorbed into the body of the women's camp like a newborn returning to his first home.

From then on, Herschel became more of a whisper in the camps than a prisoner, and for the others the camps became at least one degree less dark. He was everywhere and nowhere, while the numbed soldier from Hamburg who had held back the descending rifles from Herschel's head heard tales of further miracles that hurried the last years of his imprisonment toward their end. In the world of what he had come to think of as the *Betrugslager*, in the swindle that was his life, there were continuing legends that could never be confirmed and never forgotten, fables of hope and rescue that would carry beyond the charged wires and the fears. He heard talk of scraping sounds coming from yards in the camp that should have been vacant, of a boy sitting there alone and filing his nails on a stone until they glittered like moons, and then of his melting into the ground like so much spring water. In the latrines, where many went to weep on their own, laughter had been overheard, not bitter or insane, but the careless giggling of a child playing at hide-and-seek or a man recalling where he had hidden the lost pearls of his childhood. Everyone carried his own bowl for soup, knowing that to lose it was to die, but there was one *caravana* of minute proportions that seemed to belong to no one, yet was never empty. Others could spill some of its metal broth into their own, but still be able to pass it along to someone even hungrier, and at the bottom of it could always be found surprising bits of meat for the very old, for the frantic *Zugang* fresh from outside, for the desperate who saw the woods approaching. If a man should need to feel the sting of some wooden tobacco to help him stand, then a cigarette rolled in newspaper might appear on his bunk. If some guard in the night should ever listen through the forest for the song that his mother used to sing, then from the other direction might come singing in a language that was not German, but tonight sounded close enough. Even if the imbecile with the white armband with *Blöd* written on it – he whom everyone called *'der Lump'* – if he stood near the wire and thought of chinning himself upon it, a slip of colored paper would probably be blown up against it in a flare of hot colors that would satisfy the fool for days.

As the years passed, and as the guard found more and deeper grains in the wooden walls to explore, the boy kept flitting from place to place as if he were no more than fiction or ashes in the earth, though the legends of what he did lived longer than anyone would have ever thought possible. His name sometimes preceded him into barracks and dreams, and sometimes his deeds would linger on, long after even the throats that had repeated them had blistered in singing flames. No one in the camps, comrade or collaborator, was ever overlooked. Relatives, friends, strangers, and guards – they all heard echoes as they shouldered yokes in fields or mixed the dust of bodies into the lonely waters of the Sola River. Even those who were too weak to live would prostrate themselves on the faithful earth and pass along some of Herschel's fame to the good grass and the pebbles of light. Without the presence of the child who had forgotten how to die, the camps might have lived for ever. Only he knew of the nights he spent alone, at a window or out in the last wind, comparing the stained snow all around him with the pure snow on the moon and wondering how much longer he would have to wait before the moon itself would grow heavy enough to fall.

As for Rifka and her mother and the father who had

become a memory almost as insubstantial as Herschel himself, their lengthy survival until the end could be explained only partly by luck or cleverness. The fact that they were now even distantly connected to the ghost that materialized simultaneously at dozens of places and even in separate camps probably helped them win some favor by association and certainly raised their spirits. For Ester, hiding her son under blankets and from the more jealous women around her became the rest that made the hauling of sand and the work in the factories easier to endure. Although the boy only surfaced at her side from time to time, his large eyes breathless with excitement and fever, she still saw corners of him flickering everywhere she looked, and what she heard about him seemed to endow him with an excess of lives, or one life that would never end. And that made her as happy as any suffering mother could ever hope to be.

Rifka, on the other hand, had to be satisfied with dreams of her brother alone. Because she was always taken off to do sewing for some of the female *Kapos*, she heard less and less of Herschel until he faded away entirely, only to reappear in regular dreams that sustained her through both rains and winters. These visions were not always of their childhood together, but even when one of them might include their new village of guns and wire, the story of the dream seemed to be based upon some precious memory from an earlier town, another existence. So the phantom sight of a street illuminated by spring light helped her wade through the slime and mud between the barracks, and the thought of Herschel at a fogged window with clouds in his face made the latrine buckets glow less repulsively under the summer's sun. At times, it is true, the boy came to tell her of youth lost and promises come to nothing. Then the black smoke of grandparents and the creamy smoke of murdered children mingled sadly above her head like a smear across a fresh dress. But as she pressed on with her work, leaned into it as if a needle could ever sew anybody back together, her dreams of her brother returned almost as often as exhaustion. And his reminders of the unreal world they had been forced to leave behind kept his sister weeping long enough for her to remember how to breathe.

All this time, as the years aged and the camp decayed along with its inhabitants, Ernst Rampp did whatever he could while at the same time doing all he had to do. He brought them news of the father, now circling the extended complex like some bird of prey, searching for the end of the war by counting corpses. The soldier watched over both Rifka and her mother, keeping them less visible in the barracks and less alone in the streets and at roll call. And for Herschel he worked hardest of all, even though he glimpsed the boy only as an after-image on the edge of sight or heard of him only in tales. In some way, the German succeeded in keeping him both alive and dead at the same time, arranging that he should grow up in a part of the camp where he should not have grown at all. Before long, Herschel's death in the oven was as officially certain as a typographical error that refused to be set right. By keeping the boy remembered, on paper and in memory, he managed to keep him forgotten, until Herschel became as dream-like for the other soldiers as he was for the inmates, and so his presence in the *Lager* was overlooked as only a step in the dark or the corner of some ordinary wall.

It was then that the boy's drawings began appearing on slips of paper stuck to doors, on windows, in the clay, on the backs of sleeping children, even around the bases of the turrets where the *Posten* stood guard both night and day. At this date, there was a lot less fullness than suggestion in the artist's style. To some, the horse scribbled in the dirt and the wings fashioned among the branches of a tree were nothing more than silly freaks of nature. Others, perhaps, the more downcast, read too much into the Tarot cards on the skin of ice in the bucket, hoped too hard before the calendar of frost counting down the days to home, or fooled their hearts into believing that their own children might run back from the woods just to play with their toys made out of spit and lice. But most of the people who happened to discover a portrait of the loveliest child in their family on the crust of their bread, or an etching of their own crib in the shadow of their bunk laid across the floor, accepted the boy only as a sign of continuation, of one more life asleep but not unliving, and saved his works as if they were as irreplaceable as carrots or onions. Some even carried one or two into the gas with them, to be held up defiantly or pressed across their faces as a road map for where they were hoping to go next.

When the noise of battle finally came close enough to show a line of white caps above a rumbling of Soviet tanks, Birkenau was abandoned by its architects and by most of its walking dead, and the rest were left to find their own way back to themselves. The guard from Hamburg, caught one morning unawares behind the brick chimney where he had gone to pray, was missed just long enough to leave with himself alone. He had always been merely a transformed typist, and he would never be greatly missed by the more faithful soldiers who were now begging the mountains to fall and hide them from the coming storms. Once Ernst had burned his uniform and put on the peasant clothes that he had hidden away years ago, he ran to the hospital where Ester Silberberg had been recovering from a bout of typhus. Inside, the sick lay waiting for the Russians who would liberate them, while the dying numbered the moments until a quieter liberation. Sneaking past an observant Italian, the guard made his way to Ester's bed and found her languishing in a fever and calling for her children. It was soon apparent that she might not last the day, and in her final clear breaths she begged the German to find Rifka and Herschel and do whatever he could to help them escape. The coming Soviets she trusted less than a man who had called her by her childhood pet name and who had drained away much of his own strength to add a little to hers. After they had agreed on a meeting place, the guard left the woman behind to rest and rushed out to find the two children and somehow convince them to follow into exile one of their own former jailers.

Thus began his own strange incarceration in a month or more of endless days, circular wanderings across hostile borders, and hiding from both victors and defeated, victims and criminals. The children walked beside him as in a trance, though the girl seemed more suspicious than the boy as she hugged a black shawl around a dress that Ernst had made to replace her stripes. Herschel was in his own deep wilderness, as private as pain, stumbling along with both eyes fixed on patterns in the mud and shapes in the air. As they walked and ran, the former soldier kept promising them that their mother would find their father and the two of them would be waiting in Dresden by the middle of February. Somehow, by keeping off the roads and under shadows, he was able to lead the children to the banks of the Elbe east of the city just in time to witness the hurricane of fire that consumed the world as if it were made of hair or paper, and then he led them away. By the summertime, a fugitive camp guard was more of a hazard to the children than an aid, so Ernst turned them over to

Sophie Probst. That White Rose veteran had been working inside Europe for years, trying to lead any runaways across the Pyrenees. She told him that she would be in touch with people who would know where the liberated prisoners wound up, and also that she knew a *passeur* who could get them all into Spain, with or without papers. The last that the German had seen of the children was as they were being spirited away down a road that looked much like the one that Herschel had drawn in the gas chamber, and then he had turned back to see if he could find any signs of life left among the black bones of Dresden.

In the dark now, sitting side by side, Evelyn said that she could scarcely believe what he had told her. It was too much.

'I was there,' he said in a hoarse cry. 'I was there, and I still can't believe it myself.'

After a long silence, she added, 'What was she like when you knew her in the camp? Ester, I mean.'

'Berta?' He slipped off his goggles and stared at the rain-washed window. 'Oh, in the camp Berta was a miracle. The way she always understood everything, all her friends and their problems, all her enemies even. We used to try to meet every day at one of the corners in her barracks, a seam where the wood had come away and left an opening just big enough for a voice or a fingertip. I wouldn't have been able to make it through if it hadn't been for those daily visits. Most of our superiors,' Ernst added, shaking his head, 'saw the camps as schools where we could be taught how to suffer by making others suffer. But I never saw it that way. I thought of it only as an episode, a blank space lying between one life and another, such as what must happen on the other sides of birth or death. That was all I could think about it. Thinking too much was always our most dangerous enemy. Always.

'But it was Berta,' he went on more happily, 'who showed me that not every kind of thinking was the same. Some was good, and some was bad. She led me toward better, brighter thoughts. Every day that we knelt down together and whispered through the walls, or were lucky enough to meet somewhere outside to walk near each other or even touch, every one of those moments was a month or a year to me, a moment where I could bury myself in her and not be what I was. That's the kind of woman she was to everyone in the camp. She did everything for everyone else by not doing anything very special at all, only staying. She stayed on. And that gave all the rest of us some hope that we could stay on, too, even if there didn't seem to be much left worth staying around for.'

As he paused, Evelyn asked him the one question that she had promised herself never to ask.

'But how was she with Herschel? I know she hid him and saved him,' she stammered. 'But what about the everyday things? How did she treat him during all those daily hours when the only thing a person had to do was wait to die?'

'Simple,' Ernst smiled for the first time. 'Berta believed everything. It was the most magical thing about her. The way she treated her own children – the way she treated all of us – was just by believing everything we thought or imagined or hoped for, even when she knew as well as the rest of us that it was all a lie. In the camps, our lives were lies because nothing ever happened for any real reason. People – children – died, and everyone knew there was no point to any of it. No one ever explained anything. And in a life like that, the easiest and kindest thing to do is never to disbelieve anything, not even the most miraculous cruelty or the most miraculous salvation. Berta was the one who taught us that,' he said brokenly. 'She was the one who taught us how to be reborn simply as ourselves. Nothing more and nothing less.'

In the street below, the night had come on fully with a fair sky and a sailing moon. The normal rhythms of the apartment rose again, steadying the labyrinth of the hallways and doors into the imperturbable firmness of everyday life. Every physical detail in the entire building settled into its place, and the air felt warm and close even though there was no fire.

Just as some worries about the vanished children reached the bedroom from the restless city outside, Evelyn reached a hand out and set it on the soldier's hand where it lay upon the blanket.

'She's not coming, is she?' Evelyn asked him.

But Ernst only raised his eyes with more certainty than she had seen in them so far and studied her in the unlit room.

'No,' he said, moving closer. 'She's already here.'

No sooner had Antonio Liot left for Escorial to rejoin his mother and backtrack the missing children, than word filtered through the Jewish neighborhoods of Barcelona of 'the boy in the moon'. For two or three nights now, as the community worked as a single unit to find Herschel and Rifka, some of the more superstitious among the mix of peoples traded rumors of a vision seen against the sky at night, of a silhouetted boy who rode the full moon. No one in the relief organization followed up rumors. They couldn't afford to. The work of shifting whole populations from place to place could not depend upon anything as nebulous as gossip. But the refugees and their supporters were ready to believe anything that lifted them upward and out of their slough of exile, if even for a moment. An irrepressible joy in the fantastic overcame them and speckled the streets of Barcelona with a dancing excitement that those streets had not seen in years. Had it not been for the legend of the boy who had added his own blue mark to the blemishes on the moon, the couple from Antonio Liot's apartment might never have found themselves within listening distance of the sea. And then they would never have found a way home.

Evelyn and Ernst stood together at the foot of Montjuïc, the Mountain of the Jews, and tried to see a path up its slope in the darkness. The tangle of vegetation and the tumbling waves on the other side made the night sound hollow, and every move they made was carried upward in ripples that eventually reached all the way to the shaking stars above. Nodding toward a distant lighted road, Ernst thought they should try over there, but Evelyn refused to hear the long weariness in his voice.

'I'd rather not,' Evelyn said. 'I don't want to scare Rifka or Herschel by dragging a crowd up the hill after us. They won't want to see either one of us, probably, the way things are now.'

'If they're up there at all,' Ernst pointed out.

'I think they are,' the woman said quietly. 'I feel them.'

'You've been saying that for the past three hours, Evelyn.'

'No, no, this time I mean it. This time for sure.'

They had left the apartment as soon as the lamps outside had been lit, and walked down Balmes Street with the buildings arching above them and the moon moving overhead by not moving at all. They had talked to as many passersby as they could, asking after the children or what children like them might do and where they might go, but they did not learn enough to help them. In the city at this time, almost every road was filled with children and parents who had nowhere to go but away, and every one of them was hungry, poorly dressed, and lost about the eyes, and quite a few of them were named Herschel or Rifka. There were displaced people who had been living hand-to-mouth in Barcelona for years, making leather gloves, and men even more adrift who had escaped from the Allied concentration camp at Saint-Cyprien only to end up in the Modelo Prison here. In the busier knot of Catalunya Plaza and in the Barrio Chino where everyone went to hide, Evelyn had encountered families who had been lost for so long that not even their names would be found again. And in the ancient Jewish quarter, El Call, she had seen children starving in the depths of every shadow, and she had almost started believing her companion when he said that it might be too late for them to do anything now.

Then, after midnight, they had come upon a family of gypsies scattered upon the ground like so many grains of corn. Evelyn had bent to leave them a few coins, and as she did, the baby had made a fuss in its sleep and rolled its eyes, slitting open the lids. Inside them, the woman had caught a glint of the growing moon over her shoulder, and then she had crouched down to wake the father.

'Señor, where would be the best place to go to see the moon and the harbor around here?'

The baby's eyes had opened and closed, and the father had indicated the mass at the end of the road. 'Up on Montjuïc, of course. You can see all you want to see from up there.'

Now, faced with the long climb, Evelyn wondered if she could go any further. She was cold and scared, and there was a mountain of wilderness still separating her from the military fortress at the top where a boy might go to hide and view the night sky.

'What do you think?' she asked the German. 'If you feel too tired to do it . . .' she added hopefully.

'I've been tired since thirty-three,' he answered, rubbing his eyes beneath the respirator glasses. 'Let's go on up together.'

He led the way until they reached the battlement walks that skirted the inland side of the fortress, and then he slowed down, peering about through his goggles like a lepidopterist searching for some signs of the children's gay patterns. Even on a winter's night, the park was not completely bare and quiet. There were on every hand hints of lovers strolling, an isolated man on a bench, boys or soldiers hunting for distraction, after-images of the dead whose graves had become healed over by time. The German seemed to feel the incline worse than Evelyn, and he seemed to hear more in the murmuring of voices among the decayed leaves, and by the time they rounded the fortress she had to guide him with his arm held in hers and her encouraging voice in his ear. Even so, the higher they climbed, the more disheartened even Evelyn became, until she wondered if they would ever find Herschel and Rifka again, or keep walking until they stepped onto the surface of the moon itself.

On the other side of the fortress, separate and neglected, they came upon a low cabin that must at one time have served as a barracks. This, too, they would have passed quickly by, had not a sudden light played out of one of the boarded windows. Evelyn was the first to the door. Inside, she found one long room with three tiers of bunks on each side and a stone bench dividing the length of the room like a scar. A single bulb burned over a toilet down at the far end. Each of the bunks was narrow and bare, worse than a pull-down cot on a train, and the wooden slats were splintered and gave off a smell of earth. Tatters of sheets, some fragments of abandoned clothing hung over the outside edge of the beds like torn skin, and somewhere at the bottom of the dark scurried a panic of rodents and insects. In the sick gloom of the place, it took Evelyn minutes to find the black figure lying tucked into a bed like a log or a bundle of plaited rags.

'Rifka?'

The shadow shifted, saw them both, then moved away.

'What are you doing here?' Evelyn asked. 'Where's Herschel?'

Instead of answering, the girl only stared unhappily at

the former guard who now stood behind the woman, waiting and looking everywhere else at once. The room was reminding him of something.

'Why is he here?' she asked finally. 'And why did he come to Barcelona, pretending to be our father? Where are our parents? We thought we might be able to see them getting on one of the boats down in the harbor, but now if he's here—'

Evelyn tried to reach out to her.

'He's here to help you. To help all of us.'

'The only thing he ever did was steal our lives away from us and never give them back.' Rifka sat up, growing harder. 'He owes us, Eva. He owes Herschel and me another life!'

Hearing her voice, Ernst gradually dissolved into the darker corners of the barracks room.

Perched on the stone bench, surrounded by the ghosts of men and women and children . . . children . . . Evelyn admitted that she could not comment on that. 'But I do know,' she went on, 'that he's not so different from either one of us right now. He's lost and wounded, and he's just waking up from a nightmare that was only a few feet separate from yours for all those years. It's almost as if you were all sleeping a feverish sleep together – even me – and now it's time for all of us to wake up and get back to life. None of this makes much sense to me, Rifka. I doubt if it ever has to anyone. But I do know that we're all here now and trying to look forward instead of back and that if we don't keep moving we'll be stuck right here in this room for ever. And I don't think anybody wants that to happen. I don't know about you,' the woman sighed, 'but I sure could use a couple of new tomorrows.'

The girl considered what she had heard, but then she let her head fall back on the sunken pillow and covered her eyes with her forearm, suffocating her words.

'Eva,' she whispered, 'why do we have to do this? Why do we have to go through all this again? Why can't we just go to sleep for a long time and then wake up and start all over again fresh, my brother and I, in a new place with new people and none of the memories that make us cry in our dreams all the time? I'm so very tired of it all, Eva. Of the running and hiding and pretending to be older and braver than I am, of never being safe or happy or as hopeful as girls are supposed to be, of never having any boy for my own, someone who would know me even better than I do, someone I could look for in the future and find waiting for me there. Is it so wrong of me to want to change all this, to find a new life for myself even if I have to make it up as I go along? Didn't you feel some of these same things at my age?' she said, peeking out at the woman where she sat, listening. 'What did you do when you found out that the only life you would ever have wasn't enough to last you through to the end?'

'I don't know,' Evelyn said, and then she did know. 'I guess I just came over here and found you and Herschel.'

They stayed still for a while, and then the girl said, 'What is he doing now?'

Turning, Evelyn saw that the German soldier was no longer in the same room as they were. He was somewhere else, passing from a rag on one bunk to a message carved in another, his hands flaking in the dark air like ashes in a grate, his voice cracking when he bent over to soothe the frightened idiot who saw signs in lice or when he begged someone to turn her eyes away from the window. The women watched as he scurried from side to side, fussing here with an open sore and over there tucking a newborn into a hiding place among discarded clothing. The man's voice receded and his outline merged with the darker beams of the prison where he had lost his way, and in a moment he disappeared altogether in a black corner where the wooden wall had broken open near the floor. They heard him fall to his knees, and then they heard him press his mouth up against a crack in the wood and begin whispering promises to the night outside.

The girl sat up slowly, gathering her clothes around her in a shawl and then rising from the mattress stuffed with familiar hair.

'Herschel's up in the tower,' she said. 'You go on up alone. I'll see what I can do down here.'

Evelyn looked back as she left the barracks, but the man and the girl were still separated by the length of the room. Yet when she had made her way around the cabin and started the final climb up to the seaward turret of the fortress, a crackling as of fire or crickets or song was welling up from behind the damaged walls, and for the first time in days she began to think that everything might work out after all. And then the moon rose above the turret and reflected off a solitary window, and she saw in it the figure of a small boy who was waving his arms as if he was going to fly very far away.

Finding a stairway up to the window was not hard. The whole dark garrison was asleep, and even the guards were crouched over fires or stoves for warmth. The closer Evelyn came to the boy, the more she thought she could smell the spotless odor of young, unwashed skin lingering in the stone hallways, and she followed it as if a trail had been laid for her through a vague forest. At the top of the stairs, she found an open door where the moon shone out as an angle of gray stone dust, and she stepped through it and shut it behind her as quietly as she could.

She found herself in a small guardroom of brick walls

with a table and chairs at one end and a single window at the other. The only light in the room was the moon's, but it painted everything with a coat of soft silver, and Evelyn remembered the first time she had come upon the boy sleeping in her bed. The moon seemed to love melting him away, and even here it camouflaged him perfectly against the wall until he turned his head. Then she saw his eyes, and she was able to find him beside the window even after he had turned back to the sketch he was finishing on the glass.

'You had us so worried, Herschel. That wasn't very kind, you know. You wouldn't like anyone to do that to you, would you?'

'I'm sorry,' he said. 'But I had something else to do.'

'What?'

'Paint.'

'Paint what? Can I see it?' she asked, coming nearer.

'Not yet,' he told her. 'You'll have to wait for morning. It will look really special then.'

She looked up at the window. It was small and narrow, bound by stone and latticed with old, feeble, wooden slats. They made a frame of wood inside that matched the iron grillework outside and partitioned the glass into six sections. Each of these was about the size of the boy's face, and he had crowded the central square with a roomful of figures that would need the rising sun to make them distinct and living. So far, the moonlight made the drawing seem as if it were being viewed through standing water.

'It's very nice,' she praised him. 'But why did you want to come all the way up here just to do this? You could have done it anywhere. I can get you all the paper you'll ever need now. Your sister and I can. I don't see why—'

'Hier ist kein warum,' he interrupted her, almost angrily.

His tone made her uneasy. 'I thought there was always a why, Herschel. I thought there was always a reason for everything.'

'Not everywhere. Not where there's no more room for one.'

'And where would that be, Herschel?'

His shrug again. 'Oh, wherever there are too many people in one room, so many that you don't even have enough space to breathe. Where you always have to stand with your shoulders up by your ears as if you were never sure what you thought about anything. When you're always doing this,' he lifted them, 'eventually you don't care so much about the why's anymore. Only the who's.'

Evelyn gazed up fearfully at the boy's latest work.

'What are you using for paint? It looks,' she wavered, 'it looks almost like blood.'

'No,' he said, stealing a sip from the cup where he kept his brush of straw, 'it's only hot chocolate. Cold chocolate now. Do you want some, Eva?' She told him no, and he turned back to work, musing. 'I did try blood once, but it dried up too fast.'

Evelyn glanced at the table and chairs and said, 'Herschel, could we sit down for a moment and talk? I have something that I want to tell you.'

'If you like,' he answered agreeably.

Seated across from him in the floating light, the woman saw that a day or two of separation had made the boy seem different, older to her. She found herself suddenly regretting having missed seeing the changes as they happened, as a parent separated from a child misses his first discovery of a wicked word or the lie that finally marks his independence from the past. Herschel seemed to be exhausted as he sat swinging his legs and picking at his palm, but he was also more weathered, deeper in the grain, and she knew that she had already lost more than she could ever recover.

'Are you and Rifka all right?' she asked after a wait.

'We're fine.'

'Where did you go?'

'We came here,' he said. 'Rifka read about it in a book, and I wanted a high place to catch the moonlight.'

'But why? I mean,' she corrected herself, 'what was so wrong at Antonio's that made you want to leave?'

He stared at her, not bothering to mention the obvious.

'I know he isn't your father,' Evelyn admitted, 'but there's a long story behind that, and it's going to take a long time for you to come to terms with it. And I really don't see that you and Rifka have any other choice but to—'

'But to what?'

She paused, wondering who she was to be saying these things to this boy from nowhere.

'Well, Ernst has told me that he would be more than willing to help you two kids get to Palestine. He has money and documents and an even better reason to go than you do. I know, I know,' she hastened to add, 'he must be the last person on earth that Rifka or you would want to go anywhere with. But I'm beginning to learn that sometimes you can find little pieces of yourself in some of the most unlikely people, and that sometimes that's just enough to help you get by.'

The boy examined her closely. 'Do you like him?'

'I guess I can feel what he's been through, just as I try to see what kind of things have happened to you and your sister.'

'But why would he want to go there?' Herschel's question was not political, only the honest enquiry of a curious child. 'What about our own mother and father? Why can't they take us there? I know they want to.'

'As I understand it, it was a promise he made to your mother a long time ago. She was very sick, and the two of them had grown very close to each other, so they made a pact to see you two through all this. And,' she sighed in a bleaker tone, 'as far as I can tell, doing this might be just the thing he needs.'

'Why?'

'Well, to help make him feel a little better.'

'What's wrong with him?' the boy wanted to know. 'Is he sick from something? Is he going to die?'

'Oh,' Evelyn said quietly, 'I'm sure that dying is the least of his worries right now.'

'What could ever be worse than not being here anymore?'

Evelyn studied the hands that she had carelessly left at the center of the table in a heap and saw Ernst's head bowed into his lap and another, sadder head bowed over his. She could not think of anything to say.

'And what would he do with us once he took us to where we're supposed to be going?' Herschel went on. 'Would he leave us there all alone to wait for Mother and Father to come? What would happen if they lost their way? At least up here,' he noted with a sweep around the tower, 'we can keep watch for them. What if that man decides that he doesn't like us enough to stay? What then?'

'Don't worry,' she said, sensing his growing interest. 'Have you read that letter that Rifka got when you two were still back in Escorial?'

'She read some of it to me.'

'Then,' the woman continued, 'you know that there are families and relatives who are waiting down there for you, waiting on nice farms and in nice houses for you and your sister to come and live with them. Now if your children don't get on that boat when you're supposed to, everyone down there is going to be disappointed, and who knows when you'll get a chance to go again. You don't want to be left behind here in Spain for the rest of your life, do you?'

'It's not so bad here,' Herschel maintained with a glance at the stonework around them. 'There are plenty of castles to draw, and complete strangers have given me bananas, hot chocolate, even whipped cream. What would be so wrong about just staying here?'

Evelyn hesitated, judging the boy's strengths, and then she gently reminded him about the disappearance of Efraín. 'There are still a lot of problems here,' she concluded, 'especially for two Jewish children from villages that the world would rather forget ever existed. You'd get lost here in no time at all, or end up in some convent where they might make you pray in a way you couldn't believe in. You wouldn't want that to happen, would you? I doubt if your uncle, the rabbi, would have liked to see that happen to you.'

'Abraham?'

The fact that the woman knew some of his history made quite an impression on the boy, and he agreed that the memory of such a good man ought to be revered.

'I've done enough to him already,' he said morosely, looking shamefully away toward a webbed corner.

'That candle that you broke?' asked Evelyn.

Herschel gawked at her. 'You know about that, too?'

'It wasn't your fault, you know. It was an accident. Things fall and break all the time,' she said reasonably.

'But just look at everything that happened afterward!'

'But that wasn't your fault either.'

'None of it?' he said.

'None of it,' Evelyn reassured him.

But the boy knew better. 'I don't think you understand life very well, Eva. It's all connected, you know. You jump the wrong way once, a candle breaks, then the whole world breaks, and then before you know it all the people you love start crumbling around you as if they were made out of snow. Everyone is responsible for everything, and that's all there is to it. If not, how could any good or bad ever happen to any of us? Answer me that.'

'I don't know,' Evelyn said. 'I'm sorry. I just don't know.'

For a while, they sat in the light of the moon's window and felt the earth turning helplessly beneath them.

'And our parents?' he asked her as they both sat, listening, and the ocean washed clear to their door. 'When will they be able to meet us down there? How will they know where we'll be? If they don't follow soon, won't they have a hard time catching up? They both need a little rest, you know,' Herschel informed her. 'That last place that we were living in seemed to make both of them so tired.'

'Sit back down,' Evelyn said, as the boy's excitement propelled him up out of his chair. 'I have some things I have to tell you.'

In the next hour or so, as time turned more slowly than the moon, Evelyn and Herschel talked of things that are rarely spoken of even between friends, of memories that live too long for their own good and of hopes that are stillborn. There was no breathing warmth in the room besides themselves, but the moonlight made the hard metal of the air feel almost tender and as restful as a bit of flannel on the cheek. A long, incongruous peace came over the woman as she let the boy tell her what he could of his home, the camp where he had died and been born again and where for years he had been hidden away as a recollection of a purer time that was shared by all the women of every age. He told her of his friendships among both inmates and guards, first as a lookout and then as a go-between and confidant of both. The boy mentioned the tiny mouse that he had trained to warn them all of nearing boots, and when he scribbled its shape in the dust on the tabletop, she was amazed at how lifelike the figure seemed to be even here. She listened to his story as if she could never have enough, while he seemed pleased to show her his entire world and lead her finally through the decaying streets of its destruction.

As the early morning wore on, Evelyn clutched at every topic that the boy found the least interesting, until she knew that she could put off the inevitable no longer. Then she slowly and very quietly told him about his mother and father. In January of this year, when the Soviets had liberated the few ghosts left standing or lying about, Ester Silberberg had been found and taken out of the hospital to join a clumsy gang of wanderers who were heading generally in the direction of Katowice and the transit camp named Bogucice. It was there, in a temporary infirmary, that Ester had found the husband she had not seen in more than a year, still at work storing sutures and making names immortal. Sendel Silberberg had never been strong, but long captivity had reduced him to the crease in a wall, until he could not eat even if he tried. Ester had nursed him as long as she could, trying to feed him with her own mouth, but finally he had lost his taste for this life. When he died, his bookkeeping was passed on to a faithful apprentice who promptly recorded the father as having died three times and kept him alive as long as the memory of the camps lived anywhere.

Making her way to Dresden with a company of partisans, Ester had somehow found Ernst Rampp among the ashes, only to be told of the escape of her children – which now deprived her of everything in the world. Worse, the former camp guard was now more of a refugee and a fugitive than she was, and he had an even greater need to leave all of Europe behind him. The two old friends traveled southward, stopping only to work and eat or nurse the woman through a fierce case of typhus. Sometime during the journey, less obviously than the phases of the moon, Ernst Rampp had become Sendel Silberberg, and Ester had become precisely who she had always been. In time, letters had been written and arrangements had been planned, until nothing had remained but for the mother and the new father to run over the mountains and down to the sea. It was then, in a hut on the northern slopes, that Ester had decided that her last voyage would be inward and alone. Shielding her daughter from the truth in her final letter, she had sent the soldier in her place before turning her face to the wall. And there, in the whorls of planks brought all the way from Minnesota, she saw the two children and a man walking together over the sea and an artist's hands washing fresh greens out of a dull study in browns.

The gray of the moon had given way to the first signs of the sun when Evelyn finished telling all that she knew, and the child on the other side of the table raised his frank eyes to hers.

'Was that my fault, too?' he asked forlornly. 'What happened to them?'

'No, Herschel,' the woman said. 'It was everyone's fault.'

'And they'll never be coming back? *Morgen früh*?'

'Tomorrow morning?' she frowned. 'No, I'm sorry. Never.'

'Morgen früh.' The boy nodded wisely and looked away toward the window. Through the glass, the earliest

strokes of the sun's light were now glancing through the sticky chocolate outlines that Herschel had drawn in the night. As the sun grew more yellow, the glass broke its rays into brilliant triangles that floated in the confines of the guardroom, turning the stones of its walls into a summer morning and its icy air into peaceful breathing. A ghostly shimmering began to expand the pane inward and loosen the scribbled forms until they stepped or flowed down from the window and onto the circular floor. There, hosts of defeated women with doomed husbands and children mingled about as if they were trying to find their legs again after a long bedrest, women of profound beauty who had been whipped with belts, men with holy books under their belts who hung from poles in a torture of prayer, children as weightless as ash who dutifully followed grandmothers into the woods with handkerchiefs stuffed with toys clutched like opals in their hands. As the company of memories detached itself from the window and filled the room with light, a golden chanting started up and swelled in volume until the whole tower was overcome with warmth and the living people in it became indistinguishable from all who had lived and died before them. And when the portraits of the lost finally seeped into the red walls and went back to sleep again, they left the bones of the turret slightly separated from one another as if the light of the sun were acid and the fortress itself had originally been made of lace.

Suddenly, the boy squealed with joy and hoisted himself onto the edge of the table.

'I know what Rifka and I can do, Eva,' he shouted. 'We could go home with you! I don't know why we didn't think of it before.'

'With me?' she asked. 'Do you mean to Wisconsin?'

'Where's that?'

'To America?' she explained.

'Why not?' Herschel decided. 'We don't need any other family but the three of us. Rifka and I could go back with you. What is it? Can't you go back, either?'

Evelyn thought of everything at once. She felt her passport in her purse and remembered her silent apartment back in Madison, the bricks over there no warmer than those here and the city sky no less chilling. She saw her father and mother in the house near the railroad yards. She recalled the desk that had been abandoned in the hallway after she had taken her belongings away. She heard the few friends she had known at school and at work talking about children whose names she had never been able to keep clear in her mind. And then she heard the old Swiss gentleman back in Escorial saying that the American zones of occupation would stay open for all refugees only until the twenty-second of December, and not a day longer. That, she realized with a sudden shock, gave them no more than four or five days at the most. After that, it would be too late.

Now she looked across the table at the eager boy and felt a change occur inside her that she knew would never change again.

'Go back?' she cried, but the quiet tower around them had no voices left in it to answer.

The fishing boat was only big enough to hold twenty or thirty men at most, but tonight it plowed groaning out into the surf with a load of fifty or sixty, not counting the children who squirmed on its deck like landed cod. Josep Zacuto, the captain who had found lanes across the Mediterranean in every kind of weather, had only occasional glimpses of his bow through the masses of families and the falling, clouded night. He had been smuggling refugees out of Europe ever since the beginning of the war – ducking past patrols, skirting coastlines in the dark, pretending to fish waters where no fish had been caught in ages – and he had not lost a minute of sleep over it. But tonight he was worried. Tonight, he knew that the British would be waiting out there for him, and he knew that in a matter of hours there would rise before him a full moon with a light almost as naked and revealing as day.

On deck, tossed sick by the high winter seas, the displaced refugees shrank together into small pyramids of shelter. None of them noticed the others. The children were asleep or too tired to play. The men wished they could smoke, but had to be content with staring bravely out into the wind as if they could draw the boat forward by sight alone. The women, kept warmer beneath the bodies that were stacked up against them for support, whispered from one to the other words of encouragement and advice. No one could see very much of anything. The salt wind stung the eyes, and even in the lee of corners the night was able to steal away the shapes of their faces and the sounds of their names. A man could have been crouched next to his brother or a woman might have been speaking to an old lover, and none of them would have ever known. All true direction and velocity was lost to the dark clouds speeding above them, until even the children sometimes woke up weak and blurred, wondering who they might be now.

Just in front of the pilot's cabin, among some barrels full of salted fish, the ancient rabbi from Lithuania squinted through the sea spray and tried to make out the man who was sitting with the family across from him. He was sure that he had seen him somewhere before. The round head, the thick neck, those eyes that gaped as if they missed the spectacles that should have been protecting them from the wind – everything about the man was familiar, except the way he sat and hugged his family to him like a comforter in a windstorm. The rabbi had been through so much in the past decade that he could be forgiven his faulty memories and his thin eyesight, but even in the dark the family man seemed to be beckoning him closer, as if the familiar stranger were deaf and wanted to hear better or the rabbi were blind and late to witness an enormous secret. Still, the light and seas were so chaotic that no one could be sure of anything, least of all some old scholar who had crawled like a lion across two countries and one mountain range just to squat among these sour kegs of fish.

For a moment, for nothing longer than a missed heartbeat, he thought he knew the man hidden in his family, and the rabbi could not think. The night air turned bitter, as bitter as smoke rising from chimneys, and the whole universe became another where human reason did not apply. But then he knew that such ungodly madness was finally over and would never come again, so he laid his back against the wall and gave himself up to observing the rest of the family huddled among the shadows.

The two children, of course, were precious vessels of light. The girl, dark and brooding, was taller and more troubled by the boat's frightful leap into the night waters, and she had fastened herself to the woman's side and refused to budge. The boy seemed to be more concerned for the bundle of papers that he held like a child in his lap. From time to time, he would spread one of them out on his leg and turn it this way and that, evidently trying to study some design that had been traced on it, though in the black light off the ocean he could not have been able to see much. Even though he was small, he was more independent, and held himself in balance between his parents, sharing his pictures and heartening embraces with both his shivering mother and his father who was in a well no wind could reach. The rabbi nodded over the boy with a teacher's satisfaction. This one, he thought, will someday become a man to be remembered.

But it was the woman, the mother, about whom the rabbi would ponder for most of the voyage. She did not belong to the rest of the family, and yet she did. For one thing, those closest to her apparently could not decide upon her name. Before the crashing of the sea intervened, the rabbi had heard both children call their mother 'Ester,' but then sometime later her husband, Sendel, had addressed her as 'Berta.' Her hair and features were not the same, either. She was lighter and fairer than the girl and heavy in the body whereas the boy was as frail as ash, and she had more hair than almost anyone else on board, hair that was curled soft and of a human length. She was pregnant, too, or so the old rabbi had thought at first, until the winds that had billowed her coat subsided and left her suddenly slimmer. Now he was not so sure if she was weary of being full or weary of being empty. She had the same look that he had seen on those who passed last year's great selection, the look of someone who is going to live without much hope, but who is still against all expectations going to live.

And then he knew. It must be an *ibbur*, a soul pregnancy, the possession of a mortal body by a spirit of the dead. He had read his Isaac Luria, so he understood the signs. The woman's surprise might mean that the dead soul was using her to complete its life, or her new calm could signify that she was receiving support from an unexpectedly higher source. Either way, the presence on board of these two souls in one was a portent of good fortune, and the rabbi closed his eyes, knowing that nothing evil could stop their escape now and that all the past truly did lie behind them.

'Thank you,' he prayed to the waves flattening beneath them, a coil of ship rope as silken as his dead wife's hair keeping him warm. 'Thank you, G–d, for all the beautiful imperfections in our world and for all our perfect ignorance of them.'

The boy with the flutter of papers in his hands was the first to see the lights of the British ship. They came floating into view just minutes before the full moon was scheduled to rise, and the whole fishing boat suddenly bristled with panic. Men stood at the gunwale and dared the worst, while their women drew children into their bodies like fluids. The captain could do nothing more than keep the head of his boat steered straight and hope that somehow they might be able to pass in front of the British patrol before the moon turned the night into a day of gray mist. But the winds were against them, and before long everyone knew that no one but a blind lookout could fail to see them now.

The mother tried to hush the boy and his scratching papers, but the danger seemed to inspire him. In the rolling wind, with a pencil poking through the paper and into his leg, he scrawled on feverishly as if the buoyancy of the entire ocean depended on him and him alone. Ignoring his mother and the peering rabbi sitting across from him, the artist hurried his greatest work with hands that could hardly feel for the cold, completing it just as every soul on board saw the moon sail free above the horizon and out of the clouds, and the gunship bore down on them through the dark.

But then the moon rose red, red as copper, as blood, in full eclipse, and the light that it spread across the sea was sick and timid, as black as the shadow of a shadow, and the boat of dreams slid past the hunter like a ghost and fled into the open waves.

Then brother turned to sister and smiled, and the rabbi from Lithuania heard him say, 'Home soon,' as he had heard others say fifteen million times before, only now it would be true.

The woman looked down at the boy who was folding up all his papers and putting them away.

'Did you have something to do with that, too?' she asked, as the rusty moon climbed harmlessly above them.

He looked up and shrugged his shoulders one last time.

'Somebody did.'

And then the fishing boat plunged onward toward a land where the smoke smelled only of food and the snow lay molded into hills and valleys of living sand.

More Compelling Fiction from Headline Review

THE POSSESSION OF DELIA SUTHERLAND

Barbara Neil

'A touchingly realistic portrait of those fragile emotional bonds which give life its ultimate meaning . . . A fine writer' David Robson, SUNDAY TELEGRAPH

'A beguiling storyteller' THE FINANCIAL TIMES

'A skilled chronicler of treacherous hearts' INDEPENDENT ON SUNDAY

'Barbara Neil writes with such intelligence and seductive grace of the torments, evasions and threads spun between lovers that she silences mockery' WEEKEND TELEGRAPH

'A really mature story told with great perception and elegance' TIME OUT

'Her plot eases into place with the satisfying quiet of an expensive machine . . . A novel which stays in the mind' Jan Dalley, VOGUE

'Neil's lucid prose really captures the poignancy of the awkward and unloved' THE TIMES LITERARY SUPPLEMENT

'Beautifully written, funny and absorbing, THE POSSESSION OF DELIA SUTHERLAND is a remarkable portrait of a woman questioning her past' NEW YORK TIMES

THE POSSESSION OF DELIA SUTHERLAND is a powerful love story. In a beautifully paced and haunting narrative, Barbara Neil writes with insight and conviction, often revealing with uncanny precision that which passes unspoken between people.

FICTION / GENERAL 0 7472 4346 8

More Compelling Fiction from Headline Review

MANROOT

A. N. STEINBERG

An extraordinary novel which explores the powerful themes of identity and destiny, love everlasting and its brutal twin, violence.

In the spring of 1939, Katherine Sheahan arrives with her father, the taciturn Irishman, Jesse, at Castlewood, Missouri, seeking work. This isolated spot, which offers bathing, gambling and adultery to the passing tourist, has a small hotel where they are taken on – though Jesse drinks and neglects his work, eventually disappearing altogether.

Katherine, discovering the ginseng, the manroot, and other secrets of the foothills, finds she is a natural healer who has also inherited from her Navajo Indian mother a special but unwelcome gift for communicating with spirits.

Among the hotel's regular clientele is Judge William Reardon, a local hero who metes out justice by day then drinks the taste away at night; escaping his sterile marriage, he becomes captivated by Katherine. And is like a man reborn; but, though theirs is a union of souls, a dark magic is released.

FICTION / GENERAL 0 7472 4501 0